Praise for CUT YOU DOWN

"Sam Wiebe pulls no punches in his latest thriller, *Cut You Down*. Gripping, complex, and with an unusual play on the classic femme fatale trope, this is crime fiction at its best."

—Sheena Kamal, author of *The Lost Ones*

"Tense, turbulent, and terrific. PI Dave Wakeland is the best kind of anti-hero, riding the edge between right and wrong, creating an unbreakable bond with the reader. Wiebe's evocative prose, unexpected reveals, and riveting characters—including a contract killer who's ace with a blade—will grab you from the first page."

—K.J. Howe, author of *The Freedom Broker*

"Sam Wiebe does it again with *Cut You Down*—smart and razor-sharp, with a plot that keeps unraveling all the way to its exciting, unputdownable conclusion."

—David Swinson, author of *The Second Girl* and *Crime Song*

"*Cut You Down* begins with a simple missing persons assignment for private detective Dave Wakeland. But fans of Sam Wiebe know that nothing is ever straightforward in Wakeland's life, personal or professional. Wakeland's efforts to help an ex-lover force him to survey the hinterlands of his own heart even as the plot twists and accelerates through gangsters, corrupt police, money laundering, bleak neighbourhoods and of course, murder. A highly intelligent and satisfying page-turner."

—Janie Chang, author of national bestseller *Dragon Springs Road*

CUT YOU DOWN

CUT
YC
D

SAM WIEBE

U
OWN

 RANDOM HOUSE CANADA

www.penguinrandomhouse.ca

Random House Canada and colophon are registered trademarks.

Library and Archives Canada Cataloguing in Publication

Wiebe, Sam, author
Cut you down / Sam Wiebe.

(The Wakeland novels ; 2)
Issued in print and electronic formats.

ISBN 978-0-345-81629-0
eBook ISBN 978-0-345-81630-6

I. Title. II. Series: Wiebe, Sam. Wakeland novel ; 2.

PS8645.I3236C88 2018   C813'.6   C2017-905426-0

Cover design by Leah Springate
Cover photo © Marilyn Nieves / Vetta / Getty Images

Printed and bound in the United States of America

10 9 8 7 6 5 4 3 2 1

Penguin
Random House
RANDOM HOUSE CANADA

The sudden blow out of the darkness, which seems so far from inevitable, and which strikes down our reviving hopes for the victims of so much cruelty, seems now only what we might have expected in a world so wild and monstrous.

—A. C. Bradley, *Shakespearean Tragedy*

You must expect to receive some damage in any fight.

—Don Pentecost, *Put 'Em Down, Take 'Em Out!: Knife Fighting Techniques From Folsom Prison*

FOR CARLY

BOOK ONE

Old Flames

One

Vancouver spent its brief summer hemmed in by wildfires. Smoke from the Island and north from the interior gathered over the city, throttling us, pinning us down beneath a pale orange sky. For days the streets had been emptied, the skyline dissolved into sauna-scented ash. Even now, weeks into a damp September, the breeze carried faint traces of End Times scuzz.

In my cramped and undecorated office, I fetched my father's Maglite out of the tool kit on the floor.

"Something up?" Kay asked, watching me head to the staircase. My sister had also heard the shouting from below.

"Mugging, looks like."

She dropped her paperwork and followed me out of the office, down to the street.

Outside, a man and woman were locked in a tug-of-war over a crocheted book bag. The woman had a tight grasp on its handles, the straps cutting into the pale flesh of her wrists. The man's dirty tattooed fingers tore at the bag, so that a pair of thick textbooks threatened to spill out onto Pender Street.

The man was a neighborhood regular. As the woman pulled, he staggered forward, his gaze apologetic, hands still groping the bag. For her part the woman seemed out of place, oddly genteel amid the gray hustle of downtown.

Welcome to East Vancouver, I thought. Expect no mercy.

I approached them, casually tapping the flashlight against my thigh. "That's all right, Gary," I said. "Everything's all right."

Gary didn't look at me. He was standing still, which for him meant constant dipping and swaying, rolling the neck and shoulder muscles, as if the joints of his body had been replaced with gimbals. My free hand touched his shoulder. He unthreaded his fingers and shrugged.

The woman cradled her bag and inspected its new perforations. She unwound the straps from her wrists and studied the red marks they'd left. Gary lurched toward her. The woman looked up but didn't give ground.

I stepped between them, speaking calmly. "You're not a purse snatcher, Gary."

"No," he said, pointing with his forehead at the woman. "Was trying to help her. She doesn't realize. Trying to protect her."

"And you did good. And I'll take it from here."

Kay handed him a twenty and led him to the crosswalk. The woman seemed baffled, her curiosity outweighing shock. "Did she just pay him for attempted robbery?"

"He gets confused," I said. "A lot of people with mental illness don't get the treatment they need, they end up wandering around here. Gary's pretty harmless. But I can steer you to the cop shop if you want to lay a charge."

"Actually," the woman said, "you could direct me to 1939 Pender Street. A Mr. David Wakeland."

She hadn't struck me as the client type—but then there was no type. Desperation wears a janitor's one-piece as often as Harris Tweed.

"That would be me," I said. I nodded at my sister. "My associate River, who goes by Kay now. Don't ask me why."

I opened the door and we marched single file up the narrow paint-peeled staircase. Inside were three chairs, a filing cabinet, and not much else. A small table with an electric kettle and a tin of Twinings assorted. I explained to our guest that the head office of Wakeland & Chen Investigations was in the Royal Bank Building on West Hastings, up the street.

"This was the address I had for you," she said.

I retrieved my mug from the balcony and slid the door closed.

"This used to be my office," I said. "When I partnered with Jeff Chen we set up in the nicer building, which is where I'd be now if it weren't for the damn dress fittings."

She smiled. "Your partner's getting married?"

"And they have a kid on the way, and are high-strung to begin with. I'd rather stay out of their hair." I looked at the unsheathed neon bulbs, the dust-covered floor. "This whole block is being demo'd next year, and the landlord gave me a deal. But anyway. What can I help you with, Miss?"

"Dana Essex," she said. "I need you to help me find someone."

"Appearances to the contrary"—I swept my hand over the shabby workspace—"that's what we do here."

Two

Dana Essex sat with her bag balanced atop her knees, holding its torn flaps together. She looked a few years older than me, mid- to late thirties, dressed in tweed and slacks and a pair of scuffed laceless shoes. Her hair was hacked simply to her jawline, unstyled. No makeup or jewelry. With her thick Clark Kents and mismatched clothes, she looked like she'd been dressed by the costuming department of a Canadian TV show. A background player, College Professor Number Three.

She accepted a cup of tea and didn't speak for a long two minutes. Kay looked at me for a prompt, but I shook my head slightly. There are different types of silence; some are necessary precursors for speech.

Finally she said, in a halting voice, "The person I want you to find is a student named Tabitha Sorenson. I'm not sure if she's missing, per se. But I'd like to talk with her."

I wrote *Tabitha Sorenson* across the top of a pad of foolscap, added *student* below it. "What do you mean, you're not sure if she's missing? You've tried contacting her? Her family?"

"I couldn't bring myself to talk to *her;* how on earth could I talk to her mother?"

"Let's start with *why* you want to talk to her," I said. This engendered more silence. This time I pushed through. "Was she a friend?"

Essex nodded. "A student of mine first, and then a colleague of sorts. She served in student government, and I was on a committee with her. Yes, we were friends."

"Are you worried about her?"

"I'm worried about myself," she said. "I'm thirty-eight, and—this is difficult to say."

"Want me to leave?" Kay asked.

Essex shook her head. "Mr. Wakeland," she said to me.

"Dave."

"Dave." Essex smiled. "Are you married? I was, for two years, to a very good man who I think tried his best to make me happy. I told myself what we had must be a type of love—why else would we have gotten married? If we weren't as passionate or affectionate as other couples, well, I chalked that up to life running contrary to our expectations."

"Everyone being different," I offered, "who's to say how it should work?"

She nodded. "After a while, though, we couldn't kid ourselves. I realized I'd married out of fear—of aging, and of being alone."

Essex rubbed her eyes and the bridge of her nose.

"None of which interests you, I'm sure. I'm sorry to burden you with it."

Kay offered her a tissue, but Essex ignored it. She wasn't in tears. Rather she seemed to have drawn inward, as if strategizing how best to unpack her heart.

"Tabitha told me when she finished at the college—Surrey Polytech—she wanted to go to either UBC or Simon Fraser. I've checked. She's not registered at either university, or any other in the Lower Mainland." She took a steadying breath, adding, "I don't believe she's at school anymore—anywhere."

"Disappeared," I said.

"I couldn't locate her, at any rate."

I marked up my note paper. "Tell me about her."

Essex's face softened. "She wasn't the best student I've had. She was competent—she could take a poem apart as well as most undergrads—but more than once I could tell she hadn't done the readings. Her heart was in econ and poli-sci; lit was merely an elective for her."

"What was she like as a person?"

Essex frowned. "Didn't I just say?"

"Outside of class."

"Well, as student events coordinator she was diligent. She hadn't wanted the job—Harpreet, the woman Tabitha replaced, had transferred to Dalhousie with two semesters left in her term. The president appointed Tabitha as interim coordinator. She did well, considering the circumstances. Even through the unpleasantness she tried her best."

"Unpleasantness?"

"The scandal," Essex said.

When she saw I was going to pursue it, she clarified: "There were allegations surrounding members of student government. Misappropriation of funds. There was a forensic audit. But Tabitha wasn't involved. It started before and ended after her."

"How much money was missing?" I asked.

"Millions," Essex said. "I'm not sure of the specifics."

I wondered how well Dana Essex knew Tabitha Sorenson, and how well she thought she knew her.

"A million dollars is a million dollars," I said.

"Meaning?"

"People do a lot worse for a lot less."

"Like 'Gary'?"

"I doubt he was trying to rob you."

Her eyebrows arched in ironic agreement. "Yes, he explained more than once that he was trying to help me. Yet he watched another man make off with fifty dollars of mine, and didn't feel a Samaritan urge then."

"When was this?" I asked.

"Just before he accosted me. A man in a wolf T-shirt asked me for change for the Skytrain. I opened my pocketbook but all I had was a fifty-dollar bill."

"You showed it to him?"

"Only so he'd understand I was refusing out of circumstance, not out of tightfistedness. The man in the wolf shirt snatched the money right out of my wallet. He said he'd go make change and bring it back. I told him to stop but he'd already crossed the street. It was right after that when Gary took hold of my bag."

"He probably thought you'd be safer if he carried it for you."

"He watched me get robbed."

"Cheated."

"The distinction being?"

Before I could answer, Essex nodded. "Partial complicity," she said. "One allows oneself to be cheated by misreading the situation, being 'duped.' Robbery implies force or coercion, implies unavoidability. I see."

I looked at Kay. She was smirking.

"It's not a mistake people make twice," I said, pulling a standard Wakeland & Chen contract from the filing cabinet. "We'll find Tabitha for you, if we can. Just know going in that there's no guarantee."

"There never is," she said.

Dana Essex had parked three blocks away, in a multistory garage that charged a daily rate. There were cheaper and closer places to park, but I didn't point that out. I walked her to the mouth of the garage. She cradled her torn book bag like an injured kitten.

I told her I'd update her in three days unless I found Tabitha before then. She nodded and we shook hands. Her smile was perfunctory and timid, but she held it a second longer than necessary. She had something left to say.

"You're talking to a coward, Mr. Wakeland. I like to pretend I didn't know what I wanted until I'd lost it. But the truth is, I was simply too afraid. By the time I could accept my feelings and deal with what—whom—I wanted, she was gone."

"Tabitha."

"I just need to speak to her," Essex said. "If nothing comes out of it, I need at least to know I tried."

I walked back to the office, thinking about Dana Essex, who'd confessed more in an hour than most people manage in a lifetime. Who seemed out of her element in Downtown Vancouver, though Surrey was less than an hour's drive. And I wondered what about Tabitha Sorenson had fired her with such passion that she'd brave the evil city to employ a private investigator to track her down.

Three

Essex hadn't supplied a photo of Tabitha, but Kay found a few online. A high-resolution picture from the college website showed the student government, huddled together wearing the school colors. Behind them a red- and gold-tasseled banner exclaimed LET'S GO ORCAS!

The caption below the picture named the short man in the center Inderveer Singh Atwal, president. Flanking him were Sonny Bains, treasurer, a muscular man in a vintage orange and black Canucks jersey, and a svelte man in formal wear identified as Ashwin Dhillon, vice-president.

Tabitha stood at a slight distance from the others. An ill-fitting school T-shirt had been thrust over her black hoodie. Her face was narrow and hawkish, veiled with pale freckles, eyes reluctantly addressed to the camera lens. The photographer—or maybe the photo viewers ourselves—seemed to be wearing on her patience.

Ultimately, though, it was only a face. I imagined I could read embarrassment in its expression, sensitivity, a disdain for her surroundings. But it offered no clue as to where she had gone.

"Check this out," Kay said, tilting her laptop so I could see the screen. "Her mother has a cooking blog."

She scrolled down for me, showing the most recent posts of "A Mother of Two Cooks for Four." There were many photos, all of food.

Kay navigated to the "About" page, which displayed a short biography and several self-portraits.

"Why isn't our website this straightforward?" I asked.

Instead of answering, Kay called up a picture of a frizzy-haired woman enfolding a young girl in her arms.

"It's the only shot of Tabitha on her mom's site," Kay said.

Tabitha in braces and barrettes, hinting at the sullenness of her later self. The caption read, "Tabby and Me." Below that, pictures of an older Betsy Sorenson, still wide-grinned, posing with sunglassed men in kitchen smocks or three-piece suits.

"Celebrity chefs," Kay explained.

"We're really at the end, aren't we?"

"Of the pictures?"

"Of civilization."

I closed my MacBook. It was four o'clock and I'd promised Jeff I'd check in before the end of the day. My partner had something he wanted to ask me in person.

"How about the scandal?" I asked.

"The forensic audit report is on the college website," Kay said. "It's three hundred pages."

"Guess what we'll be reading tonight," I said, slinging my coat over my arm.

Kay's nod held less reluctance than I'd anticipated. After three months of apprenticeship, the allure of investigation still hadn't worn off. That spoke to her upbringing more than the job. My half sister had spent most of her life in a prairie town that held the national record for most churches per square mile. She'd moved to Vancouver for college, changed her name, convinced her family that what she was doing was work experience. Necessary for a career in accounting, or hotel management, or whatever she'd told them. The truth was, Kay loved the work and was good at it.

To be in the city, to be in pursuit—it hadn't yet become routine to her.

As it hadn't yet for me.

"Tomorrow I'll tackle the parents," I said. "See if they know where Tabitha is. You'll ask around the school. Tabitha strikes me as the kind of person, never walked into a room she didn't feel she was the smartest one in it."

"Reminds me of someone," Kay said.

The head office of Wakeland & Chen was a far cry from the run-down Pender Street address. Classy in an old-money way, oak paneling and brass trim, solid construction, doors that took effort to open. I wished I felt more comfortable there.

When we'd first partnered, Jefferson Chen laid out a plan to expand from investigations into corporate security and counterespionage. He'd achieved that and more. Wakeland & Chen was now an empire, kept together by Jeff's salesmanship and drive.

I went along because I didn't have a vision to compete with his. There were fewer missing-persons cases, and the ones I had took longer and longer. That myopia irked him. The hours I'd poured into the Jasmine Ghosh case alone, with no results and no bills sent to the girl's family, flew in the face of even the most obvious business sense. The search for Chelsea Loam had cost us even more. But the cases that did solve brought the firm acclaim and goodwill, and I felt the corporate work subsidized the other.

As I passed reception, Ralph scooted out from behind his desk and flagged me down. Jeff's cousin had gone off to law school and been replaced by a series of retirees, Ralph being the latest.

"A young lady was looking for you, Mr. Wakeland." It felt odd to hear someone thirty years my senior call me mister. Ralph passed me a yellow slip covered with pencil markings that could have been runes in some Tolkienesque language.

"Her name was Sonia or Sara something," he said. "She asked for you and I said you weren't here and she said when will he be back, meaning you, and I said I didn't know, and did she want to leave a number, and she said no that's fine, she'd check back later."

"Sonia Drego? Police officer, dark complexion, my age give or take?"

"That's her."

I studied the note. It didn't become more legible, or explain why Sonia had been here. I handed it back to Ralph and opened the door to the boardroom.

"Jeff around?" I asked him.

"With Marie. In your office, actually."

"Of course he is."

With the baby coming and the wedding approaching, Jeff's fiancée had commandeered my workspace for a fitting room. The sacrifices we make for our friends. In truth, I'd been glad to temporarily set up shop back on Pender Street.

I sat in the glass-enclosed boardroom and watched the printer spew pages of the audit report. I hadn't seen Sonia in a year, maybe two. We hadn't been close in six. Not since my exit from the police department. She was a lifer, dedicated to the department, and I'd become a civilian—worse, a deserter. Our relationship couldn't endure such a gulf.

More than that, though. Some people just have your number and always will.

When I'd boxed, there were opponents who'd had me figured from the opening bell, whose own movements seemed to me patternless, unanticipatable. It's a hollowing feeling, to be predicted, to be *known*, as if there should be more of you to contend with. Our relationship had been like that, only more protracted, slightly less one-sided, infinitely more damaging.

I wondered how she looked.

Jeff opened the door to my office, escorting Marie out to the elevator. I followed them. Marie kissed his cheek, and in turn Jeff placed
his hand lovingly over her slightly protruding belly. He watched as she
disappeared behind the brass doors of the elevator.

I tapped his shoulder and asked if he'd seen Sonia in the office today.

"Just to wave to. It was a busy morning. Why, what'd she want?"

"Thought you might know."

Jeff used the mirrored brass to adjust his tie. "Would you say we're
friends, Dave?"

"Far as I have any I'd count you as one."

"Then would you mind doing me a favor? My best man's having visa
problems. Doesn't look like he'll make the wedding."

"Guess I could rent a tux," I said.

"Good. Because my backup best man is ready, but I'd feel better with
a backup-backup."

That was Jeff Chen.

I sat in the boardroom while everyone left, reading through the audit
report. I'd assumed that since student government was politics in miniature, the scandal would be similarly proportioned. But the numbers
kept increasing, far beyond simple greed or incompetence. The ruling
party controlled the election budget, the health and dental fund, a number of scholarships, and the events account. Millions cycled through the
Surrey Polytech coffers every semester.

And the regulations governing it were weak already, and had been
shredded to ribbons. Withdrawing funds had required three signa-
tures, then one. Money had been loaned out on promissory notes
with no collateral. The auditors had found no records, their offices
in disarray.

What had ultimately ousted the party was chicken feed—thousand-dollar cell phone bills, the kids phoning relatives overseas. But the audit uncovered more than bad record-keeping and overindulgence. The charter forbade high-risk loans, but since risk was determined by the governors, money went everywhere—short-term deals with family friends, renovations that never occurred. Some of the governors even incorporated themselves and paid out money to their own companies.

Where Tabitha Sorenson fit in this financial mire was hard to figure. She'd spent six months as part of the student government, yet she wasn't named in the audit, and nothing specifically pointed to her. Although she had control over the events budget, so did the others. And with no records, who could say who'd been responsible for what? Complicit or oblivious, she'd remained unsullied by the scandal.

When I looked up from the report I saw a woman watching me through the blinds. I stood and opened the boardroom door.

"You were always a fast reader," she said. "Do you retain any of that?"

"Most," I said. "I can tell you how many RBIs Pat Borders hit for the ninety-two Jays, or the lyrics to 'Jesus Christ Pose.'"

"So when I asked you to run errands for me, pick up dry cleaning or groceries, and you'd say you forgot, you were—"

"Lying my ass off, Sonia."

"I suspected," she said. "It still amazes me how someone so concerned with truth can be so dishonest."

"I'm just exceedingly humble," I said. "If I didn't throw in a few I-forgots, you'd think I was perfect and develop an inferiority complex."

"Ah, I see." An exaggerated nod of her head, as if everything was finally clear. "Does your generosity extend to buying me a drink?"

I followed her into the elevator, neither of us saying anything on the ride down. Sonia was in civilian dress, her cream-colored Burberry buckled tight around her. In the reflection of the doors I studied her face. Worry. Apprehension. Something desperate behind the eyes.

Outside it was dark and the pavement gleamed with fresh rain. "Where to?" I said, shrugging into my jacket.

"Your choice. My car."

"The Narrow, then."

Four

Down a flight of stairs, in the basement of a furniture shop on Main, the Narrow Lounge was a small, unadvertised, dimly lit oasis. Its decorations blended chandeliers with hunting trophies and blue neon. The bar would've pleased the set designer of *Blade Runner*.

I set two bottles of Kronenbourg on our table. James Murphy's vocals on "North American Scum" weaved through a dozen conversations. Sonia and I clinked bottles and drank.

"You came by the office earlier," I said.

"I wanted to talk."

"There are phones and e-mails and such things."

"Does seeing me bring back sad memories?"

"It brings back memories," I said. "You look older."

"Your hairline's not exactly where it was four years ago."

"Didn't mean you don't look good," I said. "Just tired."

"It's an exhausting job. You know that. Or knew that."

"Ouch," I said. "One thing I don't miss about being a cop, the verbal abuse."

Sonia tested the strength of the stool before setting both feet on the rung. "I am tired," she said, sounding it. "Be honest, Dave. When you were forced out, you must've been relieved."

"Not at the time."

"No? You never told me the truth about what happened, but part of you must be happy how things've turned out."

"I don't know I'd change anything," I said.

Once I was gone from the department, it was inevitable Sonia and I would end. I was finding my footing as a PI, still thinking the right case or enough acclaim would restore my sense of self. It would take years to accept where and who I was, and I'd need to serve that sentence alone.

So I disengaged from her. I threw myself into work. I hardened her. And the result stared back at me with eyes like unsettled concrete.

I realized I'd begun stripping the label from the bottle.

"You know, I read that's a sign of sexual frustration," Sonia said.

"So?"

She smiled. "Unflappable as ever."

"Sonia, it's good to see you and all, but what do you want?"

"Who says I—"

"I do," I said. "And don't start with the who-says-I-have-to-want-anything shit. Out with it."

Sonia scanned the doorway and the tables nearby. Our fellow drinkers ignored us, caught up in their own intrigues. The bartender looked up to see if we needed another round, then went back to her playlist. LCD Soundsystem faded into Sleater-Kinney, "No Cities to Love."

Sonia said, softly, "I'm worried about my partner."

"I'm not a couples counselor."

"My work partner, Dave. You know Chris Chambers?"

"By reputation," I said.

I'd seen Chambers at someone's retirement party, hadn't spoken to him. I'd been new on the job, relegated to a back table with Sonia and Ryan Martz and the other rookies. Chambers had worked the room. He was a clubhouse politician, a backslapper, one of the boys. Connected. Martz told me Chambers was the only constable to regularly patronize the top-floor officers' club of the Cambie Street police station. Normally, if you didn't have your sergeant's chevrons, you couldn't even gaze through the window, let alone drink with the department's upper crust.

I remembered him as a tall blond man with pale eyes and a gunfighter mustache. Always a woman in tow. Idolized by most of the rookies. I seemed to remember him dancing with Sonia at that party.

Everything else I knew about Chambers was second-hand. I'd heard how he'd picked up his nickname. In his second year he'd been escorting two quarreling drag queens into a holding cell. As he walked away he heard a whoop from the cell and turned to see one of them remove a bent syringe from the other's eye. The rowdies in the nearby cells were cheering. "No-Frisk Chris" had been disciplined, and had never risen above constable first class for that reason. Most cops in that situation would've been eased out. Chambers, despite his lack of promotion, had flourished.

"How long've you been partnered with Chambers," I asked, "and what do you mean by 'worried'?"

"A few months. He's a good patrol officer. I've learned a lot."

"Like, 'taking pointy things away from people is optional'?"

Sonia didn't smile. "Chris has a good rapport with people. He knows downtown. He actually reminds me of you."

"Are you sleeping with him?"

"No, and go fuck yourself for asking."

"So what do you care what he does?" I stuffed the label down the neck of the bottle. "Better question: what do you expect me to do about it?"

The grooves in the tabletop were commanding Sonia's attention. She ran her fingers over them, and drank, and glanced at things that didn't glance back. Eventually she said, "I'd like you to follow him for a couple of days, see if there's something wrong, and tell me."

"You tried asking him?"

"He won't say."

"This is more reckless than I've seen you."

"I know," Sonia said, "I hate to ask."

"No, I like it."

My grin went unreciprocated.

"You don't understand what this is like," she said. "Chris is senior partner. He has the ear of people above. If whatever this is starts to affect his performance, and I have to report him, it's his word against mine. He's white and male and connected and I'm none of those things. I don't even have my ten years yet. I need to know what's going on."

"You want I should ask him?"

"No. I don't want him to know."

"I could—"

"Chris knows we're close. He might suspect I put you up to it."

"All right," I said. "Give me his schedule."

"I'll pay you."

"You couldn't afford to," I said.

She glowered at me before saying thanks. I realized it would have been a kindness, allowing her to pay. Easier for her than accepting a favor.

"You could do something for me in turn," I said. "You could run Tabitha Sorenson through CPIC, tell me if she's got priors, her current whereabouts and the like. Spelled S-O-N."

"That would be wrong," she said demurely.

"Well, you have to ask yourself if wrong in the service of a higher good—"

Sonia broke in. "You are half-smart, Wakeland, and not nearly smart enough to finish that sentence." She added, fingers starting to tear at the back label of her bottle, "I'll see what I can do."

Five

Betsy Sorenson resided in a pastel-colored duplex in North Surrey. The neighboring properties were constructed from the same kit, the same brick-patterned facades, tile roofs, satellite dishes anchored beneath the eaves. Her lawn was a strip of sculpted mulch, giving forth exotic arrays of color in the morning light. Herbs grew in gray casks near the kitchen window.

Tabitha's mother looked to be around fifty, a soft-featured woman in full makeup and heels. Her professionally cheerful smile would have been the envy of any realty office. The smile diminished when I mentioned her daughter.

"I'm trying a new recipe," she said. "If you don't mind me dashing to the kitchen every now and then, I can spare a few minutes."

"All I need, Mrs. Sorenson."

"Ms., please, and it's Betsy."

She saw me situated in a high-backed chair in the living room before returning to the kitchen, promising she'd be back in a jiff.

I smelled garlic and poultry and faded potpourri. I spotted an old-fashioned cordless phone on its own stand near the door. My fingers touched the ficus in the blue urn near my feet, verifying it was plastic.

Betsy Sorenson came back with a silver tea service, cups, saucers, and doilies. She poured chai out of a squat copper saucepan. Seating herself across from me and taking up her cup, she said, "You mentioned you're from her school."

"I'm an independent arbitrator hired by a representative," I said. I'd buttoned my flannel shirt to the collar and carried a black raincoat, and looked reasonably trustworthy if not all that prosperous. Betsy Sorenson smiled and nodded. "I need to talk to Tabitha about some of the recent events."

"You're referring to the scandal," she said.

I gave her a series of gestures that could be interpreted as a yes.

"Not that we think she's involved," I said, "but she's uniquely placed to tell us just what went on there."

"I don't see why you wouldn't."

"Pardon?"

"Think she's involved," Betsy Sorenson said. "The auditors practically accused her."

"Well, I'm not associated with them," I said. "I'd like to make up my own mind. And that entails talking to her."

"You're welcome to try."

"When did you last see your daughter?"

Betsy Sorenson sighed. She lowered her blue eyelids and regarded her cup of tea. I waited expectantly.

"Tabitha has decided not to stay in touch," she said. "It was just before the audit. Early January, a few weeks into her semester. She told me I was a—she said some bad things."

"You haven't seen her in nine months?"

"She hasn't wanted to see me."

"Do you think she could be missing? That something happened to her?"

"Tabitha is at a foolish age," Betsy Sorenson explained. "She's made choices that don't include her family. Well, what can I do?"

She pursed her lips and tapped her knees in a gesture of soldiering on.

"She's always kept me at arm's length. When we lived in Abbotsford she'd sneak out to meet people, or sneak them in when I was at work. It was one of the reasons we moved here, to get her away from people like that. A fresh start."

She freshened our drinks, centering the dishes on the tray, pausing a moment to admire the symmetry. *People like that.* I wondered who that encompassed.

Betsy Sorenson sipped and continued. "Once Tabitha started college, I didn't see much of her. She never mentioned her friends. She moved out soon after that, closer to the school. Then I saw even less of her."

"And you don't have her address."

Betsy Sorenson bit her lip. "She doesn't want me to have it."

"What about her father?" I asked. "Could she be with him?"

"Tabitha's father isn't in the picture," she said. "He has a new family and doesn't have much time for Tabitha. Once, when we were fighting, she ran away to him. I guess she thought she'd live with him. Mitch wasn't having any of it. He sent her back."

"Sounds like a very tough environment, emotionally—for everyone involved."

"We make our own world," Betsy Sorenson said.

"I'll need to talk to him."

"Of course. Would you like something to go with your chai?"

I followed her into the kitchen, using the excuse to examine the rest of the house. It was clean and bright and the furnishings had been picked out with great deliberation, but it didn't seem lived in. No one had ever shifted the rattan chairs to clear space for a drunken game of Twister. The fireplace had never been sparked for warmth or ambiance. No one had ever pushed the crockery to the kitchen floor to fuck on the cutting board island. It was a model house, built to scale and furnished for strangers.

Tabitha would have grown up feeling on display. She'd fashion her personality in opposition to her mother's, scorning and disregarding the stale middle-class lifestyle Betsy Sorenson had perfected. I felt I understood. Wherever she was, she'd be looking for something honest. Something raw.

"Did Tabitha leave anything here?" I asked, after we'd returned to the living room and I'd complimented Betsy on her chocolate zucchini cookies.

She shook her head. "Just old clothes and books. I donated them all to Goodwill when I redecorated the room. The mess I found when I cleaned it—dirty dishes, piles of paper. Cigarette butts, even after I told her not in the house. Even a couple of used you-know-whats."

"It's an awkward time of life," I said.

We chatted about food, about curries and squab and the Michelin system, and I thanked her for the hospitality. She mentioned her website and the recipe books she had for sale. "I just got the second one back from the printer's," she said. "Let me show you, you just wait right there."

"Mind if I make a call?" I asked her. "Brief and local."

Once she left I picked up the receiver. The phone's contact list was empty. In the top drawer of the stand was a gold-leafed leather address book. I trained my cell phone's camera on the book and slowly flipped pages.

Beneath the address book was a photo album in the same ornate style. The photos covered thirty years in about as many pages. A young Betsy Sorenson in wedding dress, next to a bearded, mulleted man with Tabitha's sharp features. The birth of her daughter, kindergarten, soccer practice, school recital. Photos of Betsy meeting her culinary idols.

A two-page spread near the end of the album stuck out. Every previous page, the photos had been laid out with skill, spaced perfectly, the plastic preservation film smoothed to transparency. On this spread, two photos were missing from the left page. The remaining school photo sloped diagonally, and the plastic was seamed as if hurriedly replaced.

The opposing side featured a group photo, a teenage Tabitha and classmates on a field trip to the planetarium. Bill Reid's chrome crab fountainhead loomed behind them. Two South Asian kids stood to Tabitha's right. All three were smirking. The right quarter of the photo had been cut away with multiple hacks from dull scissors, leaving a ragged edge. A fragment of black T-shirt was the only trace that another person had once shared the frame.

Footsteps. I snapped a photo of the torn photograph, then closed the album. Betsy Sorenson approached carrying two spiral-bound books, each cover white with a rudimentary stencil design in Easter pastels. *Classy Cooking,* volumes one and two. I perused them politely.

"Usually I wouldn't do this," she said, "but you seem like such a nice person. These are seventeen ninety-five each. Yours, two for twenty."

I passed her the money and she asked if I wanted them signed.

"Make it out to Kay," I said. "My sister will absolutely love these."

Six

Once upon a time, the Sorensons had lived in Abbotsford, a border town in the heart of the Fraser Valley. In a sense they still did. After the divorce, Tabitha's father had bought a three-story house in a gated neighborhood, far upscale from the home he'd shared with Betsy and Tabitha. He lived there now with his second wife and their two children.

An economist by trade, Mitchell Sorenson worked in the city as a senior analyst for a property development firm. I calculated his daily commute at just under three hours. Given Vancouver housing prices, that almost made sense.

The foyer of Dose Development's office suite featured a glass-enclosed model of the firm's latest project. A grove of white plastic apartment towers was arrayed along a relief map of the False Creek waterfront. A stack of flyers next to the model explained when each phase of the Villas Con Alma would be complete.

The receptionist told me Mitch was at lunch but I was welcome to wait. It was two-thirty. I ignored the sofas and magazines and stared out the window at the panorama of skyscrapers and cranes and scaffolding, a city launching itself higher and brighter and casting ever-longer shadows.

Eventually a quartet of middle-aged corporate types entered from the elevators. The lone woman in the group headed past the reception desk, while the others finished discussing the Lions' chances this Friday.

"Hundred says they pull it off," said a silver-haired man in a blue blazer.

"I know better than to bet against Big Mitch," another man said. "What are you, zero and fifty lifetime in the office pool?"

The three of them chuckled. The receptionist pointed me out to the man in the blazer, who turned and crossed toward me. The same face from Betsy Sorenson's wedding photo, now clean-shaven and middle-aged, solicitous yet guarded as one gets after a three-martini lunch.

His handshake was damp but firm. "Let's talk in my office," he said, leading me through the cubicle maze to a glass-walled corner suite.

Once he'd settled behind his desk, I told him I was here about his daughter. He squared his shoulders, his hand beginning a slow crawl toward the intercom. I mentioned I'd just come from his ex-wife's house.

"Ah, this is about Tabitha." His tone suggested relief and vexation—unlike his current family, trouble with Tabitha wasn't unheard of.

"No one has seen her since the end of the spring semester," I said.

"All right." He blinked, waited for me to continue.

"When did you last talk to her?"

"It's been a while—a long while."

He managed to lean back and look at the ceiling without moving his hand from the intercom.

"We talked New Years, I think. Yeah. That was when she told me she no longer wanted to be an economist. Was studying poli-sci instead. She also told me I should go fuck myself, quote-unquote, and fuck my fucking family."

It was my turn to stare and wait for him to elaborate.

"I'm guessing you're from that college," he said. "All I can tell you is, I don't have a large presence in Tabitha's life. Betsy has seen to that. And

Rita, my wife, finds dealing with them anxiety-inducing. So you see." He spread the hand closest to me atop the desk.

"Any idea where Tabitha would go? Friends of hers?"

"Sorry, no, I don't have the faintest. Now I really do have work, and it's not going to do itself."

I stood, nodding, doing my best Columbo. "Last thing, sir, if you don't mind." I held my cell screen so he could view the photo fragment of Tabitha and the other two teens. "Any idea who those are?"

"I assume her friends."

"And this T-shirt in the corner here—could you tell me who that belongs to?"

Mitch Sorenson tapped the intercom. He extricated himself from his desk and approached the door. He seemed to be working himself up to anger.

"Kid," he said to me, "I get that you have a job to do. The school probably thinks, hell, he's her father, he's worth a few dollars, so whatever she took, maybe we can get it out of him. Right?"

"I don't know she took anything," I said.

"Sure, sure. Which is why you've got that picture, trying to hold over me the people she associated with. Far as I know, she hasn't seen him since high school."

"Seen who?"

Mitch Sorenson stepped closer till his feet touched mine. I didn't back up. He was expecting me to. After a moment he withdrew and his eyes flicked down.

"I'm looking for your daughter," I said. "That person you made. She's missing, maybe in trouble. If you tell me who got cut out of that picture, it could help."

His face traveled from bluster to doubt, and was working toward credulousness when the door opened. A pair of security guards, both shorter and squatter than me, pawed my shoulders and directed me out of the office. The bluster returned to Big Mitch's face.

"See him out," he instructed.

They did.

All right, let's go, easy does it, no worries, nobody needs to get hurt. Into the elevator, please. And don't come back, next time we *will* have to call the cops. Have a better day, sir.

As the guards left I noticed the insignia on the back of their uniforms. Wakeland & Chen Security. I'd just been thrown out by my own employees.

Seven

"Do you know how long it takes to get out to Surrey from Vancouver without a car?" Kay said. "All the buses are dirty and they run whenever they freaking feel like it. And the passengers are sketchy as hell."

"It's Surrey," I said. "It's not called the New Jersey of the North for nothing."

Kay glanced at our surroundings, her look telling me we were in no position to judge.

We'd tried working in the boardroom of the head office, but Jeff and Marie had ousted us so they could confer with their wedding planner. We'd ended up back on Pender. A Styrofoam clamshell of leftover sushi was open between us on the office table. I could hear rush hour traffic outside, the dirge of a subwoofer from a car idling at the intersection.

"At least the campus was nice," Kay said. "Way bigger than I thought. Late registration is still going on. The students are mostly locals—a lot of South Asian kids, and a whole lot of white single moms."

"What'd you find out about the student government?"

Kay consulted her laptop. "There's an annual election, half a dozen positions. The campaigns get ugly. Most candidates run on a slate—four or five friends, or whatever politicians have instead of friends. The Bottom Line Party won big last year. They're the cause of the scandal."

"But Tabitha wasn't a part of their slate."

"No," Kay said. "The girl she replaced, Harpreet Kaur, was Bottom Line's events coordinator. When she got accepted to a bigger uni, the bylaw says whoever gets the second-most votes gets in. But—it gets messy here. Sure you want me to continue?"

I cleared the food to the table's edge, opened a bottle of water to fill the kettle. "Go on."

"The Bottom Liners convened an emergency session and changed the bylaws. Then the administration said you can't do that, so the party went public to say admin was interfering in student elections."

"So how did Tabitha end up in there?"

"A compromise," Kay said. "Atwal and the others met with admin. They agreed that in this case, they could appoint someone. Tabitha was that someone."

"Why her?" I asked. "Did she apply for the job? Someone suggest her?"

"Couldn't find out," Kay said. "No one will talk since the scandal. You think the election was confusing—there's no records, nobody's stories match up with anybody else's. Lies on top of lies."

I showed Kay the picture from Betsy Sorenson's house, Tabitha with friends, the severed T-shirt sleeve of the unknown fourth person.

Who gets cut out of photographs? Ex-lovers, usually. If the offender in question had harmed Tabitha in some way, abused her trust, if the sight of them would be painful—

Mitch Sorenson's response had seemed different. As if Tabitha's association with the unknown person would harm her reputation, and his own. That didn't rule out the boyfriend option, but it complicated it.

"See if you can learn who this arm belongs to," I told Kay. "Also find addresses for Inderveer Singh Atwal and the others. We'll talk with them tomorrow."

"Are you sure you don't want company tonight?" Kay asked.

I'd told her I was doing a favor tonight for a friend, leaving out that the friend was Sonia and the favor involved prying into the private life of a cop. My half sister didn't need to be involved in that. I wasn't totally convinced that I did, either.

"You'll be busy enough with the Sorenson case," I said, shuffling my notes to uncover my car keys. I had a thought. "Check out who the Sorensons knew in Abbotsford, before her mother moved to Surrey."

Abbotsford was close to the American border. Motorcycle gangs like the Exiles took advantage of that, using locals as glorified henchmen. The gangs of Surrey and Abbotsford drew their members from middle-class families no different from the Sorensons. High school kids who hung out together in the smoke pit at recess, who carpooled to karate class, who burned each other CDs and shared a resentment of their place in their parents' suburban world.

If Tabitha wasn't one of them, she'd grown up among them.

At eight o'clock when the shift change occurred, I was parked under the south side of the Cambie Street bridge, near the unpaved lot that the VPD uses for their parking overflow.

I watched Sonia leave the precinct, walk across McSpadden Avenue, and enter the lot. The strap of her gear bag was slung across her chest. Her shoulders slumped as if that wasn't all that weighted her down. She looked frail, exhausted.

A moment later her gray Mazda hybrid rolled silently out of the lot, turning down a side street that would feed her onto the bridge. She lived just on the other side, near Coopers' Park, surrendering two-thirds of her paycheck for an eleventh-floor apartment with a view of False Creek.

She'd tried once to tell me what the view meant to her.

"That this is all mine," she'd said. "That I belong here as much as any of this."

I'd looked down from her window at the condos and casino and the Science World dome, and told her she was welcome to it.

Chris Chambers came out of the precinct eighteen minutes later, in conversation with a pair of cops still on duty. The three paused just inside the gate. Chambers finished his anecdote and the uniforms headed to an Interceptor. He lingered, tapping his thumb on his cell phone, looking up to wave at the pair heading out on patrol.

Chambers wasn't the same man I'd seen at the retirement party a decade ago. He'd packed on weight, and his thinning blond hair and dark moustache made him resemble a medieval blacksmith, or someone playing one at a renaissance fair.

Still, there was an impressive confidence to his interactions. He projected solidness. Completeness. Though the other uniforms were the same rank, they deferred to him. They seemed to feel what I'd felt, what Sonia must still feel—that to disappoint Chris Chambers would be a terrible thing.

Coming off his shift he was wearing a navy blue polo shirt and tan slacks. He spoke into the phone as he climbed behind the wheel of a white Lexus coupe. He let the engine growl, then tore out of the parking lot in an exhibition of dust.

If I'd been driving the van I never would have caught him. Chambers didn't abide red lights. The Lexus slashed across town, heading roughly toward Boundary. I weaved my decade-old Cadillac sedan down parallel streets, willing to risk losing him to keep from being made.

Chambers owned a semidetached on Adanac, a faux-brick-sided building with crisp white trim. A crushed stone walkway led up from the curb through a chest-high black steel gate. No garage, the Lexus parked out on the street in view from the expansive bay window.

I drove past and parked at the end of the block. In the rearview I watched Chambers go inside.

Lights were on in the living room. At five to eleven they were switched off. A bulb in the second-story window went on, briefly, then the house was dark.

An hour passed. I waited, wondering what exactly I was waiting for. Sonia Drego and Dana Essex were essentially different—one willful and sensual, thoughtful and at the same time heedless, while the other was a construction of tiny, overthought movements, a person trapped inside an ice floe. Yet both had sent me on tasks I didn't fully understand. Maybe they didn't either.

In any case, I wasn't getting answers tonight.

Eight

Inderveer Singh Atwal stood at the end of his parents' driveway, inhaling orange-scented smoke from a vaporizer pen. The former student president of Surrey Polytech lived in a cul-de-sac near the college. His family's house was three stories of gold aggregate and whitewashed wood, set behind a brick fence topped with concrete pineapples. He swung the gate closed behind us.

"Thanks for meeting with us," Kay said.

He shook our hands. "Sure. There's probably not much I can tell you, though."

Inderveer Atwal wore beige slacks and a custard-colored polo tee, and had grown a patchy beard since the scandal had broken. He led us through the kitchen, maneuvering around piles of flyers and recyclables to reach the dining room, where his father, Sameer, was already ensconced. The older Atwal regarded us with suspicion.

Seating himself at the far end of an oval dining table, Inderveer brought out his cell phone, monitoring it as we talked. His father sat between us and his son, like a defenseman protecting a goalie. Sameer wore a similar business casual ensemble.

Hellos and offers of beverages out of the way, Sameer said, "What would you want with my son?" making it clear we'd be talking to him. Inderveer's eyes flitted glumly between his father and his phone.

"We're trying to get hold of Tabitha Sorenson," Kay said to Inderveer. "You worked with her at the school."

"He doesn't talk to those people anymore," Sameer said.

"Could you tell me the last time you talked with her?"

Inderveer looked to his father, looked to Kay, and shrugged.

"Did you choose Tabitha to replace Harpreet as events coordinator, or did someone else?"

Inderveer shrugged again, but followed up with, "Ash Dhillon sorta knew her. They grew up together."

"Ashwin Dhillon? Were they close?"

"She wasn't really close to anyone. Just did her work, didn't hang out."

I showed him the picture. Inderveer shook his head. He had no idea who the people next to Tabitha were, or who had been cut out.

"We're trying to find out where Tabitha is," Kay said. "Any ideas?"

"Why do you want to find her?" Inderveer asked.

"Just to talk to her. Don't worry, it has nothing to do with money or the school."

Sameer's eyes perked up. His body language shifted toward hostile.

"My son isn't involved," he said with finality.

"I'm not interested in any of that," Kay said, swiveling between them. But there was desperation in her voice now, which meant it was time to go.

Sameer stood up to show us out. Kay placed a business card on the table and said to Inderveer, "If you think of anything." Sameer swept up the card and herded us toward the door.

As we headed down the driveway he called to us, "My son did nothing wrong."

"I understand," I said, turning back.

"This woman, she's hiding?"

"It's possible."

"We're not hiding," Sameer said.

I tried to look past him, but his shoulder moved to block the doorway. By that time, his son had disappeared into the house.

As Kay started the van, I asked her what she'd done wrong.

"Brought up the scandal," she guessed.

"You had to mention it sooner or later."

"Answered his question instead of sticking to mine?"

"Maybe, but it's rude to ignore a question."

"What then?"

"Who were you talking to? Who were you developing an emotional connection to?"

"Oh," she said. Kay was a quick learner. "But his dad was eye-fucking me."

"He was doing that before. Once you addressed the father you accepted him as intermediary. You handed him the power to kick us out."

"So I should've ignored him, concentrated on Inderveer?"

"No guarantee, but that's what I'd've done. Jeff wrote a long and unpublished book on interview techniques which, if you annoy me some day, I'll make you read."

"Please no," she said. "Is Sonny Bains up next?"

"If we can find him. Inderveer is probably texting him and Dhillon that we're coming."

Bains worked at a car dealership on Scott Road. He lifted weights at the gym nearby. We missed him at both places, but the gym receptionist said he was at the Mumbai Sweets around Newton Exchange, drinking with two of the trainers.

The restaurant was dimly lit, televisions flashing from each wall. A pleasant smell of cumin and cloves wafted out from the kitchen. I spotted Bains. He was lounging in a corner booth with two men in track pants and tank tops, watching hockey highlights. Empty shot glasses cluttered the table like pieces of an abandoned board game.

Bains was thickset and muscular, buzzed his hair short on the sides, wore a Canucks jersey and cutoffs. His sandaled feet stuck out from the booth. There was a slow anger lurking behind his gaze. "Indy said I shouldn't waste my time."

"He's a different person than you," I said with exaggerated tact. "He's lucky to have a father that cares so much about him."

"He's a daddy's boy," Bains said. "Rich kid."

I sat down across from him. "Ten minutes. All the beer you can drink."

"I can drink a lot in ten minutes."

Bains told his friends he'd be right back. Kay and I followed him to a table across the restaurant. I ordered two pitchers of whatever Bains was drinking and told him I was looking for Tabitha Sorenson.

"You're like a private eye?"

"The best private eye."

He smiled. When the pitchers came he poured us each a glass of yellow beer. Slow pour, no head.

"I haven't seen her in forever, since I left all that school shit behind. She was all right, Tabitha. Smart. Didn't want to get into trouble." He drank, wiped his mouth. "Guess I shoulda been more like her."

Bains kept talking as he refilled.

"Y'know, I didn't even want that responsibility. I only did it for the résumé and 'cause Indy and Ash needed someone else on the slate. Politics wasn't my thing. Now, 'cause of them and what they did, I can't get into UBC. My parents are fucking crushed."

"People who don't take responsibility," I prompted.

"Fuckin' right." He drank and dropped the empty glass. "I mean, they gave me a company cell. Was every call I made on it business? It's not like I was making loans like Indy to my daddy's friends."

"Tell me about Tabitha," I said. "You get along with her?"

"Ash knows her better," Bains said. "They hooked up at one point." He realized what he'd said, and looked accusingly at the beer glass. "Shit. Don't tell him I told you."

I showed him the photo. Bains barely glanced at it before shaking his head.

"Other than Dhillon," I said, "was there anyone else Tabitha was close to? Anyone she might ask for help, she was in trouble?"

"Whatshername," Bains said. "The professor. They organized Welcome Week together. Don't remember her name."

"Dana Essex," I offered.

Bains put down the empty pitcher. "Sounds right," he said. "Not bad looking, but cold. Her thighs'd give you freezer burn."

Nine

Ashwin Dhillon was busy being screamed at when we found him at the returns counter of a clothing outlet in the Guildford Mall. He was the assistant manager, a dapper young man in a brocaded vest, silk shirt, and heavy gold watch. The customer waved an opened package of underwear in his face.

Once he was free, we approached him and asked if we could talk about Tabitha.

"My break's at two," Dhillon said. "How 'bout I meet you at the food court?"

Kay and I found a four-seat table between a Manchu Wok and a New York Fries. She read over her notes while I studied the passing crowd. Seniors, teens, workers on their break. All food courts are lonely places, even—especially—when they're busy. Life's lowered expectations brought you here. The underlying subtext to all such places is, *Let's get this over with*.

At ten past two Dhillon walked over to our table, asked us to wait while he ordered a mango Julius. He returned with his drink and sat down.

"I really hope Tab's all right," he said, punching his straw through its paper wrapper. "I feel bad for getting her involved with this, because you could totally tell she didn't want to be. She was asked to take over events, she never ran for it."

"We were told you had something to do with Tabitha getting picked," Kay said. "Why her?"

"We suffered through high school together. We weren't friends, but when we both ended up at Spew—that's what we called Surrey Polytech—we got closer. Started carpooling." His brow fell and he smiled thinly. "You talked to Indy and Sonny, right? They prob'ly told you we hooked up."

Kay said, "That's your business. We just want to find Tabitha."

"We were together for a little while, but that's not why I asked Indy to bring her in. She was an econ student, and I thought—" He shrugged.

"Thought what?" Kay asked.

"She could help right the course," I said.

Dhillon nodded. "Indy knows business but he only really cares about himself. Sonny's a nice guy, but he had no business being treasurer. It was a mess."

"Did she try to change that?" Kay asked. "Clean things up?"

"Tab took care of events just fine, but events were never the problem. The problem was, Indy set a bad example."

He removed the lid of his drink and stirred it with his straw. Behind him, four construction workers jockeyed for table space with their trays.

"Indy should've never handed out company phones," Dhillon said. "That gave everyone an excuse. Every time he tried to get hold of things, people'd just point to his own crazy-high phone bill. 'Well, you can run up that much, why can't I?' And when people found out about the loans, and the money he was making—"

Again he didn't finish his thought. He stared at his drink and the hands clutching it, his gold watch and gold ring.

"I'm not saying I was any better," he said. "I know I'm the kind of person who fits in with whatever is around. Put me in with good people and I'll be good—and the opposite. I thought Tab as an econ student would be responsible, and she'd help keep us on track. But she was so quiet, just did her job and left. Like she didn't want to associate with us."

"Who ended it between you?" Kay asked.

"I did."

"But you stayed friends."

"Friendly, yeah."

"Were you disappointed she didn't speak up about the scandal?"

"At first. Now I see how it must've been for her. Maybe she thought there was nothing she could do. And maybe there wasn't—I mean, we'd messed things up pretty good by the time she got there." Dhillon placed his empty cup on an adjacent table. "But now I'm trying to take responsibility," he said.

"Did Tabitha have other friends at the college?"

"She didn't socialize with a lot of other students," Dhillon said. "She liked to follow her teachers around—I think she thought that made her more mature. She liked Dana Essex, the English teacher, and she spent a lot of time with her poli-sci prof, Paul something. Italian or European-sounding last name, I forget."

"Mastellotto," Kay said, shooting me a sideways grin to show she'd done her homework.

"Right," Dhillon said. "You should talk to them."

I held up my cell phone and showed him the torn photo of Tabitha and her friends. "Recognize them?" I asked.

"Harv and Gurv," he said, grinning. "High school friends of ours. Damn, that was a while ago."

"Was she close with these two?"

"Not really, no. Back then she mostly hung out with—" The nostalgic grin faded.

I tapped the corner of the photo, the T-shirt and arm. "Any idea who got cut out?"

Dhillon studied it. Something clicked into place for him.

"I should get going," he said.

"Who's the T-shirt belong to?"

Instead of answering, Dhillon turned in his seat to inspect the people surrounding us. Not spying any obvious threats, he slumped in his chair, elbows sliding forward across the table.

I asked him again who it was.

"One of the Hayes brothers." Dhillon said the name warily. "Guess it'd be Cody, he was a couple years ahead of us."

Dhillon looked like he wanted to walk away from the table. He sighed. "I'm only telling you to help Tab," he told us, and himself.

"Of course," Kay said. "Goes no further than this table."

"You read about the murders in the tower last year?"

I nodded, suddenly appreciating his fear.

For Kay's benefit, Dhillon said, "One of the new high-rises near Surrey Center. Four guys our age, low-level dealers, were all found shot to death in their apartment, along with their neighbor from across the hall."

"Jesus Christ," Kay said. She crossed herself on reflex.

"You have to understand," Dhillon said. "In school we knew Cody as just another kid. We'd see his brother around town, Dalton, driving his Porsche. We didn't put it together till later, they were League of Nations."

"Meaning they dealt for them?" I asked.

"I mean they *are* the League," Dhillon said. "Dalton Hayes is the guy that started it, him and his friends. Cody's right up there, too. That kid was always big, he was top weightlifter at the school, but afterward he got scary-big. 'Roid monkey, y'know? They call him Baby Godzilla now."

"And they knew the people in the tower?" Kay asked.

Dhillon shook his head. "Rivals. Rumor is, Dalton's the one that did it."

"And his brother knows Tabitha," I said.

"Not sure how close they were, but yeah, they knew each other. We were all neighbors."

Dhillon looked relieved when I put the photo away. "Do you think they did something to her?" Along with fear, I heard genuine concern in his voice.

"Wouldn't put it past them," I said. "Would you?"

"I wouldn't put anything past the Hayes brothers. Cody especially. That kid's capable of anything."

Ten

I let Kay off at the Hastings office and swapped the van for my Cadillac, then drove up Cambie to the police station. At the front desk I asked for Ryan Martz of Missing Persons and was told he'd be right down.

I waited, avoiding the placards by the elevator, the smiling photos of dead police. My father—foster father—would be on that board. Matthew Wakeland, a twenty-six-year veteran who'd been killed off duty in a hit and run. No great glory or mystery to it, other than a general why-him, why-now.

In my brief time as a cop it had felt good, walking through that lobby beneath his photo. Now it only reminded me of a promise I'd broken, the breaking of which had made me better and happier, though not without a lingering sense of shame.

Ryan Martz didn't bother to step off the elevator, just held the door for me to join him. He grunted his version of a hello. We went up to the third floor and walked to his cubicle.

"So who's it today?" he said. "You ever gonna find somebody who's still alive?"

"Could ask you the same thing," I said.

Martz's workspace was cluttered but negotiable. The neighboring cubicle had photos of women taped to the fabric-covered walls. I recognized some of the faces. The harsh lighting and stony expressions made them look like mug shots. A person passing by might think they were perpetrators.

He sat and gestured toward the chair jutting out of his neighbor's cubicle. "Which lovely lady are you here for today?"

"Sorenson, first name Tabitha." I produced a piece of paper with her particulars, which I passed to Martz. "Student out in Surrey, family hasn't heard from her."

He looked relieved. "Surrey's not part of our mandate. That's a Mountie case. Talk to Surrey RCMP."

"I was hoping you could enter her details, see if anybody's found a Jane Doe corpse matching her description."

"Sure," Martz said. "Not like I have any actual police work to do. Anything else? Because a public servant lives to fuckin' serve."

Stuffed into his cubicle, Martz resembled a shaved bear from some east Caucasian zoo, adapting to its confines as best it could. His scalp gleamed unnaturally under the rails of neon light. There were elements of the police life that made me wistful—access to information, authority, use of force—but I'd never once visited Ryan Martz and come away wishing for his job.

I asked him how Sonia was doing.

He shrugged. "Like she'd tell me. Job's a bit rough on her."

"How so?"

"She's a tiny brown girl in a department of big white devils like myself. She got offered all kinds of details—you can imagine what the brass'd do to have her in Public Relations—but she chose to stay on the street. Constable for life. She's definitely dumb enough to fit in 'round here."

"Who's she driving with?"

He grinned. "No-Frisk Chris, the legend himself. Prob'ly got her panties hanging from the mirror of their Interceptor."

"What's he like?"

"Still got the mustache. Still friends with some of the higher-ups. Still's prob'ly fucked half the female recruits that come through here. You should see his girl—some twenty-year-old model, tight little heart-shaped ass."

"Yeah?"

Martz called up a picture on his computer. A waif in PVC vinyl, spaghetti-strap heels. She was posed looking over her shoulder, pouting, sucking in her cheeks.

"Misha Van Camp," he said. "I actually worked out a dollar figure, down to the penny, what I'd pay to have her use my tongue as toilet paper."

"How'd they meet?"

"Some possession bullshit. Chris offered to walk her through the process. Lucky sonofabitch. Women I meet are all the mothers of dead people, and they all hate me for not saving their kids from their own bad choices."

"It's tough," I said diplomatically.

Martz's co-worker entered the opposite cubicle. I gave him back his chair. He looked over at Martz's computer and hung his head.

"Ryan telling you about the number?" he asked.

Martz introduced us. "Bobby Feng, another dedicated servant of the people. This is Dave Wakeland, who used to be on the job."

We shook hands. "What made you give it up?" Feng asked.

"I don't have Ryan's way with people."

"Few do," Feng said.

"We're a rare breed." Ryan put the paper with Tabitha's particulars atop his in-box tray. "If I can wrangle a free minute or two I'll run the description. That it?"

"You know anything about the Hayes brothers?" I asked.

"Know I wouldn't want to be caught on the fourteenth floor with those boys. Why, your girl mixed up with the League of Nations?"

"All I know is she went to high school with Cody Hayes out in Abbotsford."

"Doesn't mean much," Martz said. "We all know shitheads from school. Even me. I went through the academy with you."

Feng spun his chair away from his keyboard. "I did a stint on the anti-gang task force," he said. "The League is definitely on our radar."

"Being so close to the border, they'd have to be into drugs."

Feng nodded. "Big time. The more states where weed becomes legal, there's less demand for B.C. bud. Which means the gangs are moving more into coke and synthetics, which means more risk, more deals with the bikers. Not everyone's happy kicking up to the Exiles."

"Dave knows all about the Exiles," Martz said.

"I've had a couple run-ins."

"And you're still here," Feng said, impressed. "That's something. But don't think just 'cause the Hayes brothers are small-town, they're punks. They're desperate to prove themselves. The tower killings weren't just about wiping out their rivals. That was them sending a message—the don't-fuck-with-us kind."

I thanked them and walked to the elevator alone, punched the down button. A pair of plainclothes detectives passed by. Neither returned my nod.

As the doors opened I saw Martz jog toward me.

"Dave," he said, looking serious.

"You hit on something?"

"I just forgot to tell you."

"What?"

He grinned. "Four thousand three hundred and fifty-eight," he said. "Dollars. And seventy-eight cents."

Eleven

By nine that night I was back in Burnaby, parked with a view of Chambers's townhouse. He'd repeated yesterday's movements: left work on time, raced home, hadn't left the house since. Whatever was going on with Chris Chambers wasn't interfering with his home life.

I considered phoning Sonia, threatening to quit if she didn't take me into her confidence. I knew how she'd respond. The same way I would—never mind, it's nothing, I'll deal with it myself, apologies for wasting your time.

Courage is a finite thing, and it takes so much to ask for help.

What was another night of pointless surveillance, anyway? I had the Sorenson case to occupy my thoughts. Indifferent parents, a school mired in scandal, a childhood spent living next door to future killers—Tabitha had ample reason not to trust the people around her. Maybe reason enough to hide.

Tabitha was twenty-four. At her age I'd been snugly enfolded within the structure of the police department. I'd had the job, had Sonia, had a sense of the person I wanted to be. A year later I was adrift from all of those. Had a similar rupture occurred to Tabitha? Caused by what? Had the lure of that money led her to do something rash?

All I knew for certain was that beneath what Tabitha Sorenson pre-sented to the world was a different person. More cunning, maybe more afraid.

Lights clicked on and off in the Chambers home.

Quarter to ten, Chris Chambers emerged wearing sport coat and jeans, hair slicked and repositioned. Trailing behind him, pausing to lock the door, was the woman Martz had shown me on his computer. She was model-thin and wore a sleeveless strapless white dress, lace-up sandals with platform heels. She carried a clamshell purse and paused beside the Lexus to wrangle her white-blonde hair through a scrunchie.

The Lexus rocketed back downtown, clinging to Hastings this time. Just past the fairgrounds, I ended up behind them at an intersection. Through the glass I could see the waif playing with Chambers, slapping his free hand, dropping her head onto his shoulder only to kiss him and reel back. The manic, incomprehensible gestures of love and absolute comfort.

East Hastings turned to West. The Lexus made a left and cruised into the glass-fronted high-rises of Yaletown. Chambers slowed, looking for a break in the succession of cars parked along the curb. I dropped my speed so I'd fall an intersection behind, giving them time to park. The Lexus gracefully paralleled into a space between SUVs.

I made a right and circled back to see Chambers approach a restau-rant called the Monte Carlo. He held the door for his date. It was an elegant building: elongated windows, a roof of orange slats in a vaguely oriental arch. The menu was posted on a lectern by the door, along with an enticement—*Asian Fusion Cuisine and Vancouver's Best Cocktails!*

An early evening rain had chased the patrons off the heated patio. I stood and stared through the door as if trying to make up my mind.

The Monte Carlo was doing good business. I saw couples crowded in candlelit booths. Adult contemporary music, Sarah McLachlan and the like, filtered out to the street.

I'd been in the place once, to meet the owner, Anthony Qiu. He ran the restaurant and two others, and did some loan-sharking, and laundered some money, and had some vague association with a Chinese gang connected to the ports.

One of his low-level employees had been implicated in a custody case I'd worked. Qiu and I had shared a bottle of astonishingly good bourbon, and he'd ordered me to keep my fucking distance from him and his people.

The next week Qiu's employee paid up what he owed in child support, and swore to me he'd obey my client's court order. I found out later Qiu had instructed him to do so. The instructions had been hand-delivered via an aluminum Easton softball deluxe.

That Chambers and his date chose the Monte Carlo for dinner could be coincidence. They didn't seem out of place. The maître d' seated Chambers by the window and held the chair for his date. I withdrew to the other side of the street, found an unobstructed vantage point to watch them, and tried to look preoccupied with my phone.

After the wine and tapas were delivered, a familiar figure in an ivory-colored suit crossed the floor toward Chambers's table. Anthony Qiu's weathered face seemed incongruous with his silk shirt and immaculate grooming. I trained my cell's camera on the window and zoomed in.

Qiu greeted Chambers with a palm on the shoulder. He took the waif's hand and kissed the knuckles. Turning to Chambers he lowered his head and spoke into the cop's ear. Chambers nodded. Qiu smiled and left them to their meal.

I backed under an awning as the rain intensified. Soon the street was glimmering from the reflection of the streetlights.

Chambers and his date lingered over coffee and a postmodern sculpture of tiramisu. When the couple finally left, they snuggled under a wood-handled umbrella furnished by the Monte Carlo. They zig-zagged through the slow foot traffic, back to Chambers's car.

No-Frisk Chris Chambers and Anthony Qiu. A longtime cop and longtime crook talking with familiarity. It did happen. Every cop knows criminals who never pay for their crimes. Some cops liked to intrude on their world, remind them that while the justice system had forgotten them, the police hadn't. My father's partner had told me about a college student who'd raped and murdered a fifteen-year-old, then went free when the evidence was washed away by an overzealous coroner's intern. Every year the killer received a Hallmark card on the kid's birthday, signed in the dead boy's name, courtesy of the cops who'd worked the case.

Chambers and Qiu didn't seem to be trading threats. Qiu had been cordial, even charming. Some people can veil a threat in a remark about the weather. But those two seemed to respect each other professionally.

Which meant what?

And what of this did Sonia know?

Twelve

The next morning Kay and I returned to Surrey. Kay drove. I sipped from a London Fog that was already lukewarm when we left Vancouver. I didn't think about Chambers or Qiu. I especially didn't think about Sonia. Instead I blasted Mad Season's *Above* through the van's cheap speakers and looked out the window at a city I no longer recognized.

In the last decade Surrey had done its level best to rehabilitate itself. It was no longer the car theft capital of Canada. Many of the grimy, gray storefronts had been cleaned up or bulldozed in favor of more reputable franchises. Money had been poured into the city center, and the meth dealers and petty criminals pushed back from the Skytrain stations and bus loops. The Fifties Diner, which on Sundays had hosted Drag Queen Night—gone. Skyscrapers and a brand-new civic center moved in. The major highway had been rechristened King George Boulevard, enough stoplights installed to slow down traffic and give the impression that Surrey could be a destination rather than a waypoint between Vancouver and Seattle.

South of the city center, in a cluster of professional buildings near Bear Creek Park, was the office of Martinez, Burrows & Chatwood, the accounting firm that had performed the forensic audit on Surrey Polytech. Since the school had made the results public, the auditors had agreed to entertain questions, though they regretted they might not be able to answer them.

Kay and I were shown into a small meeting room on the second floor. Large windows provided a dazzling view of sights that didn't warrant a dazzling view. A coffeemaker burbled.

After eight minutes, a woman joined us, introducing herself as Jaswinder Pahwa. She wore a green double-breasted suit with matching skirt, silver bracelets on her wrists. I put her age around forty.

"Mr. Baker is running a little late," Pahwa said. "I can perhaps help you with some things."

"You prepared the audit findings report," I said. When she nodded: "We'd like to know what didn't make it into the report."

"We pride ourselves on being thorough," she said.

"Not challenging that, only asking if there were other avenues you didn't have time to explore." Levelling with her, I said, "Like Tabitha Sorenson."

"Right," Pahwa said. She poured a coffee and added various powders to make it white and sweet. She seemed to use the time and the ritualistic movements to decide something.

"What is your concern with Ms. Sorenson?" she asked.

"No one seems to know where she is. I'd like to find her."

"So this isn't for legal purposes?"

"Well it's not for illegal purposes," I said.

She didn't smile. "You know what I mean. I can tell you my opinion, but as far as using any of this—"

A man stepped in, offering apologies. He wore a short-sleeved dress shirt and a tie covered in explosions of orange and green. Hair rimmed his gleaming pate like the petals of a sunflower.

"Ray Baker, senior auditor. You've met Jas already."

His hand patted her shoulder, his thumb over her collar and brushing her neck. He sat down at the head of the oval table. "Don't let me interrupt, Jas."

Kay was sitting next to me, but the window occupied her gaze.

"I was just telling them we stood behind the report," Pahwa said. She stirred her coffee with a metal spoon that made a sandpapery sound as it scraped the edges of the Styrofoam.

"Absolutely," Baker said. "Wouldn't put our names on it if we didn't. Accurate to the best of our abilities." He tapped a duo-tanged copy of the report. "It's all in here."

"Tabitha Sorenson's not mentioned much."

Baker looked at Pahwa.

"Interim events coordinator," she reminded him.

"Right, right. Our feeling was she was on the outskirts. Not a player."

"Based on what?"

"Lots of various factors."

"Race?" I asked. No response from Baker. "Only white person on a predominantly South Asian government."

"If you want to play that game," Baker said boldly, "you go right ahead. But the fact is, she was appointed after and wasn't part of the original slate of candidates. She was never issued a cell phone. Never drew a check on her account that wasn't co-signed, even though Atwal dumped the three-signature rule." He touched Pahwa's stockinged knee. "Jas examined her accounts just like the non-whites'. No different treatment. All in the report."

"Either of you aware that she and Ashwin Dhillon were a couple? Or that they went to high school with the Hayes brothers?"

Both looked suitably startled. Baker's stray hand went back to rest on the tabletop.

"There are time and budget constraints to every investigation," he began.

"All I care about is finding Tabitha," I said. "You investigated her. You must've come across something that didn't make the final draft. Something you couldn't prove—given your timing and budget constraints."

"I hope this girl's all right," Baker said, "but us sharing unsubstantiated rumors won't help anyone."

Kay turned away from the window and said to Pahwa, "Do you mind it when he touches you?"

Flustered, Pahwa said nothing for a moment. Baker looked eager to respond but paused and listened for her response. "I hardly notice," she finally said.

"She doesn't like the way you touch her," Kay said to Baker. "You shouldn't do that." And she stormed out.

I'd had a few ruses and end runs planned, but Kay's speech ruined them all. I lingered a second to see if the interview could be salvaged.

Baker gestured at the open door. "Unbelievable," he said. "Five minute interview, I'm called a racist and a sexual harasser. Un-god-damn-believable."

I wanted somehow to reach out to Pahwa, to get back to where we'd been before Baker's entrance. He wanted me out, and she wasn't going to fight him. I left them each one of my cards.

In the parking lot Kay leaned against the hood, grinning. I stalked past her to the driver's side. When we were both inside and I'd slammed my door, I said very, very quietly, "Don't bring personal shit to an interview. How many times we go over that?"

"Dave, listen—"

"You listen," I said. "He knows something we need. You want to right wrongs, you do it after we get what we came for. And you never leave a talk so you can't go back."

Calming down, I added, "But I understand where you're coming from. Guy's a creep, you got emotional. Happens to me sometimes. Don't make it a habit. Now. Would you like to drive or should I?"

As we were changing seats I saw Jaswinder Pahwa exit the building, spy us, and head in our direction. She was clutching something small in her hand. I rolled down the window.

"I talked to Ms. Sorenson," Pahwa said. "In that same room. She seemed very withdrawn. But every dollar of every event she oversaw was accounted for. That's why we excluded her."

"So nothing amiss?"

"The exactitude. The fact that she could recall those transactions despite the records being removed, and her personal computer suffering a hard drive failure. The interview felt wrong, but the problems we had with the others overshadowed our doubts about Tabitha. My doubts," Pahwa added.

"Putting the evidence aside, and going on your gut."

"My feeling is, there were two scandals," Pahwa said. "Call them above and below ground. Above is flashy and wasteful, taking what it wants, disregarding the paper trail or what might happen later."

"And below?"

"Quiet, patient, playing her cards—its cards, sorry—close to the vest. Above draws all the attention. Below, no one really sees what she's doing. By the time they catch on, she's gone."

"You're saying Atwal and the others didn't suspect what she was up to."

"Right. The cell phone bills and overpayments, even most of the loans—it's all amateurish. Spoiled rich kids writing each other unencrypted e-mails on a public server about how they should be careful the next time they take a few thousand. It's really quite funny."

"Tell me about the second scandal," I said.

"From what I reconstructed of the bookkeeping, funds had been transferred between student-government-controlled accounts with no signature. For instance, we found a hundred and sixty thousand dollars of the operating budget dumped into the elections account. That's in addition to the three hundred and seventy thousand that somehow ended up in the dental fund. Only Inderveer Atwal should have control over large transfers from those accounts, but with no written authorization needed, it's unclear who moved it. Or when."

"What's the significance of when?"

"Well, what if that money was withdrawn and invested for six months and then deliberately misplaced? The accounts would match, more or less, but whoever did that would have access to the interest earned off that money. A hundred and sixty thousand at ten percent would yield eight thousand."

"Not much," I said.

"That's eight thousand that exists nowhere, and isn't missed, provided the principle is returned. Now say it was more, half a million, and say the person got an exceedingly high rate of return, twenty-five or even thirty percent. That could very quickly add up to something significant."

"Enough to run away on," I said.

"Right. If the scope of our audit had gone beyond the student government, who knows what we might have found? As it is, this is speculation."

"So there could be someone out there with a hundred thousand dollars."

"Or millions. The right investment, or something less than legal."

"But you uncovered nothing to prove that."

Pahwa shook her head. "Ray wasn't fibbing about deadlines and limitations. The school wanted it done, but done quickly and cheaply. Hopefully your client wants it done right."

Pahwa reached through the window and passed Kay the black leather wallet my mother had given Kay for her birthday.

"I appreciate the sentiment," Pahwa said to her, smiling. "You put up with male bullshit for so long, you almost forget. Almost."

She walked back inside. Kay began explaining how she'd left the wallet on purpose, knowing if she insulted Baker it would be Pahwa who'd bring it out to her. "I know it was a gamble but you're always saying go with your instinct, so I did, and—"

"When you get tired of being right," I said, "you can drive us to the school. Coffee and apology's on me."

Thirteen

We wanted to see Paul Mastellotto after lunch, but were told by the instructor sharing his office that he didn't teach Tuesdays. Mastellotto would be in tomorrow after class.

"I'd come early," the instructor said, taking down my name. "This close to midterms, His Eminence always has a lineup."

Dana Essex's office was down one floor in the English department. Her door was locked. I phoned her as we headed to the car, but didn't leave a message. On the drive back to Vancouver, she returned my call.

"Sorry," she said in lieu of salutation.

"Were you in class?"

"No, just indisposed. Has there been any news?"

I filled her in on the investigation, leaving out for the moment the darker possibilities.

"What do you know about Paul Mastellotto?" I asked.

"He's an instructor here. But you probably knew that. He's ABD—all but dissertation. Meaning he doesn't have his doctorate."

"What's he like as a human being?" I asked. "Good guy? Sleazebag? Popular with the kids?" Essex didn't respond. "All three?"

"He's very passionate," she said tactfully. "Some students appreciate that about him."

"And the rest?"

"I've heard complaints."

"Sexual?"

"No," she said, almost scoffing at the word. "Just that he has very strong political convictions, and doesn't perhaps enjoy the dialogic element of teaching."

"Meaning the back-and-forth? He more of a this-is-how-it-is type?"

"And as I said, some students are very drawn to that."

"Anyway, I'm talking to him tomorrow afternoon. Might see you on campus." I hesitated. "There's a good chance we'll find Tabitha, and this whole thing will be over nothing. She'll be on a Greenpeace barge, or backpacking through the Ardennes, or whatever twentysomething kids do."

"I got the impression," Essex said, "that you yourself were recently of that age group."

"I'm thirty," I said, "but I'm not exactly in step with people my age. Ever read William Gibson?"

"I'm somewhat familiar."

"He has that line in *Neuromancer*, 'Don't let the little shits generation-gap you.'"

"Right. So?"

"Well, they generation-gapped me."

Essex's laughter seemed to contain surprise at its own existence.

"I have confidence you'll find Tabitha and that everything will be all right," Essex said.

"I'll try to keep my billable hours low."

"See you tomorrow, Dave."

Fourteen

Back at head office, I commandeered the boardroom, opened a company laptop, and researched Dalton and Cody Hayes.

Both brothers still lived in their parents' three-story house in Abbotsford, a fifteen-minute drive from the subdivision where Tabitha's father lived. Dalton had been arrested twice for possession with intent. Months ago he'd been shot at in the drive-through of a Dairy Queen. The bulletproof windows of his Cayenne Turbo had saved him. There'd been another attempt, where an associate of his had died, shot three times at a strip club in Surrey. Dalton had made it out unscathed. No one was in custody for either shooting.

Cody had served six months for aggravated assault and dodged another complaint. He'd been implicated in a nightclub incident where three people were wounded. No witnesses, despite the crowd, and the victims couldn't ID him. Or wouldn't—the news articles seemed to imply the victims feared speaking out.

Brains and muscle, and both living with their parents. Their father taught high school gym. Their mom had been a teller at a credit union before taking early retirement. Dalton was thirty-one, a few months older than me, and Cody a couple years younger. I found myself wondering, if I'd had a few more advantages early in life, would I have ended up like them.

Spoiled kids these days, wanting everything and wanting it now: I could see the appeal of that line of thinking. I thought of my small office on Pender, which in a few months would be dismantled, the building pulled apart and carted off in pieces. Condos filled with wealthy singles and their pedigreed dogs would stand in its place.

So where do you go, and what do you do, when the world has no place for you? When the idea of owning a home, the cornerstone of your parents' security, is only a cruel joke?

To live in Vancouver in the twenty-teens, and maybe to live any-where, you had to accept two facts. That you lived in the best pos-sible period of history, and that it wasn't going to last. That didn't excuse gangsterism, but the Hayes brothers might have sensed that the middle-class stability their parents preached wouldn't be there for them. Not the way drugs would. And when even that began to change—well, at a certain point, you figure out what you're willing to die for.

I stood up and stretched, trod down the hall to Jeff's office. For once he was alone.

"I need you to talk me out of doing something stupid," I said.

"What else am I here for?"

I sat down and outlined to him the direction the Sorenson case had taken, the roadblock waiting for me in Abbotsford.

"You have the address for these brothers?" Jeff opened a drawer and began pulling out wallet and keys. "Through Burnaby's probably the fastest route there."

"I can't ask you to go with me," I said.

"Didn't you get beat up, last time you pulled something like this by yourself?" When I didn't answer: "I wasn't getting much done today anyway."

Ten minutes later we were in the elevator, going down. Jeff paused at the entrance to the parking garage, noticing a figure between us and the company van.

"Was hoping to avoid him," Jeff muttered. To the man he said, "Hello, Tim."

Arms crossed, his sunburnt wrists emerging from the confines of a cheap tan suit, Tim Blatchford looked as if he'd be more comfortable wearing pelts. Taller and wider than me, Blatchford had the look of a brawny primitive dropped into modern society. Last I'd heard, he'd been working for Aries, one of our less than reputable competitors.

Blatchford said to Jeff, "We had an appointment."

"You asked to see me," Jeff corrected, "and my assistant told you I was busy."

"'Mr. Chen is very busy but he'll try to fit you in.' That's how the geezer put it. Hiring senior citizens, that could only be a Jefferson Chen penny-pinching scheme." Talking to me, he said, "And when I asked for you, that nice old piece of prune-tang said, 'Mr. Wakeland is currently indisposed.' That right, Dave? You look plenty disposed to me."

"What do you want, Tim?" I asked.

He rubbed the rim of his nostrils. "Job, of course. What else? I figured since we all used to be close, you could spread some of that wealth around."

"Are you licensed?"

"Think my ticket lapsed."

"Lapsed, or was taken away?"

"Does it matter?" His belligerent expression mellowed into a confident smirk. "You and Jeff sign me on, the licensing board'll print me another."

"We'll think on it," Jeff said. "Leave us your number."

Blatchford pointed at Jeff but spoke to me. "'Bout what I 'spected outta him. How 'bout you, Dave? Your first years, who was it showed you the ropes?"

It was true. I'd been in limbo after resigning from the police. It had been Tim Blatchford who'd helped steer me toward the PI business. Who'd taught me what to do, and shown me by example what not to.

"How 'bout it?" he said. "You know I'm a worker and I'll hustle my own cases. Just the ticket and insurance is all I need."

I looked at Jeff. Jeff shook his head.

"No," I told Blatchford.

"Why?"

"It's a joint decision. Jeff's not on board."

"Don't put this on him," Blatchford said. "You won't go to bat for me and I want to know why. Don't hold back on account of my feelings."

"Because we don't need you," I said. "Because you're a liability. Because waiting down here for Jeff is your idea of tact. Because you're only listening to this so in a minute you can make a point about how it's us that've changed, and not you that stopped caring."

He made a show of pressing his knuckles into the van's side mirror and flaring his nostrils. "I'm better than the pair a you put together and you both fucking know it."

"You're right," Jeff said. "We're sorry we can't accommodate you. Best of luck, Tim."

"That's tact," Blatchford said to me. He removed an orange pill vial from his jacket and poured its contents down his throat. I noticed the scars on his cheeks and hands, his forehead a latticework of pink slashes beneath the suntan. He hobbled past us, toward the door.

"You did change," he said.

Jeff's face was impassive, but his eyes followed Blatchford's back. Once he was gone, I unlocked the van.

"Would it really hurt us, helping him out?"

Jeff shook his head. "Just 'cause we started with him doesn't mean we owe him. He's too aggressive for this business. Anyone who spends his weekends getting smacked in the head with a chair for fifty bucks lacks common sense." He started the engine. "And anyways, you can't save guys like that. They drag you down."

We rolled up the ramp into a bright rectangle of sunlight. I half-expected to see Tim Blatchford waiting for us on the sidewalk. He was gone, though. Another ghost with claims on the future.

Fifteen

Ridgewood Crescent was the name of both the street and the subdivision. Narrow houses on yardless tracts filled the winding cul-de-sac. No ridge, no wood. Traffic from the freeway lent a baritone rumble to the still neighborhood.

We drove a slow loop around the crescent. No cars in the driveway of unit 14. Parked opposite the house, on the curb, we saw a black sedan. Its windows were tinted and I couldn't see inside.

"Cop car," I said, pointing at the exposed spokes on the wheels. Police vehicles didn't have hubcaps, due to the fear they might fly off during pursuit. Even unmarked cars were easy to spot by the absence of chrome on the tires.

We rolled past, stopping three car lengths up the street. The front door of unit 14 was just in our sightline. Jeff killed the engine.

"Doesn't look like they're home," he said.

"Someone is." I pointed to the lights on in the upper window on the side.

"Think the Hayeses know the cops are set up on their house?"

"Might be the point."

Jeff opened the takeaway bag from Budgie's on Kingsway. He unpeeled and bit into his burrito. He said through a mouthful of cabbage and cheese, "What d'you think their connection is with Tabitha?"

"I had to hazard a guess, I'd say she went to them with money. She had access to millions in clean currency."

"And then what—double cross?"

"It's possible. They're both gang-connected."

"You bring your gun?"

The question surprised me. Jeff knew I'd bought a pistol last year during another case. He hadn't approved. Our security guards had firearms, and we were both licensed, but guns had never sat easy with Jefferson Chen.

I shook my head and pulled the Maglite out of the passenger's side footwell.

"Gonna swat bullets away with that?"

"We're just asking friendly questions," I told him and myself. "No need for things to escalate."

We waited twenty minutes. Nothing disturbed the stillness of the street. At five I nodded to Jeff and opened the car door.

"What's our play?" Jeff asked as walked up the drive.

"Let's try the direct approach."

"Honesty," he said. "Something different, at least."

We stepped onto the ratty welcome mat and I rang the buzzer. Discordant chimes went off inside the house.

Jeff nudged my shoulder and pointed toward his feet. Beneath our shoes the letters on the mat spelled F C RIGH FF. I shifted my right foot and uncovered a K.

"Fuck right off," Jeff said.

The door was opened by an old woman carrying an axe.

Her clawed bare feet stuck out from beneath what looked like a nylon kimono. She was tall and solidly built, her hair dyed a blackish red and piled up in a sloppy bun. Her face showed pissed-off curiosity, wondering who'd dare intrude. The axe was new, still price-stickered, and she carried it with a fist clutched below the head, as if the blade was the fancy ornament to a dandy's walking stick.

"Yuh-huh?" she said to Jeff and I.

"Mrs. Hayes?" I asked. "We're looking to speak to your sons."

Her expression melted into a sneer.

"We're looking for a young woman who went to high school with Cody. If we could—"

"You fuckers leave or I'm calling the cops."

I craned my neck and looked at the unmarked car across the street, wary of a sudden broadside from the axe.

"We could walk over to them," I said.

She followed my gaze. A momentary confusion settled on her, as she worked out who would ask for her sons and know the police but not be associated with either. Jeff solved it for her by holding up his card.

"We're private investigators, Mrs. Hayes."

"Hold it closer." He did and she squinted and read off his name, her lips moving.

"You remember Tabitha Sorenson?" I asked.

"Nope." She spoke quickly before the recollection hit her. "Oh, you're talking about Mitch's kid."

"That's right. She's missing and I wanted to ask your sons for their help."

"They don't know her," Mrs. Hayes snapped. "That's years ago, anyway. What happened to her?"

"What we're trying to find out."

She nodded at the cop car. "Should catch real criminals, 'stead of framing my boys. Making 'em look bad."

"Where are they tonight?" I asked.

"Fuck you's where."

I was tempted to ask directions. Fortunately Jeff said, "If we could talk to them for five minutes we could clear this up and maybe help the Sorensons."

"Full of themselves," she said. "Too fuckin' good for us, 'specially that new wife of his. Little Miss Big Time."

"Tabitha is still missing," Jeff said delicately.

Mrs. Hayes seemed flummoxed, caught between resentment and sympathy and matriarchal protection. Not caught for long, though.

"My kids are good kids," she said. "They should be allowed to play their games same's anyone else, 'thout people casting 'spersions on them. Like you're doing."

"No aspersions," Jeff said. He handed his card to her. "We just want to find Tabitha."

She struck the door with the head of the axe and it swung shut.

As we walked back to the van, I thought I saw a red light blinking behind the tinted windshield of the unmarked car. I nodded in its direction.

"Guess that could've gone better," Jeff said. "Think she's put that axe to use?"

"Wouldn't put it past her."

"It looked new. Meaning maybe she wore out her last one."

We entered the van. Jeff had another bite of his burrito. "Home?" he asked.

"'Play their games the same as anyone else,'" I repeated. "Kind of games you think she means?"

"Christ, Dave, she's not the fucking Riddler."

I plugged an address into the van's GPS.

"Let's take a look here, and if we don't see anything, we'll go home."

"This is your show," Jeff said.

The Fun Time Palace was five minutes down the highway, a dilapidated, selectively maintained arcade and mini-golf built a quarter-century ago. Caution tape and maintenance signs were strung across the go-kart track. A covered walkway led over a bridge to a front entrance beneath a plastic facade of castle turrets and spires.

"Think I was here for a kid's birthday once," I told Jeff as we circled the parking lot. "Looks about the same."

"Guess every town's got to have a place for high school kids to get drunk on the weekends," Jeff said. "Aw, shit, look."

Parked across two spaces near the entrance was a Cayenne Turbo.

Sixteen

Just inside the arcade we found a concession booth and ticket stand, stuffed animals and bags of popcorn shelved behind the cashier. The overhead lights were dim, illumination supplied by the neon piping along the walls. Machines for buying and spending tokens spewed noise and light as we passed. *Street Fighter II, Cruis'n USA.* Clusters of teens and ironic young men danced and drove and shot dinosaurs and blew up Russian tanks.

"*Bad Dudes,*" Jeff said. "Remember that one?"

Near the entrance to the batting cages, a half-dozen men were gathered in an alcove, drinking and talking loudly. They were arranged around a punching machine, where for two tokens you could swing at a speed bag suspended from a metal bar and it would tell you how strong you were.

I motioned for Jeff to hang back as I approached. They were all in their late twenties or early thirties, wearing matching black shirts with THRIVE OR DIE in gold glitter on the chest. Two wore black bandanas. The largest wore camouflage pants and a bulletproof vest over his shirt. This was Cody Hayes.

"Baby Godzilla" was apt. More simian than reptilian, Cody Hayes wouldn't look out of place amid the city-devouring monsters of Toho

Studios. He had a bodybuilder's torso and arms, melting into a thick waist and wide-calved legs. Skin pale pink and rubbery. His face had the perennially sleepy look of a stupid, violent man.

As I watched, Hayes slurped to the dregs of his soft drink and handed it to one of his cronies, who began dumping Jägermeister into the plastic cup with the subtlety of a carnival clown. The others watched Hayes with admiration, calling for him to fuck that bag up. Hayes squared up to the machine, wound back a big right fist.

His punch jolted the bag but the machine scored it a paltry 740. Cody fumed and pulled out more tokens.

"It's the angle," I told him. "It's measuring force, not impact."

He ignored me, wound further back, and took a running lunge fist-first at the machine.

Clang and the machine rattled and Cody howled in pain. He'd missed the bag entirely, connecting with the metal bar. To add further insult, the machine posted a score in the low four hundreds.

One of his pals attended to him earnestly. The others held back from snickering with greater or lesser success.

Cody flexed his fist. "Broken piece*ashit*." I couldn't tell if he meant the machine or his hand.

He looked at me, slowly deciding I wasn't mocking him. "Think you can fucking do better?"

I nodded. He stepped back with facetious courtesy, waving me toward the machine.

One of his cronies dumped two tokens into my palm. I fed them into the machine and pulled the bag down.

"Like this, see?" With an icepick motion I arced the bottom of my fist down and through the bag. It pattered against the roof of the machine. The score read 960.

"It's the angle," I said. "How hard it swings, not how hard you punch."

He nodded. "Show me that again."

More tokens were tossed toward me. I readied the bag and turned back to show him the movement. As I did I saw Cody throw a punch aimed at my head.

I crouched and stepped back into the machine, brushing my head on the bar. He came forward and I sidestepped, turned and waited for him to swing.

Years spent boxing had taught me a few important things. Namely that getting punched hurts. But every punch thrown takes something out of the thrower. Tossing haymakers like he did, Cody would exhaust himself soon. What worried me were his friends, and whatever weapons I couldn't see.

Cody swung at me again and I took it on the arm and clipped his nose. He regrouped and charged forward. I evaded, keeping him between me and his friends. After his next lunge I swung at his temple with the same motion I'd used on the bag. It landed and sent a sting through my wrist. Cody flopped forward like a buffalo shot through the brain.

And then the others swarmed.

I kept my hands out to keep distance. Behind me was a staircase leading down to the entrance of the Deep Sea Adventure mini-golf. I backed toward the stairs, watching for weapons, hoping Jeff had secretly packed a flamethrower.

Hands seized me from behind. Someone interposed himself between the mob and me. A thin white man holding a golf putter motioned for the mob to step back. He walked to Cody, nudged him in the ribs and asked what the fuck was going on. It wasn't a question and no one replied.

Dalton Hayes was shorter than his younger brother, narrow-shouldered, and wore a THRIVE OR DIE T-shirt under a leather vest decorated with Asian characters and a gold glitter yin-yang symbol. His head was shaved on the sides, and the long neck of an Asiatic dragon crawled up his throat in green and red ink.

The man who'd grabbed me was the size of Cody. I stopped struggling as Dalton Hayes walked toward me, pointed the end of the club in my face.

"Who're you?" he said.

"A private investigator from Vancouver. Also the current high score holder, though as I was saying to your brother, it's all in the angle."

"Fucker swung at me," Cody told his brother.

"Not what happened," Jeff's voice said behind me.

Dalton looked from Cody to Jeff and me. "You two are together?" he asked.

"Partners," Jeff said. "Looking for someone you know. Tabitha Sorenson."

Dalton knew the name. He made a shoo-shoo gesture with the putter to the others behind Cody.

"We'll talk," he told us. "Down here." He gestured at Cody to come too.

The four of us descended the stairs, followed by the bodyguard, into the Deep Sea Adventure.

Seventeen

"I will straight-up kill you if you touch my brother again," Dalton assured us. Unlike Cody, his face registered little in the way of emotion. He spoke as if offering to lend us a barbecue.

"Last thing we want to do is hurt anyone," Jeff said. His eyes followed the golf club in Dalton's hands. "Like I said, we're looking for Tabitha."

The Deep Sea Adventure had coral and starfish on its wallpaper and a swinging entrance gate lashed with life preservers and a glossy ship's wheel. A ramp led to a low-ceilinged mini-golf with blue Christmas lights strung from the roof. The first hole was a basic rectangle of green turf, scuffed and stained and cigarette-burnt.

A teenage double date evacuated the course as Dalton leaned on the slope of the second hole. His wrists spun the club as if it was a martial arts weapon.

"I respect your culture," Dalton said to Jeff. "All Asian cultures. I've studied tae kwon do and aikido. I'm a big fan of Miyamoto Musashi; but I guess you can tell." He held up his forearm, showing a tattoo of an armored samurai swinging a katana, the portrait surrounded with Asian sayings and five red rings.

Jeff acted impressed. "The code is important," he said.

"Fuckin' A it is."

"Which is why finding Tabitha matters. Whatever happened, it's our job to find out."

Cody scoffed. He paced behind us, occasionally stepping close so I could feel his elbow scrape against my shoulderblade, smell his sweat and the foul licorice scent of his breath.

"All we're interested in is finding her," Jeff repeated.

"Good," Dalton said. "Fact is, I want to talk to her myself. We had some things going on."

We didn't press him. Dalton sat down on the hill and lit a cigarette, offering Jeff the pack.

"Let's say Tab was doing something for us," he said. "Not really important what. We finished what was like our trial run, and we were gonna talk later. Only no one knows where she went."

"When'd you see her last?" I said.

"Not for months. We talked on the phone—mostly texted. Then she stopped answering."

He threw his cigarette down after two deep pulls. His bodyguard hurried to stamp it out. As he did I noticed the pistol on the bodyguard's hip, underneath his hoodie. A similar bulge beneath Dalton's vest.

"I deal with a lot of shitheads," Dalton said. "Cody and me both. It's rare someone's reliable. For her to be so on point, and then poof, just nothing—it's fucked up."

"Really fucked up," Cody said.

"Reliable people, you want to use them again, y'know?"

"Any idea what she was up to?" Jeff said. "Know anyone she hung out with?"

"She brought one guy with her once, when we met. Indian kid. Nobody I recognized."

"Was it Ashwin Dhillon?" I asked.

"Said he didn't fucking recognize him," Cody said.

"I know Ash, wasn't him." Dalton ground the end of the putter into the turf, scratching out a furrow, then another. "Preppy kinda kid. I don't think he knew what he was there for."

"Tabitha handled finances for her school government," I said. "Was she working on something along those lines for you?"

Instead of responding, Dalton said, "I want you to find her, put us in touch."

"We can't promise to do that," Jeff said.

Dalton stood up, dragging the putter behind him as he approached us. "Why not?" he said, almost a whine. "This about money?"

"We already have a client."

"So?"

Dalton swung the club up to his shoulder. He tapped it impatiently against his neck.

"Makes no sense," he said. "You want to find her and so do I. So where's the problem?"

"I don't know why she's disappeared," I said. "Or whether she's in danger. I do know, telling anyone where she is, other than our client, could add to that danger."

"It's our code," Jeff said.

Dalton stared us down. He blew his nose into his knuckles and looked over at his brother. Cody circled us to stand at Dalton's side.

"Not for anything," I said.

Dalton nodded. "Tell you what. You'll pass on a message for me, you can do that?"

"That's fine," Jeff said.

"Good. There's a guy I sometimes deal with, has a farm down on Zero Avenue."

"That's on our way," Jeff said.

"No." Dalton jabbed the head of the putter into Jeff's throat. "You don't get to go there. You never go close to there, understand?"

He pulled the stick back once he was sure Jeff and I comprehended.

"I'll talk to this guy, this friend of mine. He's out of town right now. When he's back, I'll ask him about Tab."

"How does he know her?" I said.

He struck my arm with the club, hard enough to leave a welt. There was no anger in the stroke; I took it.

"I'll talk to my friend and get back to you," Dalton said. "What's your digits?"

His bodyguard took down our cell numbers.

"'Spect to hear in a couple days," he said. "And you find her, you give her our message. Tell her we're happy, we want to go again. Thanks and I hope she's okay."

He pointed up the stairs. We took the cue.

"See you fucks around," Cody said to our backs.

Eighteen

Still wired from the confrontation in Abbotsford, Jeff insisted on accompanying me as I followed Chris Chambers home from the police station. My partner threw back the last half-cup of coffee from our thermos, and drummed on the van's steering wheel each time the Lexus sped out of view. Chambers's route home was familiar. I told Jeff to take Hastings over to Boundary, then make a right.

"I'm not saying I enjoyed that," Jeff said. "Fact, I never want to see them or that place again. But I think I get why you did it."

"Just nice to get out of the office," I said.

"Right. You think Hayes will talk to that friend of his?"

"I don't know."

"What was Tabitha doing for them?"

"I don't know, Jeff."

He considered it. "Money laundering. That or some kind of loan."

"Fits with what I learned about her school." We passed Chambers and parked the van up the block from his condo. "The auditor said someone might've used the scandal to withdraw money, lend it out, then replace it before anyone noticed."

"Someone being Tabitha."

"Right, and pocketing the interest or fee. Half a million that the audi-tor knew about, and could be much more."

"Why replace any of it? Why not pocket it all and vanish?"

Chambers exited his car, stretched, looked up the block briefly in our direction. He waved to a neighbor who passed by our van. Then he headed toward his front door.

"My guess?" I said. "Tabitha figured she wouldn't have to vanish. She worked this pretty slick."

"But something went wrong."

"As it does. And now she's in hiding."

"Or dead."

"More than possible," I admitted.

Chambers met his girlfriend at the threshold with a deep kiss and affectionate strokes to the cheek and chin. They disappeared into the condo. I started to wonder if I'd read too much into the meeting with Anthony Qiu. Chambers didn't seem troubled. He seemed to have everything.

As the lights in the condo blinked off, Jeff said, "Just what's this all about?"

"A favor for Sonia."

"You hoping if you do this, she'll want you back?"

"Never crossed my mind," I said. "Just helping out a friend."

We stared at the dark building for a while.

"Bringing anyone to the wedding?" Jeff said.

"Hadn't thought about it."

"You could ask her."

"Sonia?"

Jeff looked at me as if to say, who else?

"I think that bridge is pretty well torched," I said. "And anyway some-one's gotta watch the office."

"Which is suddenly your specialty," Jeff said, "seeing as you all but moved back into your old one."

"Hard to get work done with so much going on."

"So much work going on, you mean?" He turned in his seat to look me in the face. "What it really is, you think we're too big now."

"Maybe, yeah. Guess I always saw us as Townes Van Zant, 'stead of the bloated Kenny Rogers we've become."

"I think we've proven a large firm can retain a small-business inti-macy," Jeff said.

He'd spoken it free of irony or salesman's guile. Jeff Chen's earnest-ness in business matters was one of his better qualities, and hard for me to argue with.

"What the fuck do I know?" I said.

I finished my burrito and told Jeff to drive home. Whatever Cham-bers might be up to, he wasn't coming back out that night.

Nineteen

In the morning I drove alone to the Surrey campus, taking my Cadillac and a Sharon Minemoto album, *Live at the Cellar*, the late Ross Taggart on tenor. Surrey Polytechnic occupied a block in the middle of Surrey, a series of older concrete buildings fronted by a glittering prefab registrar's office and convocation hall. The quad was small and enclosed a duck pond. A couple of fat mallards and a heron struck poses for the students, who caught it all on their cameras. The steel tines of a busted classroom chair emerged from the water like so many Excaliburs.

The Humanities offices were on the top floor of D Building, which looked imposing and dour from the courtyard but was a maze of laboratories, auditoriums, and at the top, small cubbyholes with desks jammed in, four to a room. I joined two students waiting outside Paul Mastellotto's office. The door was open and he was speaking to a third.

"This is not something I can help you with now," he was saying. "The list is the list."

The kid looked on the verge of blubbering. She said, "I understand, sir, I just thought because I'd taken One-Oh-One with you, you'd—"

"Make an exception?" A caustic grin spread over Mastellotto's face. "You took first year with me and you still cling to notions of preferment?

That says I'm not doing my job. Now I have this man to see, Vancey. So go with God, but please go."

The students took a few paces away from the door. Mastellotto used thick arms to spin his wheelchair out from his desk. He was middle-aged, with unkempt hair that was flared silver from the temples out, his beard dark black and shaped to a mildly devilish point. Wearing an unbuttoned gray cardigan over a Metallica *Master of Puppets* T-shirt, dun-colored slacks and velcro-laced shoes. A pop-art print of Mao Zedong hung over the row of books that ran along the surface of his desk, propped up on one end by a chunk of crumbling peach-colored concrete.

"Berlin wall?" I asked.

"It's from the rubble of an office building in Cuba," he said. "Shelled during the Battle of Santa Clara. Liberated by a former student of mine. The brick, not the country."

I nodded. "You have devoted students," I said.

Mastellotto rolled his neck. "Sadly. Like everyone they love hearing the truth so long as it doesn't cause them to question their orthodoxies. Living the truth is much harder."

He swiveled his chair and nodded toward an unpadded stool placed parallel to the desk.

"One thing I won't do is set myself up as an example," he said. "I tell them I'm as much a hypocrite as anyone. I like cigarettes, single malt, Starbucks, pornography. How can you not?" Mastellotto smiled. "One thing about having a stroke: it's tremendously helpful in clearing away sentimental bullshit."

"So what happens when school is out?"

"Then it's for others to take the next step," he said. "I'm Henry the Fifth standing by the breach in the walls, urging them forth but in no hurry to go himself. A hypocrite, like I said. But if I can spur a few of them through . . ."

He didn't finish the sentence, but shifted his chair to look me in the eye. Conviction and confidence were what his pose was meant to convey.

"What might that next step entail?" I asked.

"Any manner of civil disobedience, from pamphleteering to you name it."

"Would you mind naming it for me?"

He rubbed his cheek. "Corporate vandalism. Sabotage. I don't think I've inspired any assassinations yet."

It couldn't have been said unironically, but there was a current of sincerity running through his words. Mastellotto's confidence came from that supreme ambivalence. Any objection you could raise had already been considered, answered, and incorporated, while simply picking a side, establishing a right and wrong, would sound childish and petulant. Like the image of Mao, his words were chosen to stupefy and outrage. The more he confessed his own hypocrisies, the more he'd seem to have risen above them.

I said, "I'm a private investigator looking for Tabitha Sorenson. She was a student of yours. I get the sense she might've been one of those through-the-breachers you're talking about."

"Yeah," he drawled noncommittally, pushing back from the desk.

"You remember her?"

"I do. I like her."

"Mind talking about your relationship?"

"I didn't fuck her, if you were so insinuating." His expression was a challenge, a demonstration he could withstand any question with honesty and no shame. "Tabitha was looking for purpose. Direction."

"And you gave her that?"

"I gave her some skills for decoding the culture. And I don't mind answering questions, but I'd like to ask you one."

"Shoot," I said.

"I researched you," Mastellotto said. "When you left your name with my office mate, I looked you up. You didn't last very long on the police force."

"That's not a question," I said.

"It is, by implicature. What did you do that was so bad you were kicked out, or off, or wherever ex-cops get kicked?"

"I resigned," I said.

"Of your own volition?" He held up his hand, smiling. "If you don't want to answer, you don't have to." But he waited, testing me.

I said, "I'm not a fan of bullies."

"Is that an accusation?"

"It's the answer you wanted," I said, adding, "I may have hit someone who was hitting someone."

"Bullied them, you mean."

"You want to put it that way." I shrugged. "I'm a complicated man. Like that other private eye."

Mastellotto slowly grinned.

"It's good for a person to discover their threshold for truth. Please continue the interrogation."

"What do you remember about Tabitha?"

"Fearless and inquisitive," he said. "Not my best student but maybe my most thorough. She went through a typical freshman falling-out with her petit bourgeois parents. Only Tabitha followed through. She moved out to avoid living with that degree of compromise."

"Where did she move when she left home? Do you have an address?"

He wrote something down on a lime-green Post-it pad. "The Lincoln," he said, tearing off the sheet and handing it to me. "It's a low-rise a few blocks from here. A lot of students stay there."

"What else did you encourage her to do to show her commitment to *la causa*?"

"As I said, I merely—"

"Right, you just lay out the truth for them," I said. "You don't think encouraging a confused woman who's just out of her teens to forsake her mother and sister makes you a bit of a—"

"Defiler of innocence?" he said, grinning. "Misleader of youth?"

"Douche," I finished.

"But is it on par with beating a man with a nightstick?"

I leaned forward, over the desk, till the grin on Mastellotto's face had been replaced with a sort of gleeful apprehension. He was enjoying the fact of his own instinctive fear.

"Riot baton," I said. "And I guess that depends on what condition I find Ms. Sorenson in."

I'd hoped that was the kind of response to sober him, leave him mulling things over until I could come back and find him more cooperative. But it was a game to him. He'd impacted her life, maybe in some way cut it short, and still she wasn't real to him. He flung his own rejoinder at my back as I passed out of the office, steering past the same hopeful students lurking near the door.

"When you live in the shadow of the gallows, it's but a matter of time before the rope finds your neck."

Twenty

Dana Essex was in her office this time, back to back with a balding man who seemed to have been folded in three and molded around his desk. She seemed nervous when I showed up, perhaps at having the investigation in close proximity to her work. But then she always seemed nervous, anxiety dripping off her like cheap sunblock.

"I'm just going to walk my friend to his car," she told Slouch.

As we took the stairs down I told her I'd spoken to Mastellotto.

"Do you think Paul knows where she is?" Essex asked.

"I get the feeling he knows something," I said. "He's charismatic and knows how to make a game out of the truth. I could see Tabitha, young, impressionable, falling for it."

"I'd like to think she was stronger than that," Essex said.

The bell sounded. We crossed the courtyard through a throng of gabbing students. The heron was gone.

"Did she ever mention Dalton or Cody Hayes?" I asked. "Or the League of Nations?"

"Not that I recall." Essex covered her mouth. "The street gang?"

"They're involved," I said. "I'm not sure exactly how. But you might want to brace yourself for certain possibilities."

"Death, for instance?"

The parking lot had filled to capacity. Cars streamed into the hard-packed dirt lot nearby.

"I've considered that prospect," Dana Essex said. "Quite often, actually. I accept it. All the same, I'd like you to keep looking."

At my car, I leaned on the Cadillac's side panel. Clouds sped across the sky, colliding into one another. Dana Essex rubbed her shoulders. Without looking at me she said, "Everything's become so muddled. I don't know how I ended up here. Maybe this whole enterprise is foolish."

"I don't think so," I said.

"If I knew I was passionately in love, willing to dive into the grave like Hamlet, that would be different. But I honestly don't know what I feel. Passion? Concern? Talking with her, knowing she's so much younger and more worldly—the idea it could be mutual and that I've not completely misread the situation, as I'm wont to do." She put on an embarrassed smile and wiped at her tearless cheek. "I don't know what I'm doing," she concluded.

"Maybe that's a positive," I said.

"I feel new to myself. It's one thing to accept the sexual preferences of your friends and colleagues and another to confront that within yourself. I know I have nothing to be ashamed of, but I'm battling my upbringing." She laughed ruefully. "Dana Essex, the Human Dialectic."

"I used to have feelings about the drummer from Alice in Chains," I said. "Even now, the right guy comes along, who's to say?"

"You don't have to patronize me."

"No, I'm just—"

She reached to touch my shoulder and she nodded.

"It's strange, you're the first person since Tabitha I've felt comfortable talking to. Really talking."

"For the rate you're paying me you should expect some comfort."

It was the wrong thing to say. She nodded and smiled but the connection was broken. I watched her walk back to the campus, shouldering her cares and worries, joining others headed inside who no doubt shouldered their own.

Twenty-One

I drove four blocks to the apartment Tabitha had lived in, and waited for the landlord to come back from lunch. The Lincoln was a prefab block-long building with only the most minor architectural embellishments. Mold streaked down from the gutters like black eyeshadow marred by tears. The lobby was as impersonal as a government office, overseen by a seated guard in a neon-yellow windbreaker.

Gaspar Boucher showed up forty minutes later. Native or Métis, he wore his black hair tucked under a foam-fronted cap with USS CONSTEL-LATION in gold lettering above a gold-garlanded naval insignia. We shook hands. His forceful grip quivered the flesh that hung off his forearms. He led me into a carpeted office on the third floor, sat behind his desk, and regarded me with amiable indifference.

"Can't say I remember her specifically," he said. "Though I sure know the type. College kids aren't the most dependable."

"She take a run-out on you?"

"More than possible," Boucher said. He turned his chair and dug into a filing cabinet, coming up with a gray file he slapped on the desk.

"After a year they're allowed to take off with a month's notice, else they default their deposit." He scanned the file. "This one never gave her thirty days."

"She leave a forwarding address?"

"'Course not. I phoned around, talked to the credit agency, but that was that."

"Her possessions?"

"Auctioned off what we could to recoup the rent she owed, then dumped the rest at the Sally Ann. She's still in the red"—he squinted at the page—"three hundred and some odd cents. For a college kid, that's halfway almost respectable."

I opened my wallet and began peeling out twenties. "I have a proposition," I said. "I'd like you to hire me to get your money back. I'll give you the three hundred right now. Deal?"

Boucher looked at the pile of money on my side of the desk, at my face. He nodded to himself. He spun the file around and picked up a sheet.

"'Course," he said, "this is what you're looking for. Her sig on the credit check form. I hire you, makes it easier for you to check her credit history."

"And her account's in the black. Win-win."

"Could be," Boucher said. "Who's looking for this girl? She have a rich daddy?"

"It's more about romance than finance."

He nodded. "Romance is all well and good but it doesn't 'zactly feed a family, does it. I think this sheet's worth another five." He smiled. "If you don't have it on you I don't mind waiting."

I got comfortable in the chair. "I'd maybe go an extra fifty."

"I'm betting you'll go the full five hundred."

"There are other ways of getting the info," I said. "But I guess a hundred and fifty wouldn't exhaust my expense money."

"Keep going, hoss."

"One sixty, makes it easier to take out of an ATM."

Boucher laughed. "I got the time to wait."

"Not me, I'm very popular and busy. I leave this room you get nothing."

He shook a toothpick out of a jar and inserted it between his bottom row. "Guess I could agree to four, let you save some face."

"You're a shrewd bargainer."

"We're the best bargainers," he said. "Best thing Hudson's Bay ever made are those point blankets they sold to us. Highest quality 'cause they knew we couldn't be duped." He studied the toothpick. "That's why that stereotype bothers me, the dumb Indian, doesn't understand the value of things. You people"—he said it friendly—"want to think you put one over on us, rather than using force to take what you wanted."

"Other words, you got robbed, you didn't get cheated."

His laugh was a sharp quick grunt. "Yeah. 'Zactly. I like that. Might use that."

"I might go three."

"Then you'll go three sixty."

I counted out twenties, tens, and fives, and pushed the pile across the table.

"Five short," he said.

"It's what I got."

Boucher's arm swept the bills up. "Anything for love," he said.

Twenty-Two

That evening, parked under the bridge, I watched Chris Chambers and Sonia Drego walk out together, talk, part, and head to their respective vehicles. No sign of unease between them.

I followed Chambers across the bridge and onto the off-ramp. On Pacific Boulevard he sped through a lingering amber, disappearing into the stream of luxury sedans pouring out from the financial district.

I made a right on Pender, reasoning that Chambers was headed home. Traffic was heavy on Hastings, but moving. When I turned onto Skeena I began looking for Chambers's white Lexus. It wasn't parked in the area around his condo. No lights on inside.

As I parked, I dialed Sonia. She answered and said breathlessly, "I have two minutes before my class starts. Is it critical?"

"I lost Chambers in the corridor," I said.

"He's not at home?"

"No one's there."

"His girlfriend works the odd modeling job. He might be with her."

"Where would that be?"

"You're the detective," she said.

"What's her deal?"

"Misha? They've been together almost a year. She moved in a few months ago."

"They seem in love."

"They do," Sonia said. "Nauseating, isn't it?"

"Think she's the source of his stress, or whatever it is?"

"I don't know."

"Ever hear of Anthony Qiu?"

"No."

"He's worth running through CPIC," I said. "Loan-sharking and probably a lot more. Chambers and his girl ate in Qiu's restaurant two nights ago."

"Interesting."

"What class are you taking?"

"No-gi," she said. "Advanced combat defense. Judo and jiujitsu."

"What do you wear for something like that?"

"Bruises," Sonia said. "I have to go."

I coasted back downtown, traffic lighter now. On Main Street, activists had painted slogans over the old police building across from the courts. AFFORDABLE HOUSING NOT CONDOS, GENTRIFY THIS, and the like. A crew with stepladders and buckets were busy erasing the graffiti. By tomorrow it would be washed away. Some crimes vanish.

There was a martial arts dungeon off Alexander. I headed toward it thinking Sonia probably wouldn't be there, and when I saw her car I thought I'd just drive past. But I found myself descending the steps and slipping off my shoes, enveloped in the humid air of the studio.

Class had wrapped and half the lights were off. I watched Sonia toss a demonstration punch at a short Brazilian man with hairy wrists. With a smooth motion he caught up her arm and flung her across his body, dumping her onto the floor with sickening force. She went limp and rolled to one knee, a defensive pose.

Her instructor noticed me and waved. "We're finished," he said.

"Thanks, Roland," Sonia said. She was wearing a purple sports top over drawstring yoga pants. The bruises were there, especially her back and left shoulder. "What are you doing here?" she asked.

"Just in the neighborhood," I said. "You fall pretty well."

"Ex-boyfriend," she explained to Roland.

Her instructor nodded. "I'll finish my paperwork," he said, withdrawing into a back room.

The gym had posters on the walls of Gracie fighters and way-of-the-warrior type sayings. The mats and equipment had years on them. Scuffs on the floor.

"Take off your socks," Sonia said.

I started to comply. "Any reason, other than you like the sight of my feet?"

"I need an untrained sparring partner, and like you said, you're in the neighborhood."

Sonia watched while I shed my coat and placed wallet and keys near my footwear. I'd boxed in my teens, working out of the old Astoria basement. As I approached her, my feet fell into the stance.

"What do you want me to do?"

"Attack me," she said. "Like you mean it."

I swung a lazy left near her ear. She caught it and stepped into me, mimicking her instructor's moves. I tumbled over her and landed badly, my head smacking the wood beneath the mat.

"Don't fuck around, I want you to really try." Sonia held out her hand. I took it, feeling the pulse in her wrist. I stood.

"I can't do that," I said.

"I want you to."

"Swing at you."

"And hold back nothing."

I shrugged and moved in. I jabbed at her. She caught the second one and tripped me. I landed on my ass.

"You're not trying," she said.

I stood up. This time instead of throwing a punch I got my hands over her shoulders and shoved. It was a hard shove and she back-pedaled, taken aback but nodding. "Again."

"No," I said. "I'm not comfortable with this."

"Hit me like you would if I was Ryan asking you to."

"You don't want that," I said.

"Hit me, Dave. You can't hurt me."

"Get someone else."

She approached me and kicked my thigh. I backed up. She aimed another kick toward my shin. It missed but her foot stamped the floor with all her weight.

I reached out and she slapped me. I grabbed for her and she trapped my wrist, ducked, coming up behind me with my wrist trapped. I shook her off, easier than she would've liked.

"I know you think this is going to make you invincible," I said. "My father would say, a good big man will always take a good small man. The whole reason they have weight classes, Sonia—"

"Shut up," she said. "Come at me."

I did. I swung at her and found myself on the floor. I pushed up and bulled into her, propelling her backward. She rolled and came up on my left. I was breathing heavily.

"You don't want to lose to me," she said. "Well, I don't want to lose to you. Or anybody. Can you do better?"

I swung hard. The fist caught her bruised shoulder. Pain welled up in her face, her dark eyes on the verge of tears. I dropped stance.

Her kick caught me in the solar plexus and rattled my lungs. I stepped back and held out a hand to keep up distance. She seized it and began another throw. I let myself become dead weight and collapsed her knees, bringing the both of us down.

I had her wrists. She was struggling. I pinned them and sat atop her. Her legs thrashed beneath me. Her jaw locked in a grimace. She tried every movement, but I was clamped down for good. I could hear our breathing and looking down I saw her nipples erect through the fabric of her shirt. She was staring at me with raw hatred. I felt sick, like watching the throes of a small animal attempting to escape a hunter's trap.

I let her go and rolled off. She sprang up. Wiping the hair out of her face, she said, "I shouldn't've put you in that position. I'm sorry."

I stood and rubbed my back. "Impressive moves," I said. "If the size difference wasn't so—"

"Yes, I understand, all right. Let's not keep talking about it."

I walked her out to her dust-caked Mazda. Sonia still wore her gym getup, her coat and gear bag under one arm. She dug in the bag for her keys. Teens passed us on the sidewalk, midweek revelers, leaving a contrail of dope and tobacco and fading laughter.

Sonia stored her bag in the trunk of her car. Coming around to the driver's side, she paused and looked at me, waiting on the pavement.

"What's Chris Chambers got on you?" I asked. "Or you on him?"

She shook her head and shrugged, eyes wide, as if scanning for extra meaning in the nearby world. "I don't know. I don't understand why I do some things. Like back in there. I don't know what I wanted out of that."

"To kick my ass?"

"Maybe."

"You don't have the worst claim in the world for it," I said. "How long do you want me up on Chambers?"

"I'm not sure. Maybe it was a stupid idea."

Sonia got in the car. Lit by the interior light her face looked beyond physically fatigued, as if the workout had tapped into her reservoir of hope.

Twenty-Three

Chris Chambers's Lexus was parked in front of his house, amid the dark sedans of his white-collar neighbors. Lights on in the kitchen, television flicker from the upstairs den. Other lights snapped off individually. Shutting down the house for the night.

I wondered what their bedroom ritual was like. Did they wear pajamas, did they brush their teeth or piss with the bathroom door open. Who initiated sex. Who doled it out. Oral? Toys? It wasn't voyeuristic. It was time-passing. Like wondering what they'd ordered in for dinner.

When the last light blinked out I started the engine. I was pulling up the block when Chambers left the house.

He'd donned a leather bomber jacket and a baseball cap, and what looked like steel-toed work boots. I pulled over and killed the lights but let the engine idle. Chambers passed me, driving his customary thirty over the limit.

I followed with the lights out, glad when he pulled onto Hastings. Traffic slim but enough to keep a few cars between us. Back into the city we went.

I was half-expecting a turn into Yaletown, another meeting with Qiu. Instead Chambers drove to Main, to the stretch of bar-hotels that began with the Waverley and ended in Chinatown. Chambers parked on the street and stuck something on his dash. I waited till he ducked into the Cobalt, then parked a few spaces behind him.

He was all of six minutes, and when he came out he started walking down Main toward the waterfront. A one-person foot tail was dicey, but the only option.

All kinds of desperation huddled under the awnings. Chambers nearly collided with a dreadlocked man pushing a shopping cart, its casters squealing as Chambers shoved past.

He was asked for change and cigarettes and so was I. Chambers didn't look back.

I crossed the street and watched him turn in to a by-the-slice pizza joint. He came out sans food or beverage, went up another block and ducked into the Electric Owl. A moment later he was back outside, this time heading for the Crossroads Inn, sharing a gruff hello with the doorman as he entered.

I loitered by the bus stop and wished I still smoked cigarettes. Two weeks of breathing wildfire smoke had cured me, at least temporarily. The urge flared up as I watched the door of the Crossroads.

A bus shuffled by. Chambers didn't come out, which meant he'd found whatever he'd been chasing. I headed inside.

A karaoke party in full swing, drunken warbling and peals of laughter from the corner stage. Flock of Seagulls bleeding into Paula Abdul. Scattered barflies at the tables. The bar itself was a battered wooden island holding tubs of ice and beer. Behind it, a mosaic of liquor bottles on the shelves, lit by naked bulbs framing a greasy mirror.

No Chambers.

At the bar a slim young man in a suit monopolized the bartender's time. He was drinking from a pint glass filled with something silty and yellow. His suit was rumpled and the hat he wore seemed to have been fetched from the closet of an elderly relative. He kept up a steady patter, punctuated by nods and yuh-huhs from the bartender as she filled a tray with shot glasses.

I sat down and had a beer brought to me, left the change on the table. The room was dim, what light there was tinged green. Heat and volume beyond comfort. A few singles talked and made sorties to the bar.

The man in the suit rapped on the counter and grabbed his crotch, smiling and still speaking. He made what he thought was a straight line for the toilets.

He was intercepted by a hand reaching out from a booth. It settled firmly on the suit's shoulder and shoved him toward the back of the club. The hand belonged to Chris Chambers.

The cop's face was a blank, his jaw clenched as if holding back disgust. The suit's grin was pure fear.

Chambers marched him down a hallway and out the service door. I followed, putting on a drunk act in case anyone was watching Chambers's back. The door was wedged open and I could hear the sound of a hat being knocked off someone's head.

"—and then three days later here you are drinking imported beer with his money, 'stead of paying him back."

"Chris, not like I was—"

"Shut up and turn your bitch pockets out."

A rustling sound, coins hitting concrete. Then a fabric swish as the suit bent over to retrieve them.

"Where's the rest?"

"What rest, if I had more don't you think I'd give it to you?"

"This goes easier I have something to show the Restaurant Man."

The sound of clothing being adjusted, the revealing of someone's hidden cache.

"Kind of mutt buys dope with his boss's money?"

"I know I got problems. Please. One more day, everything's squared. I've got things playing out."

"Let me see that hand, Miles."

"Please. One day."

"Double. One day."

"Sure, of course, I swear."

"Good."

"Thanks, Chris. Thank you."

"Welcome. Now your hand."

"Please." The word stuttered and blubbered out in half syllables.

"Stick it in the door. Whole hand."

I stepped back as Chambers's foot kicked out the wedge. I saw a hand placed tightly on the frame. The door opened slightly and swiftly swung closed. A scream carried inside and the fingers retracted.

"Put it fucking back," Chambers's voice said.

The hand was replaced. Chambers stamped the door. Three heavy bootfalls on the hollow metal along with the agonized whimpers of Miles.

The door opened. Two heavy hands inspected the mangled one. Chambers shushed him.

"Lucky the Restaurant Man didn't send someone enjoys this shit," Chambers said. "Else it wouldn't be your hand, Miles. Count your fucking blessings."

A rustling sound I could barely hear over the drone of the music. "Pizza napkins'll do till you get your ass to St. Paul's, get a real bandage." Chambers's voice held some concern. "Holding?"

"Nah."

"I search your pockets—"

"All right, all right. Shit."

A vigorous snort from Chambers, one from Miles.

"Good. Get yourself fixed up and I'll see you tomorrow."

"Okay."

"I don't care how. And don't make me hunt for you."

"Won't, I promise."

"Make me waste my goddamned time tracking you down. You should fucking know better, Miles. And you're running out of hands."

"I know. Won't happen again."

"This shit isn't fun for me."

"I'm sorry, Chris."

I backed out of the hallway and turned away. Chambers passed and entered the washroom. The bartender asked if I wanted something and I asked if I could call a cab. She said that was against the rules, that drunks tended to get sentimental and dial Mom and Dad in Saskatoon, but she'd order me one if I wanted.

In my peripheral I watched Chambers head toward the front, dropping a brown paper towel on the dance floor as he passed. I put two twenties on the bar.

"Order one for the guy in the alley," I said. "Give the cabbie one of these up front, tell him St. Paul's."

"Do I want to know?" she asked. Then, answering her own question, she picked up the receiver.

Twenty-Four

Sonia wasn't answering her phone. I thought of leaving a message but figured she wouldn't want that. But then I wasn't sure I cared what she wanted. Images came to mind: Miles's mangled hand and the nauseating way he'd apologized to Chambers. If Sonia had known—and if she hadn't known—

I stayed with the Sorenson case. It was more manageable, if no less perplexing. A picture was emerging of Tabitha Sorenson. Clever and foolish, furious and ironically detached. She'd see the injustices of the world as justification for fraud. When the opportunity to borrow the money was practically dropped in her lap, it was too good to pass up.

That was the key—opportunity.

Tabitha was smart, maybe brilliant. She'd executed her scheme well. But she'd planned it on the fly. Emotion had guided her—exhilaration, fear, and something else that I couldn't think of.

In the small office on Pender I cracked the window, allowing the chill and the sound of rain to lull me to sleep. When I woke someone was coming through the door. Kay, carrying coffee and a paper sleeve holding a bagel.

"Your phone's dead," she said. "You weren't at your place or Hastings."

"Something up?"

"Just worried," Kay said.

"Don't be."

I dumped the remnants of last night's tea in the trash and plugged in the kettle.

Stringing a tea bag around the handle of the mug, I said to Kay, "Sake of argument, let's say Tabitha made off with half a million dollars. What would a young, somewhat educated woman in her twenties do with that kind of money?"

"She doesn't seem like she'd be into ponies."

"Is that what you'd do?"

"Well, I'd never work again," Kay said. She thought about it. "I do like horses. Travel, maybe. You?"

I took the seat by the window. "Get a house. Maybe buy this building, fix it up."

"My half brother, the landlord-slash-private eye. Or would you quit?"

"I'd probably pick my clients more carefully."

"You'd never quit," Kay said. "Without this job you'd be like that old guy from *Shawshank*, end up hanging from a ceiling beam somewhere."

"Thing is," I said, "it's not that much money. Whatever Tabitha did, she'd have to be careful. She could get out of the country, but where would she go? Did she use a false passport? Or sneak into the States?" I thought of something. "You know if Tabitha took a language course?"

"Which question did you want me to answer?" Kay said.

"Last one. How much French did she learn?"

"As much as you need to pass high school in Vancouver," Kay said. "Which is—"

"Next to none. And college?"

"Spanish Zero Nine Nine, 'Intro to Latin American Culture Through Film.' That's all."

"Tabitha's not a career criminal," I said. "She's getting by on brains and audacity. Remember, she didn't high-tail after the scandal, she was around for the first part of the audit."

"And then split after because why? Waiting for the right time?"

"Maybe," I said.

"Or maybe something scared her," Kay ventured. "Like what if Tabitha was in on it with one of the others. Dhillon, maybe, they were close. They could've had a falling out. Or they could all be in on it together."

"If she did have an accomplice, I'd bet on Mastellotto. More of a political angle than a financial one. That's who she looked up to, her last couple semesters."

"What about Dana Essex?" Kay said. "Don't laugh, she would've seen a lot of Tabitha, same as Mastellotto. Plus she was on that events committee."

"Possible," I said, "unless you've met her and seen she's the type who looks both ways before crossing her own driveway. She doesn't know Tabitha well. And I don't think she has the first clue about money."

"She's paying us," Kay said.

"Which tells you plenty."

Down the other end of the street, a tour bus rolled by at full speed. Detour, maybe. Or maybe they were including this area in a "Seamy Side of Vancouver" tour. Not too much seaminess in the middle of the day.

"This point it's all conjecture," I said. "She might've had help, but she kept her family and schoolmates out of the loop. We'll learn more from her credit report than we did from them."

"All those people we talked to," Kay said, "and we still don't know who she is. How can someone hide so much of themselves? It's like maybe even she didn't know who she was."

Twenty-Five

The credit report finally came in. After lunch I walked over to the Hastings office. I picked the form out of my in-box along with the rest of the correspondence and locked myself in the boardroom.

Tabitha Sorenson's credit score was in the high 700s. Good for anyone and miraculous for a college kid. She'd made regular credit card payments. Same with her student loan. No other borrowing, no serious delinquencies, zero cases of fraud. Credit card paid to nothing and then canceled. Except for her apartment, Tabitha had settled all her financial affairs before she disappeared. The document told me little.

I phoned her credit card company. It took patience to get through to a human, and the tiniest of deceptions to speak to a manager with the authority to pull up a client's records. I asked about large purchases, anything out of the ordinary.

"One sec, sir." *Clack clack clack*. I tugged at the corner staple of the leatherette covering on the boardroom table.

"Mostly just bookstores and coffee shops," the manager said. "Two thousand eight hundred dollars to something called Surrey Polytech."

"Tuition," I said. "Anything else?"

"Forty-two hundred dollars paid to a Luxuria Travel, also in Surrey. Hmm."

"'Hmm' what?"

Clack clack. I pulled out the staple and tried to reinsert it. The holes in the leatherette wouldn't line up with those in the wood.

The manager came back on, saving me from a second chorus of "Highway to the Danger Zone."

"The purchase was made on March seventh and then the same amount was refunded on April third. Five months ago."

"Her last purchase?"

"May twenty-eight, coffee shop. Her balance was one thousand eight hundred and forty and thirty-two, with a minimum payment of forty-eight fifty. Then came the refund, and on June fifth the balance was paid down completely."

"Can you tell if that was by check?"

Clack clack. The Danger Zone segued to Black Velvet in that slow southern style. "Online payment through her credit union," she said. "No activity since."

I thanked her and hung up.

On June fifth she'd paid her debts in full. It was hard to know what to make of that. There were enough credit card alternatives that it didn't explain where she was or what she was up to. However Tabitha Sorenson was making her way in the world, it wasn't by paying eighteen percent.

As I was thinking about how to proceed, Jeff knocked and entered. He tapped his phone and held it so I could view the screen. A text from a number I didn't recognize.

NEWTON XCHANGE

TONITE @ TEN

ALONE

Jeff sat next to me. "From Hayes, I assume. How are we gonna play this?"

"Much as I'd like to sit back and let you go, it has to be me. You don't know the case. Plus it's your wedding tomorrow. I'll take the Hayes brothers over what Marie would do to me, you got hurt."

"So what do I do?"

"Hang back, plan your wedding."

"Dave," Jeff said, "you know there's a good chance this is them trying to hurt you."

"I've been hurt before."

"Which taught you nothing?"

Jeff stood up abruptly, put a hand on his stomach. He shushed me when I asked what was going on with him.

After five slow diaphragmatic breaths, he returned to his seat. "Chest pains. Doctor says they're brought on by anxiety."

"I can take care of myself," I said.

He moved his gaze to the floor and said, "It's more to do with the wedding. I just want it to go well. I mean, for Marie's sake. It means a lot to her."

I suspected there was more of Jeff vested in the wedding than he'd admit, but it wasn't the time to pry. I told him to leave the meeting to me.

Twenty-Six

Luxuria Travel was on the lower floor of the Surrey Central Mall, sandwiched between a TNT supermarket and a passport office. The sandwich board outside the travel agency offered a list of airfares in red, with PLUS APPLICABLE TAXES AND FEES below each quoted price.

"Weird," Kay said. "It's cheaper to fly to Paris than to London."

"Different airlines," I suggested.

"But you fly over England to get to France."

A woman in a brightly colored chunni sat behind the laminate counter. On the wall was a business license and a community service award for Bhavya Brar, owner-operator. She smiled and shook our hands.

I asked her about the two transactions from Tabitha's credit card, the purchase and return. She opened her spreadsheet program and scrolled down.

"I know who you mean," Brar said. "She come in a second time and I know, one day, I have this conversation with you."

"She just felt wrong to you," I said.

"Yes. When she come the second time she look different. Her hair is shorter and much redder. She's very worried."

I held up Tabitha's photo. Brar nodded, it was the same woman.

"Where was she going," I said, "and why'd she cancel?"

While she was looking it up, a customer entered the store. Brar asked us to come back in half an hour and excused herself.

We bought London Fogs at the Waves Café and sat outside on the concrete bench. It was raining lightly. The only people around us were smokers, huddled under the small patch of awning away from the doors. We watched a woman in drawstring sweatpants drag a ten-year-old toward the parking lot while pushing a two-child stroller.

"This place makes me never want to have kids," Kay said.

It was after four o'clock when we drifted back. The customer had gone and a child in a dress shirt and a black patka sat on the edge of the counter. Bhavya Brar came out of the back office carrying a two-page printout.

"Why I remember that woman," Brar said, "is because she canceled her booking to Costa Rica, then make it again."

She showed me the itineraries and a photocopy of a check. Two passengers on a June flight to San Jose, Tabitha Eleanor Sorenson and Sabar S. Gill. Same flight, adjacent seat numbers. The first booking paid for by credit card, then canceled, the second booking by corporate check. The company's name was Mi Mundo and it had a Kingsway address.

I tapped Gill's name. "He come in with her?"

Bhavya Brar said, "First time, he give his details over the phone. Second time we copy paste."

I asked her for a copy of the check. As we headed to the parking lot, Kay said, "'My World.' That's what Mi Mundo translates as."

"You'll have to follow up on this," I said. "I've got to meet someone later."

"Fine," Kay said. "But if you have to go look for them in Costa Rica, you're not leaving me behind."

Twenty-Seven

Mi Mundo was a paper company, incorporated by Tabitha Sorenson in March before she disappeared. It held no assets and the corporate head-quarters was a post office box in a Shoppers Drug Mart. No company taxes had ever been filed.

At eight o'clock I walked home to my flat on East Broadway. I cooked a veggie patty and served it over rice with a can of green beans, smothering the mess in sriracha. After choking that down, I poured a tumbler of Bulleit bourbon and spun a Muddy Waters record. Drinking TNT and smoking dynamite. When it was time for the shift change, I phoned Sonia and told her I needed to see her.

She still had her key and she let herself in. I took her coat and offered her a drink.

"Food first, if you have any."

"I've got cereal, corn bran and generic Rice Krispies," I said. "The milk's still got a day or two on it."

"What a gourmet," she said, choosing the corn bran. As she ate I told her about Chambers.

"He's moonlighting as muscle for Anthony Qiu," I said. "I watched him bust up the hand of a guy named Miles. Definitely a beef over money."

Sonia nodded, continuing to eat.

"Not quite the reaction I expected," I said.

She set down her bowl. "I looked up Anthony Qiu when you men-tioned him. He's the son-in-law of Vincent Leung. Leung has all sorts of gang connections, especially heroin and guns. But Qiu seems limited to loan-sharking. His place is a front to wash Leung's money."

"I had a run-in with Qiu a while back," I said. "He could've made things much more difficult than he did. Got the sense he was playing it safe."

I took Sonia's bowl to the sink and brought back the bourbon and another glass. I stared at the bottle.

"I should be mad you're lying to me," I said. "I wish you didn't feel you had to."

She stared at me. I mimicked the demure expression on her face: "'Lying?' she intoned, with wide-eyed innocence. 'Moi?'"

Sonia didn't smile.

I changed tack. "How can I do what you want, Sonia, how can I help you, when you're holding back on me?"

"I told you you didn't have to," she said.

"So it's either trust you implicitly and question none of this, or for-sake you completely?"

"You know how the job is," she said. "I don't have a lot of channels open to me."

I said, "What do you want me to do about Chambers? Let's start there."

"What are the options?"

"Ignore him."

"No."

"Turn him in."

"No."

"Talk it through with him."

"I can't," she said.

"That doesn't leave much."

"Can you stay on him for another week?" she asked. "I know it's asking a lot. I need the time to work something out."

"Another week," I assented. "With two provisions. You run Sabar Gill through CPIC. He's on a flight itinerary with my missing girl."

"I'll try. And second?"

I poured. "Some time in the future, we sit down over a bottle not unlike this one, and we tell each other everything."

"I'd like that."

We finished our drinks and she left. Her kiss before she wended her way through the patio to the street was one part whiskey, one part something else.

Twenty-Eight

Small shops and an antiquated youth center surrounded Newton Exchange, a transit hub in the middle of industrial Surrey. People crowded under the bus stop awnings, waiting, ignoring the beggars and dealers who circulated between clusters. I stared through the windshield of the van at the empty parking lot, listening to the wiper blades and the skitter of rain on the roof.

Nine thirty turned to nine forty-five. A teenager in a black bandanna and thick survival jacket approached the van, knocked, told me he had what I was looking for.

"What you need?" Small inside his jacket, eyes wide and tentative.

I shook my head, I was fine. He wished me a nice night and walked back to the turnaround.

I'd debated with Jeff about taking a gun. He hadn't advocated for it, but he'd been puzzled at my reasoning. Introducing a firearm wouldn't improve my safety, I told him. So far they hadn't threatened me. That was no guarantee, but Dalton Hayes had seemed somewhat reasonable.

Beneath Jeff's question, though, was the deeper one, the one I'd never been able to answer. Why go at all?

Tabitha Sorenson was unknown to me, and all I owed Dana Essex was her money's worth. A nice little show of effort followed by a shrug of the shoulders. Sorry, ma'am, gave it my best. Make the check out to Wakeland & Chen, and don't forget the ampersand. If anything comes up I'll let you know.

As I waited I tried out my usual responses, knowing they were all insufficient.

The possibility that doing this made a difference.

[in what?]

The satisfaction of work done to the utmost of one's ability.

[to what end?]

I'd never articulated an answer that had passed my own bullshit detector. Maybe there were no answers. Just momentum and curiosity, a lack of sense and a need to know.

A white Denali swung into the bus loop and jumped the curb. It stopped a few feet from me. The back door opened. The interior light showed Cody Hayes sitting sideways across the back bench, holding something pink and plastic in his hand.

I stepped out of the van and walked toward the truck before he could order me to. I leaned my head inside.

"Where's the other guy?" Cody asked.

"Not here," I said, wondering the same thing. Dalton Hayes had the authority and the temperament to reason with; the look Cody gave me meant he hadn't forgotten our last encounter.

He slid his feet off the bench, making room. "Got something you need to see."

I waited for him to elaborate. Cody jabbed whatever he was holding into the carpet and idly pulled it out. I realized it was the handle of a machete. He was stabbing the floor out of restless boredom.

"You coming?" he finally said. "I'm 'sposed to take you there. If you want. If not, go fuck yourself."

"Where?"

Again no elaboration.

"I'll follow you," I said.

Cody stabbed the blade to the hilt into the cushion next to him. "Into the fucking car," he said.

Bus passengers ignored us. It continued to rain. I thought about it and then climbed inside, closing the door behind me.

Twenty-Nine

Zero Avenue.

We took the highway that led to the border, through farmland and swaths of undeveloped properties. Cow shit and ocean scented the air. The driver turned off onto an unlit strip of asphalt. More farms, a gas station. We passed Matsqui prison.

Nearly half an hour later we made a turn onto gravel. The driver cut the headlights.

I'd asked Cody where we were going, who was at the other end of the trip. He didn't speak. He kept his hand gripped over the pink plastic handle of the machete, favoring me with his best scowl.

The driver was South Asian, his head shaved and a thick beard covering his jowls. He glanced at his rearview constantly as if worried. Our eyes met. His showed something like pity.

My phone buzzed with an incoming text. Cody took it from me before I could answer.

"No phones," he said.

The truck stopped and the driver exited. Through the windshield I saw him unlock a thick chain that was barring the road. It landed on the gravel, making a sound like spilling coins. He rejoined us in the truck.

We passed an unlit house as we headed into the heart of an untended field. Down a steep hill, over a black and corrugated landscape. The rain had stopped.

I'd assumed Dalton Hayes would be waiting for us, that he'd asked to see me. As the truck braked I saw nothing around but farmland. Cody told me to get out.

"And go where?" I said. "Where's your brother?"

I wasn't prepared for the kick. It caught me in the ribcage, doubled me over and jolted me into the door. I fell forward. A wet hand pulled me from the truck, dropping me onto the spongy soil.

Boots came down and I was told to stand up. Before my vision could clear, a fist caught me, the glint off steel the last thing I saw. I stumbled and collapsed into the mud.

"My brother asked you nicely, tell us where she is." Cody's boot struck my thigh, stamping down, grinding me into the dirt. "You fucking tell us. Understand? Do you?"

I needed five minutes to clear my head. Ten seconds, even. Cody made sure I didn't have either. I was dropped and spun, prodded, hit where I couldn't defend myself.

Mud and water and pain were constants. I thought I heard the crunch of tires. My eyes focused on a distant light, cut off, my vision spoiled.

It was an open field, the ground furrowed with long pools of rainwater. Cody was herding me away from the truck. I couldn't tell where the driver was.

The flat disk of steel knuckles struck my collar bone. I turned over, staring face down into the water.

"Stay there," said Cody.

I tried to disobey but my body didn't give me a choice.

The sound of spilling liquid. The water near me took on a noxious benzene smell. I breathed and coughed. Heard the *scrup scrup* of a lighter being struck.

The puddle near my face exploded.

Cody was laughing as I spun away from the flames. "We can do this all night," he said. "Get the answers outta you."

"What answers?" I managed.

"Like you don't know."

Something struck my hip with more force than the other blows combined. I screamed, thrashed.

As I crawled backward I saw him clutching a baseball bat, strolling toward me, the trenches behind him burning.

He darted right, swinging the bat playfully, forcing me toward the fire. "Having some fun now," he said.

A gunshot stopped us both.

The driver marched forward, hands held up like he was about to fall on his face. Behind him, Jeff Chen, holding a small black pistol to the driver's ear.

He told the driver to lie down. After the driver complied, Jeff calmly stepped over the burning trench, holding the bunched-up tails of his overcoat with his free hand. He motioned for Cody Hayes to toss down the bat.

"Tailed you from the bus loop," he said to me. "You okay?"

I could stand, though I wasn't sure what damage I'd sustained. Everything hurt, which I took as a good sign.

"Where'd you get the gun?" I asked him.

"Bought it," Jeff said. "Think I'd bring a kid into the world and not be able to protect him?"

In answer, I hunched over and threw up.

Thirty

Jeff asked Cody why they'd brought me here.

"Dalton said to. Said he talked to his friend and he wanted you scared off."

"The friend did, you mean." Jeff gestured to the bat, the steel knuckle dusters and the dying flames. "Your idea of scaring off?"

"Dalton's friend said this guy doesn't scare easy."

"No," Jeff said, looking at me. "He really doesn't."

At gunpoint Cody's manner became deferential. He explained how Tabitha had come to him with the deal. Seven hundred thousand clean and untraceable dollars, loaned out for six months. Her return was twenty-two percent.

She'd told them if it worked out they'd be able to do it again, maybe perpetually. Lending them cash, then laundering their returns. This would be a trial.

"What did you use the money for?" I asked. My breath had returned and I'd wiped off my chin as best I could.

"Buy product," Cody said. "The fuck you think?"

When he saw we weren't impressed, he added, "Chemicals. Fucking government makes them tough to get, got to pay our ephedrine guy in advance. Once we off-loaded, the money went back to Tab."

"But you don't know where she went."

"That's why Dalton wanted you to find her. No one knows where she is."

"Who owns this place?" I asked.

"Dalton's friend. Lets us use it sometimes. Guy's a biker."

"His name."

"Terry Rhodes," Cody said. Even at gunpoint, he half-smiled at the reaction the name brought from us.

"Tabitha was never out here?" I asked. "Never had dealings with Rhodes?"

"Fuck no. She only dealt with me and Dalton. We were hoping—" he caught himself.

"Hoping what?" Jeff asked.

"That this would be our deal," Cody said.

I said to Jeff, "He means Tabitha's operation would be strictly League of Nations. They weren't going to kick up to the bikers."

"We weren't," Cody said. "Have to now."

It had been too good to be true: a financial operation all their own. Maybe Tabitha had sold a long-term plan to the Hayes brothers, knowing she could only perform the scheme once. The possibility of repeating it would ensure her safety through the first transaction.

The driver was still facedown in the mud. The gasoline fire had long gone out. I could close my hand without too much pain.

"I'm parked close to the gate," Jeff said. "Followed you out here and cut my lights. You ready to leave?"

"Almost," I said.

I stripped off my jacket, now ruined by mud. Walked over to Cody.

"Is this going to end here?" I asked him. "Stay between us?"

"Yeah," he said. "Yes. I promise."

"And we never see each other again. Your word."

He nodded vigorously. "Swear to god. Swear on my moms."

"Good. Then Jeff won't have to shoot you. You feel like it, by all means, defend yourself."

I hit him below the cheek and dropped him. Cody looked up with a child's what-was-that-for innocence. Behind me Jeff said something, but I was concentrating on getting hold of Cody's shirt front and hitting him again, splitting open his mouth.

Cody scooted backwards, away from me, across the mud. I lunged forward and struck his left eye socket. I sat on his chest and hammered at his face. Slowly. Considering each blow. Swatting away his hands when they tried to ward them off.

"Enough," Jeff said.

But it wasn't. I hit him again. I hit him until I was sure I'd broken his jaw. Until I was panting and a fresh round of nausea was poised to erupt out of me. Until Cody Hayes had been reduced to a whimpering, quivering thing.

He was sobbing. Snot mixed with black blood. I stood up and wiped my knuckles.

"I'm good now," I said.

Thirty-One

The shower stall of a one-bedroom flat in East Van isn't the ideal convalescent space. I made do. A long scalding shower, several ice packs, a double slug of cask-strength bourbon and a fitful night's sleep.

At ten the next morning I was back at Hastings, doused with ancient liniment from my bathroom cabinet and nursing a pot of Earl Grey. I needed to talk with Sabar Gill.

The flight purchase connected him to Tabitha Sorenson. A boyfriend, maybe, or co-conspirator. Maybe the cause of her disappearance.

There were plenty of Gills in the Pacific Northwest. I narrowed by age and location. None in Surrey but one likely candidate in Vancouver.

The Vancouver Gill was twenty-six and held a masters degree in Library Science. He worked in the Special Collections department of the Vancouver Public Library's central branch. His picture on the VPL website showed a handsome man with short-cut hair and beard and pensive eyes.

I phoned the library. The cheerful male voice in Special Collections told me Gill wouldn't be in till one. I asked for his phone number, but the voice wasn't comfortable with sharing that information.

I was flipping through the audit report when Jeff entered the boardroom. He made a show of locking the door and unfurling the blinds so that we were secluded. He said, "We should talk about last night."

"If you want."

"I don't remember much of what got said on the ride home. But the way you hit that guy—" He looked at me as if inspecting glass merchandise for hairline cracks and chipped edges. He spread his hands. "And here you are, drinking tea."

"Coffee after breakfast fucks with my bladder."

"Worse than a baseball bat?"

I pushed back from the table and rummaged in the bottom drawer of the file cabinet. "If you want me to say thanks again."

"Not about thanks, Dave." My partner spoke with a hint of exasperation. "You hit him when you didn't have to."

The knuckles on my right hand had swollen to red burial mounds. I used my left to fetch the parcel out of the back of the drawer.

"We're gone tomorrow on our honeymoon," Jeff said. "Which means you're in charge. I'd like to think things'll be okay while I'm gone. Like very much to think that."

"So think it."

"Hard when last night you nearly beat a guy to death."

"We're never going to agree on that," I said. "So let's not hash this out again."

"I think we should."

"All right. You were the one who pointed a gun at Cody Hayes."

"To rescue you."

"Yes, and thank you again. But Jeff, he's afraid of the gun, not of you. He's a bully. His whole point, the fire, the weapons, was to scare me. Intimidate us into doing what he wants. We needed to show we can't be intimidated."

"So what's to stop him from getting a gun of his own and coming after us?" Jeff said.

"There's no guarantee, but he's afraid now. Bullies prefer easy targets."

"Know what I think?" Jeff said. "He did scare you, and you wanted to pay him back for that."

I handed him the parcel, a square the size of a hand wrapped in cheap brown paper.

"What the hell is this?"

"Your wedding present."

He tore away the paper, revealing a mocked-up book jacket. A giant magnifying glass on the cover, the lens raising details on a fingerprint and a Sherlock Holmes hunting cap. The words *"Advanced Techniques for the Contemporary Interviewer* by Jun Fei Jefferson Chen" in a bland default font. I'd wrapped the cover around an old copy of *Tai Pan* someone had left in our waiting room.

"Not the actual cover, of course," I said. "There's a publisher on the North Shore. They mostly do cookbooks. Got the idea from Tabitha's mother. They'll work with you and put this out professionally. No money, but such is the writing life."

He held the book up and grinned. "Holy shit."

Jeff was a notoriously difficult person to shop for, and it felt good to hit the mark. At Christmas the year before, he'd walked into the office on December twenty-third holding a copy of Nomeansno's *Small Parts Isolated and Destroyed*, the same album I'd just finished wrapping to put on his desk. "Look what was on sale," he'd said, and I'd taken his present home with me.

Now he turned the book over in his hands. "This is great. Thanks, Dave. Thank you." Suddenly serious: "So's this mean you're gonna stop teasing me about writing it?"

"Not a fucking chance," I said.

Thirty-Two

I had two hours to kill before Sabar Gill's shift started at the library. With the office abuzz with last-minute wedding preparations, I headed out early, walking up Beatty. Past the viaduct, past the decommissioned tanks outside the drill hall. The bruise on my hip meant each step was accompanied by a jab of pain.

As I neared the sandstone coliseum that housed the library, I detoured into Yaletown, stopping outside Anthony Qiu's restaurant.

The Monte Carlo attracted a lunchtime crowd of yuppies and swells. A few couples lingered on the heated patio despite the light spatter of rain. Music blared from inside the restaurant, some radio station playing all your soft-rock favorites.

I took a seat on the patio with my back to the glass. The lunch menu presented an array of thirty-dollar salads. I ordered a double Bulleit with an ice water chaser and told the waitress I wanted to see Anthony.

"Mr. Qiu is very busy," she said. I gave her a business card to take into him. She looked at it and smiled and disappeared into the restaurant. I never got my drink.

Before Qiu showed himself, two heavies came out and took up position at a nearby table. One was Chinese, acne-pitted, with the bulge of a gun under the breast of his burgundy suit. The other was white, in khakis and suede, with a face like a ruined holiday. Neither made any pretense of ordering anything.

Eventually Anthony Qiu strolled out. He draped his tan blazer over the back of the aluminum chair opposite me. The top button of his dress shirt was undone and his sleeves were rolled up. A handkerchief spotted with diamonds bloomed from his breast pocket. His smile showed patience and poise and very little humor.

"David," he said pleasantly as he sat. "You moved up in the world. Business is brisk, unh?" His grin was a gleaming white parody of cheerfulness, a botched take on warmth.

"It's picking up," I said.

"Good, good. I'm happy for you. What'd you want to see me for?"

"Just to visit," I said. "How's Mr. Leung doing?"

Qiu's smile tightened, gained a remonstrative edge. One of the two men behind me shifted his chair.

"He's fine," Qiu finally said. "Has some issues with his health. You know him?"

"Of him. Doesn't surprise me about his health. Crime has to weigh on you, doesn't it?" I scratched my cheek idly, watching Qiu watch me. "All that added stress, spending your time wondering what other people know, when the other shoe will drop. 'Less you're a psychopath. Then I guess it's easy."

"I wouldn't know," Qiu said. "I just run my restaurant."

"Of course you do." I looked at his hired muscle. "Who are these charmers?"

"Waitstaff," Qiu said.

"They do look like minimum-wagers." I nodded to the one in khakis. "'Specially that one. He looks like he'd be a very dangerous man to someone tied up and unconscious. Which with a face like that is probably what he calls dating."

The man in khakis rattled his table getting to his feet. He shoved his chair out of the way, moving toward me.

"Nagy," Qiu said, holding up a hand. "Have a seat."

"Yeah, Nagy, have a seat." Nagy didn't move. To Qiu I said, "How much of your crew do you actually control?"

Qiu's eyes hadn't left his subordinate's. Nagy blew out a sigh and returned to his chair. The diners left on the patio avoided looking at us.

"What exactly did you come here for, David?" Qiu asked.

"I heard you do a splendid salmon penne."

"Be serious."

"Every year this city changes," I said. "Developers move in. We lose whole neighborhoods. Rate of change like that, sometimes I wonder who I actually know that's still here."

"I'm not likely to leave Vancouver," Qiu said.

I shrugged and stood up. I looked at Nagy like I wasn't impressed. Back to Qiu to nod and make my exit.

"Is that it?" Qiu said. He was scrutinizing me like a poker player watching for tells. "Last time we spoke longer."

I smiled at him. "Last time you were more generous with the whiskey."

Thirty-Three

Sonia once told me I had a knack for completing the kind of tasks that shouldn't be started in the first place. I'd set out to frustrate and mystify Anthony Qiu, and to do so without breathing a word about Chris Chambers and what I'd seen behind the Crossroads Inn. What remained was to see how Qiu would jump.

As I opened the front door of the library, a sparrow brushed past my ear. It fluttered and gained altitude, sailing up to the heights of the crescent-shaped concourse. It settled above a large reading-is-good banner featuring a quote from Milton. I walked past the pizza and coffee shops and through the scanners. I zigzagged up the escalators to the seventh floor.

Near the help desk, a bearded man in a starched paisley shirt and suspenders was laying out a display under glass. History books with black-and-white photos on their covers showing haggard Sikhs, placed next to a model of a cargo vessel turned on its side. The man adjusted a piece of Bristol board with the title pasted to it, "Rethinking the *Komagata Maru*."

I leaned over his shoulder to examine the display and to make sure I was talking to Sabar Gill. "What's to rethink?" I asked. "Wasn't it a bad decision?"

"It was a horrific decision," Gill said. "A Japanese ship full of Indian passengers denied entrance into the country for no reason other than they were the wrong skin color, spoke the wrong language. British citizens, but of the second class. It's an event that's still being reinterpreted, hence the display." He grinned. "But if I have to explain the title, maybe that's not a good sign."

I examined the craftsmanship of the boat, which lacked only a miniature crew and passengers.

"A local artist," Gill said. "She donated it for this exhibit. Did you need a hand finding something?"

"I'm looking for a Mr. Gill," I said. "Unfortunately I dinged a car in the underground lot. Someone told me it was his and he'd be up on this floor. Know where I could find him?"

"That would be me." Gill's expression soured a little. We shook hands and I noticed the wedding ring.

"I think I only kissed the fender," I said. "Why don't we take a look and then decide how to make this right."

Sabar Gill replaced the glass lid of the display. I looked around baffled and said, "Mind leading the way? I'm not even sure how I got up here."

"There's an elevator this way," he said. When we were on board I asked him how long he'd been working here.

"Close to four months," he said. "I was part-timing during grad school. I finished and took some time off, but then a position opened. It's pretty much the job I've always wanted."

There was an element of self-conscious irony to his dress and mannerisms, but Gill spoke with a genuine reverence for his vocation. He was almost bashful about it. Curating library displays and wading through the stacks wasn't everyone's dream. But it was his, and he accepted that.

"What does a librarian do when he takes time off?" I asked.

"See a bit of the world. Relax." He stared at me. "What do you do for a living, Mr.—"

"James," I said. "I install security systems. I know that might sound boring, but it's actually fascinating work. Are you in the market? Because I can get you a honey of a deal. Person can't be too careful."

"Maybe," Gill said.

"We should swap insurance info." I dug out a Manitoba driver's license in the name of William J. James. I took Gill's and copied down his details. The 400 block of Quebec Street. A Mount Pleasant address, not an apartment.

I followed Gill as we threaded through the parking level, an ominous maze of concrete and flickering neon. He stopped by an SL-series Mercedes and crouched down to examine the fender.

"Not a scratch," he said. "No harm done. Where's your car?"

I looked at the oil stains on the concrete. "I feel pretty stupid about this. The car I touched was a Honda. I think I'm parked on the other end."

"I don't know anyone who drives a Honda," Gill said. "Hope it works out."

"I'll muddle through."

Thirty-Four

Jeff and Marie had rented the dining hall at the Shaughnessy Golf and Country Club for the wedding reception. The décor was classy and the food was a hodgepodge of traditions and styles, from shark fin soup (Jeff's mother insisted, even though it was illegal and damn near tasteless) to filet mignon. The Bon Ton Bakery outdid itself with a tiered matrimonial cake, topped with figures that vaguely resembled the bride and groom.

The newlyweds shared a microphone, mangling Marvin Gaye and Tammi Terrell. Jeff's uncles traded cigars and dirty stories. His cousin Shuzhen, our former receptionist, emerged from the law library long enough for the ceremony and left after the second dance. Kay skulked by the bar with one of Marie's cousins.

I'm not a party person. I mingled as long as I could, then drove to Hastings and took the work van over toward Mount Pleasant. I parked opposite Sabar Gill's house on Quebec Street. Seated in the back on a milk crate, I could stare through the tinted panel at Gill's front door.

Gill lived in a renovated Vancouver Special, a facade of masonwork below a gray-painted top story with a Juliette balcony. All lights soft, all curtains drawn.

The rain slid over the windshield and crackled off the roof. I'd liberated a flask's worth of Macallan Ten from Jeff and Marie's open bar. Gill's television glowed through the curtains. He stood and moved left, his frame appearing in the kitchen. Simultaneous movement in the living room. Another form stood up in front of the television. Gill's date, maybe. Popcorn and late-night TV, probably what Chambers and the waif were doing.

I opened the back door and climbed down, putting my feet in a stream of runoff from a clogged storm drain. I crossed to the sidewalk in front of Gill's house. From here the shade in the kitchen seemed feminine, the other shade, slinking back onto the couch, more closely resembled Gill.

I took two steps onto the lawn and was bathed in cold white neon. Motion-activated lighting. I stepped back and walked to the corner, hooked left and then down the alley.

At the back of Gill's small untended yard stood a rotting garage with one door hanging askew. The same drapes hung on the house's rear windows as out front, no movement behind them.

In an adjacent backyard I spied a dog's chew toy. I hopped the low fence and retrieved it. No lights, no alarms. I returned to the van.

The Wakeland & Chen work vans contained audiovisual equipment, a camera and tripod, microphone and field recorder. I extended the tripod legs and threaded the camera onto the base, training it on Gill's door. The window of the van had a slight overhang, which kept the glass clear. I adjusted for low light, zoomed in, and focused.

If only Kay or anyone else had been free—but they were all busy living it up. The entire population of the world was paired off, reeling drunkenly toward the doors of their rented suites, to fuck and tell each other sweet nothings.

This was how I spent my time—peering through strangers' windows. How I spent birthdays, holidays. Alone with the work. It was sick, perhaps, but it was a choice I'd made. Like Gill and his love of books.

I waited for a commercial break, a bathroom trip, something. At last the couple stood up and stretched. The shapes diverged, Gill this time heading to the kitchen. I felt the weight of the rubber toy. I jogged toward the house, hucked the toy at the living room window. I saw the throw was good and ran.

Two blocks up I paused, shivering. I went right, a long circuit to Broadway, past the darkened storefront of Mountain Equipment Co-op with its windows advertising backpacks and skis. Before I turned back down Quebec I made sure no one was waiting outside of the Gill house, no extra lights on. All told it was twenty-three minutes since I'd thrown the toy.

I crept back to the van, then drove a few minutes before stopping to check the camera. In the viewfinder, I saw myself throw the toy and run out of frame.

A moment later the curtains parted in both kitchen and den. It was clearly Gill in the kitchen window, but the woman was out of focus, and she quickly snapped the curtains closed.

The shades reconverged. I swore. Drenched to the bone and nothing to show for it.

Then the front door of the house opened and Gill stepped out, triggering the motion-activated porch light. He studied the ground and found the toy, smiled, relieved by such a harmless explanation for the noise. He turned toward the door and held up the toy.

And framed in the orange light of the doorway, evidently sharing his relief, Tabitha Sorenson smiled back at him.

Thirty-Five

That it was her, no question. The face and eyes and freckles hadn't changed. She'd altered her hair—darkened it, cropped it Jean Seberg short. She was holding a wine glass and dressed in flannel and sweats. Shorter than I'd expected, with a more mature and slightly weary posture.

The biggest difference from any pictures I'd seen of her was that Tabitha seemed happy. When Gill returned to the house she kissed him and they went in, arms around each other.

That was the case. And yet finding her begged a whole series of other questions.

It was Dana Essex's money I was taking, so she'd be the first to know. How to tell her would be the problem. She'd seen Tabitha as her romantic salvation. But Tabitha was involved with someone, which Essex would also have to learn. However I broke it to my client, the news meant a broken heart.

Well, hearts break. They break and break. Hers was no different.

I hunt-and-pecked out my report, then saved it to the company's cloud storage. I thought of Tabitha and the modest house on Quebec Street. What was that saying about fortunes and crime? Some fortune. All the risks and manipulations had been done so that she and Gill could live in a real house, in a real neighborhood, like their parents had done. It put her suburban rebellion in perspective. But it also served as a sad commentary on the city and the times. You want to live here, on your own terms? Be prepared to steal.

I was reading over the report, sitting near my window on Pender Street, when a knock on the office door interrupted. I opened it, thinking it would be Kay, hungover and looking for clerical work to kill the afternoon.

Instead, Chris Chambers leaned on the frame, grinning down at me. Dressed in slacks and a suede jacket, a peaked tweed cap on his head. He had a brown paper bag in his left hand.

"Dave," he said, grabbing my hand. "You remember me? We met a couple of times when you were still on the job. Rough deal, that. Feel like a taste of Glenlivet?"

I showed him in. Chambers took in the room, not impressed but keeping it amiable. I poured some of his scotch into two office mugs and took mine to the chair behind the desk.

"Main office is on West Hastings," I said.

"And this is your fortress of solitude?" He showed his capped teeth. "Place to get away. I understand. *Sláinte.*"

He raised his mug and drank to my health, refilled and topped mine up liberally.

"Might seem funny," he said, "but I feel I know you pretty well. You're the subject of a lot of conversations I've been having."

"Oh?"

"From what my partner tells me, you and she are close. Sonia Drego?"

"I know Sonia," I said.

"From what I hear." He mock-saluted. "She's a fine girl. And not a bad little police, either."

"Much better than I was."

"You feel safe going through a door with her, which is not something I can say about every female officer I've served with." He drank quickly and shuddered. "Male either. Also knew your foster father a bit. He was still walking the Sixth when I was coming up. Good man and a goddamn shame what happened to him. Car accident, wasn't it?" I nodded and he reiterated, "A damn shame."

I sipped the whiskey. It burned pleasantly. I waited for Chambers to come around to it.

"You must miss him," Chambers said at length.

"Sure."

"He raised you."

"Him and my mother, foster mother, yeah."

"Nice you found Sonia," he said, "the two of you both not having much family and all."

I nodded, thinking of the way Chambers had mangled Miles's hand. My expression remained neutral.

"I was like that myself," Chambers said. "Father not around, mom working and splitting her time 'tween me and her other family. Rough world."

"And it doesn't get easier," I said.

"Surely does not." Chambers tipped another shot into my glass, refilled his own. "Cheers. So tell me about work. I hear you and your partner have just about cornered the market. How'd you manage that?"

"Jeff's a lot smarter than me," I said. "I just try and keep my head down."

"Smart." A touch of sarcasm to the word. "Let me get to why I'm here, Dave. I'm not that far off from my twenty. On account of past mistakes I don't see myself rising much higher. It's not worth it to wait till I'm sixty-five. Not if I can do something else. I was hoping you could give me a glimpse into the life, so to speak. Tell me about a few of the things you're working on."

"Current cases?"

"I won't blab. Fact I might be able to help. I've got a few more years logged on the job than Sonia or your buddy Ryan Martz."

"Glad to share," I said.

I took him through some of what Wakeland & Chen was working on, leaving out names. Industrial insurance cases, a few pieces of litigation. I explained our corporate security contracts in minute detail, surprising myself at my own level of understanding.

Chambers ate it up. Moses wasn't a more attentive listener.

"So it's a mixture of things," he said. "Just like on the job. I like that. Nothing else on your plate?"

I shrugged. "Jeff keeps talking about expanding into repossessions, but I'm not sure I have the desire to take some poor bastard's—"

"What about alimony cases?" Chambers said, as if just thinking about it. "I heard something about a tough one you had. Something about a gangster. Asian last name. You and him had some sort of showdown?"

I played it as if I'd almost forgotten the incident. "Right," I said. "Qiu. He had a deadbeat dad on his payroll. He told me to leave the guy alone."

"And you didn't?" Chambers grinned.

"I got the money," I said.

"Someone threatened me," Chambers said, "I'd want to even the score."

"I'm in no hurry."

He nodded, tilting his head confidingly. "You must at least have thought about it. What was his name again? Chow?"

"Qiu," I said. "I think it's about as even as it'll get."

"I'm just saying if it was me." All humor draining out of his voice, his eyes narrowing, putting aside his mug. "I'm saying if there was some way I could help you get retribution, you let me know."

"Truth is," I said, "and this humble abode doesn't bear it out, but I'm making money hand over fist with corporate clients. I might roll past Qiu and put the scare into him, just so he doesn't think I've let my guard down. But I don't have the time or inclination to start anything. Retribution's expensive. Up for one last drink?"

Chambers smiled.

"Let's kill it," he said.

Thirty-Six

I didn't tip my hand to Chambers. I wanted him to report back to Qiu on our conversation, tell him I was all empty threats and money talk. I needed time to figure out how to play them. To learn what Sonia wanted and what I could live with.

But first I owed Dana Essex a meeting. I called her and told her I'd found Tabitha Sorenson and she was alive.

"She's okay? You saw her? You have an address?"

The hope in her voice, the giddiness—I told her I'd give her a complete report and debriefing in person.

"I live in the West End," she said, surprising me. I'd thought she'd lived closer to the school, and been a stranger to Vancouver. "There's a Ukrainian place on Denman Street. Could we meet there in half an hour?"

I took a cab and found her already at a table, spinning an empty wine glass by the stem. The smell of the rich food was tempting, creamy borschts and steaming cabbage rolls. But Essex wasn't eating and I wasn't staying longer than I had to.

I'd printed a few hi-res frames of the video. Essex shuffled through them, a grin breaking out on her face. "It's her," she said. "Tabitha. And she's living in this city?"

"That's right."

Essex was wearing a dark pants suit and smelled of lavender soap. For jewelry, a plain gold watch. She poured wine from a small decanter and went through the pictures again, more slowly, pausing to study each one.

"Maybe she doesn't look like much to you," Essex said softly. "Some people contain worlds within them. Isn't this strange." She wasn't smiling. Her joy came across as nervous anticipation.

"She's living with someone," I said. "A man named Sabar Gill. From what I observed, they're a couple."

Essex nodded. She kept her eyes on the photos. "You have evidence of that?" she said.

"I could play you the video, show you their body language."

"Not just good friends? Close friends?"

"Kissing. Cuddling. Sharing a bedroom."

"You have video of them together—physically together? Sexually?"

"I'm not a pornographer."

"No. Of course not." Essex bit her lip and leaned back in her chair. She played with her hands, as if suddenly unsure what to do with them.

"Tell me what happened to her," she said.

I told her. "Tabitha was brought into a student government that was falling apart. The officials were crooked and petty and disorganized, in charge of millions of dollars, with the only restraints what they themselves decided. In comes Tabitha with economic smarts and a political cynicism she learned from her poli-sci prof. She found a way to lend out money illegally, then replace it and pocket the interest. She ran a very smart scam under cover of very stupid scams. The auditors caught a whiff of it, but no more than that."

"Where did she go?"

"I think her original idea was to flee the country," I said. "She stayed here, though. Her partner was offered a job he couldn't turn down." I gestured to the report. "In any case, there they are."

Dana Essex spread the photos on the table. "How does Tabitha live like this?" she said. "Homebound, out of touch with friends and family. She was so active."

"I have two ideas on that," I said. "Either she's very careful—"

"Or?"

"Very scared."

"Of what?"

"I had to guess, I'd say the Hayes brothers. She led them to believe this would be the first of many loans. They're not happy about the deception."

"I'd like to read the full report," Essex said.

While she read I stared out the window at the rush hour traffic on Denman. A procession of neon-attired bicyclists, silver coupes, and midsize sedans. The occasional lurch of the Downtown Express as it crouched to pick up passengers. People, and more of them all the time. You'd think making connections would become easier.

I noticed Essex wasn't reading anymore. She was gripping the page tightly, but her eyes were focused elsewhere, on other things.

"I think I need a drink," she said. "Will you have one? On me, of course."

"How about a bit of a walk first?" I said. "The rain's let up. We can catch a drink at the Sylvia on our way back."

We paid up and left. Walking against traffic, we crossed Davie and turned onto the gray sand of English Bay. Luxury apartments and upscale franchise restaurants had encroached on the waterfront. The West End breathed money on display. The cloud cover and the late hour kept all but the most dedicated walkers off the Seawall. We strolled in the direction of Third Beach.

"Are you going to talk to Tabitha?" I asked.

"I don't think so, no. Not if she's happy."

"It cost you a lot to find her. Maybe she should know that."

Essex gave an abrupt, derisive laugh. "Tabitha would probably find it funny. Or think it was the gesture of a stalker."

"Or a friend."

"It wasn't friendship," Essex said, drawing her coat around her. Rounding the corners of the Seawall, you could be met with heavy wind and foam spray, or an eerie, preternatural calm.

"The fact is," she continued, "we weren't friends, we were colleagues. I wanted to find her to assuage my own feelings that I've wasted my life, and that I'm destined to be solitary. It had very little to do with her and everything to do with what she represented."

"Love," I said.

"Or something less noble." She paused at a bench and looked out past the beach at the rusted hulls of the cargo ships anchored in the bay. A face full of wind was a convenient excuse to wipe her eyes.

"When I was in grad school, I'd pass certain professors in the halls and know that, as learned as they were, they'd never lived. Some were bureaucrats, some socially inadequate. Some simply lived through the books they studied, and I liked those the best. Many were waiting for a proletarian revolution that wouldn't happen in their lifetime. Those people were ghosts. I told myself I'd disguise myself as one of them, but I'd never become *like* them. I would live. And now, however many years later, here I am—I've deceived myself into a spectral existence no different from theirs. Only I knew better, and chose it anyway."

I didn't know what to say. On the beach, a woman and a white-stockinged lab treaded the edge of the surf.

"Have you ever read Ishiguro?"

I shook my head. "Any good?"

"Brilliant," Essex said. "You'd like *When We Were Orphans*. It's about a private detective. The more success he has, the more he realizes his entire life is supported by the crimes he's trying to solve."

"Listen," I said. "Whether you talk to Tabitha or not isn't up to me. But for her sake, it might be a good idea to put someone on her house. Just in case."

"Security?" She thought about it and nodded. "As a precaution. I owe her that much."

The wind relented. Turning back, we soon reached the Sylvia Hotel.

"I'm not up for a drink just yet," Essex said. "Would tomorrow night be all right? I realize consoling a client is an imposition but"—her face scrunched up, then blanked—"I don't know anyone else I could commiserate with."

"Consoling and commiserating is part of the job," I said. "What'll you do in the meantime?"

"Find a way to live with myself," she said.

Thirty-Seven

In the afternoon I listened to an irate Don Utrillo, president of Solis Solutions, gripe about the hygiene of one of the guards we'd sent his company for a corporate fundraiser. "His ass was practically hanging out, like a goddamned plumber."

I assured Utrillo I'd speak to the kid about proper grooming. His name was Greg, and I made him drive down to the office to tell him in person he needed a shave and a good pair of suspenders.

"Appearance is important," I told him. Me, wearing two days' stubble and a perforated Hanson Brothers T-shirt.

"But you—" he began.

"—are a genius, and for a genius rules are meant to be transgressed. That's how society develops new ideas and inventions. The liberties that Jeff or I take must be seen against a backdrop of competence. That means suit and tie and proper-fitting clothing."

Greg scratched the fuzz on his chin and nodded. Looking at him closer, I recognized him as one of the guards who'd turfed me from Mitch Sorenson's office. Evidently Greg recognized me, too.

"Sir," he said, "I'd like to apologize—"

"Don't. That was your job. I'd be pissed if you did anything else."

"Thanks, sir."

"Now let's talk about what you're doing next."

I assigned him the van and told him to station himself on Quebec Street, watching the home of Sabar Gill and Tabitha Sorenson. Report anything strange to me.

"Keep out of sight, but close enough to help if something happens."

"Are you expecting it to, sir?"

"It's a precaution," I said. "A client's peace of mind. But that doesn't mean you don't take it seriously."

"Understood, sir, and thanks."

When I was done with him I took a video call with Jeff. His vacation attire was a straw fedora and an unbuttoned sunset-pattered shirt. His cabana opened onto the beach.

"Any problems?" he asked.

"Nope. Everything's running fine. Admit it, you think you're irreplaceable."

"One of us thinks he is," Jeff said. "How's that missing student case coming?"

"Turned out she stashed herself a few dollars and was hiding out with her librarian lover over in Mount Pleasant."

"As one does. You ought to come out to Maui. It's hot. No rain. People are friendly. Kind of the opposite of Vancouver."

"What's the fun of that?"

Jeff shook his head. "I'll phone next week, before we leave."

"You'll be calling tomorrow," I said. "You miss me too much."

"That must be it," he said.

At nine I locked up the main office and called it a night. Walking down Hastings, I saw a beige Navigator creep past me, abruptly shifting lanes toward my side of the street. The SUV stopped at the light.

I changed direction, heading west toward Burrard. As I turned a corner, I saw the Navigator swing around, stop, its passenger door opening.

Up Burrard and into a throng of people on Homer. Past low-rise apartments, opulent hotels, drab shopfronts and diners like weeds between the gray monoliths. I darted across the street, moving purposefully. In my peripheral I saw a man in a dark suit follow.

I headed south toward False Creek, staying amid other pedestrians. The man followed. I'd assumed it would be Chambers, but the man was shorter and broader, his tail work too conspicuous. I needed a better look at him.

Near the water I took out my cell phone and snapped it open truculently, as if objecting to a call. "What?" I said, turning to face the street. "You're serious? This can't wait?"

The man in the dark suit halted and stared into a storefront window. He was contemplating the glass with a window-shopper's scrutiny, but the building was for sale, and the glass looked in on a few discarded tubs of drywall plaster.

"I hear you," I said into the phone. "Twenty minutes. Phone you from the office. Just have the wife ready to talk."

I headed back the way I'd come, fast, and staring at the street, with my eyes focused nowhere. Certainly not on Nagy as I passed him. No mistaking the off-kilter nose and the slightly porcine eyes. He waited until I was twenty paces ahead of him before he fell in step.

Nagy would have a pistol. He looked the type to carry more than one. His tail work was pitiful, but I had no doubt he'd shoot me if the order came down from Qiu. Or maybe if the chance arose.

I caught a taxi on Robson, told the driver to take me down Water and then right on Clark. I got out two blocks from my apartment. I didn't see Nagy or the Navigator again that night.

Thirty-Eight

An energetic morning rain drowned the patio outside my apartment, giving my view of the trees beyond the fence a gauzy texture. I phoned Sonia and didn't get through. I wondered if she was blocking my calls or all calls or if something had happened.

I dressed and wrapped my coat around me. Walked to Cambie Street and over the bridge, through Coopers' Park, to the high-rise where Sonia lived. I saw scattered boats on the turbulent water, a few drenched hobos milling about the park. Shivering under the awning, I hit the buzzer.

Her voice on the intercom, guarded and interrogatory. "Who is it?"

"Delivery."

"Please leave it by the door."

"It's me."

"Why would you—"

"You're not answering my calls," I said. "Can I come up?"

"Rather you didn't."

"It's goddamn cold out here," I said. "At least make me a cup of tea."

Up in her apartment I took off my coat and wrung out my shirt. A large stainless steel espresso machine dominated her tiny kitchen. Sonia tamped and frothed and put together two cappuccinos.

She was wearing her gym pants and a threadbare off-the-shoulder sweater. Her cop gear was laid out on her living room table—sidearm, handcuffs, stun gun, baton. A white Kevlar vest was draped over one arm of the couch.

We drank standing on opposite sides of her kitchen. I waited for her to speak.

After a while she said, "I should've told you not to come."

"You could tell me what's going on."

"I can't," she said. "I'm sorry I got you involved."

"So we're done then?"

"There's nothing you can do," she said.

I wiped my mouth. "Almond milk doesn't froth for shit, does it?"

She didn't respond.

"Are you in danger?"

Sonia sighed. Put down her cup. Her hands went to her hips.

"You love to help people," she said. "Especially women. Nothing makes you happier. But did it occur to you, Dave, not everyone wants your help?"

"You asked me—"

"Yes. And now I'm asking you to stop."

"It occur to you, Sonia, I want to help because I can see you're in trouble?"

She took deep breaths and stared at her feet. "I'm being followed," she said.

"You too?" When she looked up, I added, "Why do you think I've been trying to contact you?"

"Were you followed here?" she asked.

"No."

"You're certain?"

"I walked here," I said. "Halfway over the bridge I paused to look down at the water. No one was around."

"No one else would be dumb enough to do it in the rain," she said.

"I like the rain."

"Do you know who followed you?"

I nodded. "Guy named Nagy, works for Anthony Qiu. He did a craptastic job, too—which may have been the point."

"Intimidation," she said.

I nodded. Like I'd tried to explain to Jeff, people like the Hayes brothers and Anthony Qiu trafficked in fear, along with whatever else they were involved in.

"Your partner works for Qiu," I said. "After I visited his restaurant, he sent Chambers to suss me out. Chambers all but interrogated me on my plans for Qiu."

"Does Chris sense that you know they're connected?"

"I don't think so," I said. "Did you recognize your tail?"

"No," she said, "but I got a license number. The car was registered to a Wong Jian Ye, also known as Winslow Wong. A couple charges for receiving stolen goods."

"Well dressed, slender build, acne scars?"

Sonia nodded.

"He's another of Qiu's. I saw him with Nagy when I paid my visit."

"They could be watching my place," she said. "That's why I didn't want you coming up."

"Might be sheer egotism," I said, "but I think they're tailing you to find out what's motivating me. They're confused about why I dropped in on Qiu's restaurant."

"So am I," Sonia said. "I wish you hadn't."

"Seemed like a good idea at the time."

"Which is what they'll put on your tombstone, Wakeland."

Sonia bussed our empty cups to her sink and collapsed on the couch with a sigh.

"When I started riding with Chris," she said, "I lied to him. Well, he assumed you and I were still a couple, and I didn't correct him."

"A girl's allowed to dream."

"You don't understand. When I partner up with someone, half the time they think I don't belong. That I didn't get here on merit, that I can't do the job the way they can, that I'll put them in danger. I don't get the assumption of competence their privileged white male asses do. But Chris seemed to know you, and that made him more comfortable with me."

She sat forward on her couch, hunched with her chin on her fist.

"I'm so fucking tired of having to prove myself," she said. "Chris is part of that old boys' club. What he thinks of me matters to others, it affects my career. If he tells someone I'm good police, or 'she's all right for a girl, I guess,' that distinction matters. I hate that it matters but it does. I want to make rank, but I don't want to be one of those paper bosses that none of the rank and file respect. I want people to know I earned it."

"I don't know why Chambers would remember me," I said.

"You're white. You're male."

I thought about it. "Maybe he thinks I'm bent like him. He heard I was forced off the job. That's the rumor around the cop shop, isn't it?"

No answer. Which was its own answer.

"Chambers is dirty," I continued. "He sees me as being the same. And if you're with me—"

"—then he can trust me." Sonia's eyes widened.

"What?"

"Nothing, not important."

"You have to tell me," I said.

She laughed mirthlessly. "Only you, Dave, could demand someone open up to you completely at the same time you dance around your own guilt."

"My guilt's not the issue," I said.

"The last time we spoke you said you hoped there'd be a time we could be totally honest with each other. Hold nothing back."

"Right."

"I hope that comes soon," she said.

Thirty-Nine

I got to the Narrow early, waited at the bar for a table to open up. Business was conducted around me, the circulation of dollars and beers. Mark Lanegan on the sound system, "Ode to Sad Disco." I was watchful for Nagy or Chambers.

Sonia's words had stung. I chased a double Bulleit with a bottle of beer and wondered what exactly I'd expected out of helping her: gratitude, sex, an alleviation of guilt? It didn't work like that. I thought of Shay, the woman I'd seen briefly last year. I'd wanted to help her, too. Shay's demons had been different than Sonia's, and no amount of care, of love, could rid her of them. Maybe Sonia was right, and I was addicted to playing savior. I wanted to believe there was more to me than that—but maybe that was the point.

Dana Essex showed up on time, wearing a pleated skirt and a tawny jacket which she slipped over her stool. She seemed amused by the surroundings.

"I'm not much of a beer drinker," she said. She ordered a gin Collins and I bought another Kronenbourg.

"You look like you're surviving," I said.

"I'm enduring," she said. "Like Dilsie's family. My affection for Tabitha was a bit abstract, I recognize that." She took a long drink and shuddered. "Tonight I'm going to enjoy myself."

Liquor loosens tongues. By the second round Essex was holding court on various authors, most of whom I'd never heard of. She seemed shocked my reading list hadn't included Tomas Tranströmer, that my exposure to Atwood and Richler had been strictly compulsory.

"But you do read?" she asked.

"Sure—books on boxing, the odd crime novel."

She brought her lips together in what was either distaste or resignation. "Have you heard of Mo Yan? Elfriede Jelinek?" I hadn't. "Nobel winners. And unread by almost all North Americans. Unless we're giving an award to a pop singer, we pay it no heed. Why does the only truly international book award mean nothing to us?"

"Why would you trust a book award given out by the guy who invented dynamite," I said, "when none of the books involve people dynamiting things?"

She shut her eyes, laughing. "You may have a point," she said. "Tabitha never read anything but those eight-hundred-page fantasy novels—unless it was some anarchist tract assigned by Paul Mastellotto. And my ex-husband, if it wasn't Restoration poetry or the contemporary English novel—which reminds me."

From her purse she produced a slim volume.

"Ishiguro," she said. "Slow-going but worth it."

"Thank you," I said politely.

"He writes with an English sensibility, Ishiguro, and yet his books build to these moments of sadness and recognition. You're familiar with *mono no aware?*"

"Will you think less of me if I say no?"

She shook her head earnestly, happy to explain. It was a Japanese term, an apprehension of the transience of all things. I drank my beer and enjoyed listening to her digress.

"In the West we ask impossible things from our artists," she said. "Everything is disassembled and commodified. People take quotations from Shakespeare's characters and repeat them as if they're words of infallible wisdom. They miss the inherent irony of a line like 'To thine own self be true.'"

"Those rubes," I said.

"Sorry to drone on." She took up her new drink and tasted it through the half-sized straw. "I must be a complete boor."

"No, it's fine. It's interesting. Tell me more about Shakespeare."

She thought for a while and abruptly resumed laughing.

"I just remembered how a graduate instructor of mine referred to him," she said. "It was after a few drinks in a bar similar to this. We were talking about the Anti-Stratfordians, the dullards who think Shakespeare was too uneducated to be the writer he was."

"So who do they think wrote *Hamlet* and all that?"

"There are a few candidates, all invariably drawn from the upper crust. My friend responded that they'd be horrified to know the real Shakespeare. And I of course asked what he was like."

"The answer?"

"'A tight-fisted, status-obsessed, alcoholic pussy hound with questionable sexual history' is how she phrased it."

Around midnight Dana Essex complained of a headache. "It's the air," she said. "Mind if we walk a bit?"

"There are other bars around, quieter ones."

"How far away is your place?"

"Half hour," I said.

"And you have alcohol there?"

As we walked she slipped her arm around mine and leaned against my shoulder. I thought of the first time I'd seen her, how indeterminate she'd looked. Now she seemed more sexualized. More playful, too. It was a costume she was trying on, one that didn't quite fit. But then neither had the other.

At my door she kissed me. We stumbled into the dark apartment and as I reached for the lights I felt her hands ensnare mine. Her lips moved over my face and neck.

"Bedroom," she said. I nodded in the direction.

Unbuckling my pants she said, "This isn't payment. I don't want you to think I'm thinking about it that way."

"I won't," I said.

"I've been thinking about this since I first saw you. I felt the same way about Tabitha. You're both strong and self-assured. I want this to be perfect. I want this to please you."

"All right."

"Tell me what to do. What you want, how and where. Tell me, Dave."

In the end I didn't need to say anything.

Later, with the morning sun making overtures through the blinds, she got up naked and retrieved the book. She wanted to read to me. I liked the sound of her voice and the play of her free hand over my body. We made love again with the reading light above us. After, lying on our sides, I saw someone looking back at me, a person, a woman I'd never seen before.

It was noon before I could summon the energy to fall out of bed. She was still asleep, her breathing cool and measured. My phone was vibrating in the pocket of my jeans, which had been abandoned in the kitchenette. I put water on the stove, slid into the pants, and afterwards decided I should answer.

"It's Kay," she said. "I've been hitting your buzzer for the last twenty minutes."

"Come around the patio side."

She did. I opened the sliding door. We stared at each other from opposite sides of the screen.

"You're not gonna let me in?"

"Company," I said.

"Ah." She smirked. "I was wondering what I'm supposed to do, now that Tabitha's found."

"Good work on that," I said. "You can relieve Greg from out front of the house."

"Sure. Or I could just hang out here for a little while—"

I shut the door.

Dana Essex emerged from the bedroom wearing a T-shirt. She smiled awkwardly and maneuvered around me to the washroom. In the mirror she inspected the love marks on her shoulders and throat. "You wouldn't have an extra toothbrush?"

"Under the sink," I said. "Breakfast? I make a pretty decent instant oatmeal."

The kettle whistled and I took care of it.

"Thanks," she said between rinses. "I have proposals to mark and a lesson plan to write. But I enjoyed that."

"Some other time," I said.

"I hope so."

Forty

At one I walked to Hastings. Before I could enter the building, I heard someone hail me.

Chris Chambers was approaching, waving at me. Out of uniform, suede jacket over turtleneck and cords, the jacket halfway zipped up, bulky enough for a shoulder holster.

"Time for a brew?" he asked.

Seated in the basement at Steamworks, over a pitcher of house lager, Chambers pitched a job to me.

"I've a friend who's looking for a top-notch PI," he said. "After our whiskey session the other day, only one name came to mind."

"What's the job?"

"You'd be on retainer, 'case something came up. He's a pretty high-profile businessman, but generous to his friends. All you need is discretion and a willingness to make money."

"This wouldn't be Vincent Leung, would it? Anthony Qiu's father-in-law?"

Chambers's mouth formed a worldly, confiding smile. "He's thinking of appealing his sentence again. There'd be canvassing and re-interview work. Plus all types of corporate gigs might come up with his other businesses." He reached into his suit pocket and withdrew a folded check. "Best of all, here's the retainer."

I looked at it. High five figures. "And that's yearly," Chambers said, "on top of the bread you make now."

"Chris," I said, pushing the check back to him, "how deep are you in with these people? You know how they operate?"

"Mr. Leung is a good businessman."

"He's a lot of things," I said. "But he's not good and he's not a businessman. If he has something over you, there are ways to get shut of it."

Chambers's mouth opened. Whatever his response would have been, he killed it, snapping his jaw shut. His gaze lost its warmth and became clinical, an appraisal.

"This is going to get ugly," he said. "Answer your own question, Dave—do you know what these guys are capable of?"

He smoothed out the check.

"Now. We have a mutually beneficial way out. Everybody gets paid and everybody gets left alone."

I picked up the check and stared at it.

"Call it a consultancy fee," Chambers said. "Your partner doesn't even have to know."

My phone buzzed, Kay texting me. *Van trouble.*

"I've got to deal with this," I said. "Are Qiu's guys going to keep tailing me?"

"That really depends on you, Dave."

I refolded the check and put it in my wallet. A broad relieved grin spread across Chambers's features.

"You're making the right call. Knew you'd see that." Chambers emptied his glass. "I gotta ask, though, what made you rattle Tony's cage the other day?"

"Honestly? Sheer fucking boredom."

Chambers laughed and bought himself another pitcher.

Forty-One

"Van trouble" was company code for "assistance needed ASAP." I sped away from the restaurant, hoping I hadn't tipped as much to Chambers.

I drove an erratic route to Quebec Street. Over the Burrard Bridge, through the parking lot of Vancouver General Hospital, weaving down side streets and alleys. I parked on Ontario, walked a long circuit to the van.

Kay sat on the milk crate in the back, watching the front of Gill's house through the tinted glass. Greg sat on the floor next to her. Both jumped when I opened the back door.

"What's going on?" I said.

Kay looked at Greg, who seemed to defer to her despite being more experienced. "We think something's up," she said.

"Based on what?"

"It just feels wrong."

"Did you see Tabitha or Sabar Gill leave? Or anyone else enter?" Both shook their heads. "Then what?"

"We think the house is empty," Kay said.

"I didn't see anyone last night," Greg said, nodding. "No movement at all. And I didn't fall asleep, sir, I swear."

I leaned against the back door. "Why are you still here?"

His face reddened. "Just thought Kay could use some help. Gets boring doing this yourself."

"But neither of you actually saw anyone."

"Think about how weird that is," Kay said. "It's three o'clock and no one's left or come home since last night. If they haven't gone away, then something has to be wrong."

"We don't know that," I said. But I reached into the front, found my flashlight where I'd left it. "Might as well know for sure."

I told Kay to follow me, Greg to wait in the van. We walked up the steps and knocked on the front door. There was no answer. I couldn't see through the curtained windows.

"It's probably nothing," Kay said, with as much conviction as she could summon. "Everything's probably fine."

Leaving the porch, we walked around the side of the house. There was no path. Leaves covered the neglected lawn, crunching under our feet.

Around back we found a gray sagging porch, bolstered with a skeleton of fresh timber. No guardrail on the weather-warped staircase. The property looked different in daylight, its disrepair in stark contrast to its professionally maintained neighbors.

Newspapers and empty cans were piled near the back door. I unlatched the outer screen and reached for the handle. The door swung inward at my touch.

"I knew it," Kay said.

Gill and Tabitha could have left out the back at night, if they'd been careful. With the blackout curtains drawn, the lights dimmed, they could have packed what they needed into Gill's Mercedes and been gone before anyone noticed. Why they'd do that, and how they'd been tipped off, was anyone's guess.

The kitchen was cold, painted yellow, the counters spotted with grease. Trays of wheatgrass arrayed along the windowsills. Empty mason jars on the floor near the heater. A doorway led from the kitchen to a dining nook, Formica table matched with lawn chairs. A small library, its shelves made of cinder blocks and planks.

Kay uttered a grunt of shock and disgust. A body was sprawled on the floor, head against the baseboard, legs threaded between the table's. Sabar Gill. A coin-sized slick of blood had formed on the floor, issuing from the side of Gill's head.

"Our father in heaven," Kay said, the prayer breaking off in a shudder.

I crouched and turned Gill on his back, shoving the table aside. "He's still alive."

Crossing herself, Kay knelt on her heels and took Gill's hand. She found his pulse, her shock abating as she watched the slight rise and fall of his stomach.

Gill was dressed in a pressed white shirt, dark pants, suspenders. His left shirt cuff was stained with blood. His wedding ring was missing.

I dialed Emergency and gave them the address, told the operator my sister would stay on the line. Kay took the phone, describing the unconscious man's condition.

"Be right back," I told her.

Upstairs the house brightened, light filtering in through the half-drawn curtains. The staircase turned sharply, then opened onto a T-shaped hallway. A bedroom and bathroom, doors open, between them another closed door. Behind it, what looked like an office.

Tabitha Sorenson leaned forward in a leather swivel chair next to her workspace. Head tilted downward, as if she were scanning the floor for something and poised to pick it up. She wore pyjama bottoms and a sweater, the fabric darkened over her right hip. Her slashed throat had soaked the gray carpet with blood. A bundle of cords lay draped over the edge of the desk like severed tendons.

An inner voice whispered that there was no returning from this, for any of us. I stepped carefully out of the room.

Forty-Two

In the aftermath:

An ambulance and patrol car arrived. The officers searched the house, then returned outside to take our information. I asked them for cigarettes but neither of them smoked. From the front lawn we watched the EMTs cart Gill out to the ambulance and the ambulance race away. Lights, sirens.

More officers materialized. Scene preservation began. Tape was stretched along the perimeter of the house. Neighbors gawked. Kay and Greg were separated, their stories taken down.

At last one of the cops found a cigarette for me, a menthol. I inhaled it while giving my statement. I left out Dana Essex and made it my idea to enter the house. Otherwise I was honest.

The techs arrived and donned white Tyvek suits to begin processing the scene. We were driven in separate cars to the Main Street station. Fingerprints and fibers were taken, shoes removed. All done to eliminate us, we were told. I was allowed one more smoke.

In a pleasant blue-painted interview room, a detective named Triplett thanked me for my assistance and said she and her partner would be back as soon as they could. She asked if I needed anything. I told her I was fine.

The door shut, leaving me alone with the thought that while I'd been fucking Dana Essex, someone had slipped into Tabitha's home, intent on killing her.

Panic, shock, fear, anger, sorrow—guilt—none of those would help Tabitha now. (Nothing would.) It all came back to breathing. I closed my eyes, forced myself to inhale—a luxury she'd never have—I couldn't help that now—couldn't help anything, ever—dead—

As my breathing slowed my thoughts took a more logical shape. Priorities asserted themselves. Find her killer, which meant telling the police what they needed. More important was protecting Dana. I'd have to speak to her first, alone. She was entitled to confidentiality, to protection as a client, as well as whatever else we were to each other.

I opened my eyes as the door opened and Triplett and her partner walked in.

Both wore gray overcoats and drab dark blue suits. Triplett was taller, had short silver hair and a slightly stooped posture. Her partner, McCurdy, was squat, red-headed, his gruff body language announcing he'd be playing the antagonist. They sat down.

I told them what I'd told the officer at the scene. Hired by an unnamed client. My decision alone to enter the house.

"What makes a person think he can trespass where he pleases?" McCurdy said.

"Had a feeling someone was in trouble."

"They were. Lucky for you."

Triplett turned the conversation to Tabitha. "Had you talked to her before?"

"No."

"Seen her."

"Once, two days ago."

"She was under surveillance?"

I nodded. Triplett waited to see if I'd elaborate. When I didn't, she smiled, as if conceding I knew the tactics and now we'd move beyond games.

"Who's your client?" she asked.

"Before I tell you," I said, "I need to confer with them."

"Get your stories straight," McCurdy said.

"My client's not involved, I can guarantee that. Once we confer, if they agree, I'll arrange an interview."

"Way to avoid those goddamned adjectives," McCurdy said.

"Gendered pronouns, you mean."

"Up your ass is what I mean."

Triplett placed her hand on McCurdy's chest. "If it has to be that way," she said. "We'll talk again soon. In the meantime, Mr. Wakeland, it might be best not to make any travel plans."

Forty-Three

There wasn't time to mourn. Once I'd left the station, I dialed Dana Essex, then thought better of it. I walked up to Broadway, bought a prepaid phone from a convenience store, then made the call.

I told her the news. It was pointless to apologize, but I did anyway.

"It's not possible," she said. "There's simply no way."

She spoke softly. I could hear the collective murmur of voices behind her.

"I have class in a moment," she said. "Why don't I end early and call when I'm finished?"

"Best to stay off phones till we get a chance to talk. Can you meet me tonight?"

"I can be back in the city by nine. How about we meet by the wharf on Granville Island?"

"That works," I said.

"Am I—are we in trouble, Dave?"

"Right now we're just careful. See you tonight."

After the interviews, Kay and Greg had headed back to the main office. I found them in the boardroom, searching online for information about the killing. They looked to me for answers I didn't have.

"You both should take some time off," I said. "Don't speak to anyone. If you're pressed, call our lawyer. Then call me. Don't mention our client to anyone."

"This isn't my fault, sir, is it?" Greg said.

"It's mine," I told him.

"Does Dana know?" Kay asked once Greg had gone. "All that waiting, and then heartbreak. She'll want you to work on this, find who did it."

"It's not our job to solve murders. Right now it's to protect our client. You're sure you didn't mention her?"

"Cross my heart," she said. "And Greg doesn't know. So what next?"

It was a good question.

"I need to phone Jeff," I said. "Help Ralph re-encrypt the storage drive and then get some rest."

Jeff understood why it was important, going to the wall for a client. That didn't mean he liked it. I told him I'd advise Dana Essex make full disclosure to the police, unless she gave me a reason not to.

"What possible reason could there be?" he asked. Waves breaking on the shore in the background.

"Protection," I said. "The person who killed Tabitha might be after her, too."

"Dave," Jeff said delicately. "What percent sure are you this woman didn't do this?"

"One hundred."

"Or have it done?"

"Ninety eight. She's not the type to get worked up into a white-hot rage. And if this was about money, well, you don't teach English at community college because you harbor a deep desire for wealth."

"So who did it, then?" Jeff asked.

I was getting tired of being asked questions I was already asking myself. "Someone who got a look at the report, either in the office or on our client's end."

"Unlikely it came from us," Jeff said. "Our office staff doesn't leave info lying out."

"It's a zoo, Jeff. There's a million ways you could get a glimpse."

"This isn't your fault," Jeff said. "You know that, right?"

I couldn't answer him.

Tabitha Sorenson was dead. She'd died badly, and in some way I'd led the killer to her. The report I'd written for Dana Essex was a murderer's blueprint—address and schedule of the only person who knew where Tabitha was. The document was saved to our cloud storage account, which meant anyone in the Wakeland & Chen offices or anyone with the password would have access.

And it wasn't a small company anymore—a full-time office staff, part-time guards, Jeff and Kay and anyone that any of us knew. Someone in the waiting area could have over-the-shouldered Ralph and seen him enter the password. To say nothing of decryption. To say nothing of anything.

If Essex and the office were protected, the smart thing was to let the police take over, the professionals with the databases and the lab equipment and the sanctioned use of force. I could harm the investigation and wreck any chance of her killer facing justice.

So often what you know to be a stone-cold, irrefutable fact sits in opposition to the kind of truth that comes to you through intuition and surmise. The head and heart work different terrain. Perched in my mind was the image of a faceless someone who wielded a knife with precision and skill, who had no qualms about applying that blade to a twenty-four-year-old woman. I saw that someone standing over her, listening to her weak pulse speed her toward death. Getting what he or she wanted and killing her in an instant, with no more emotion than a creditor balancing accounts. I couldn't let that go.

Before I left to meet Essex, I checked the news sites. Already the *Sun* had an article up about the mysterious death in Mount Pleasant.

The neighbors had seen nothing. None of them had ever met Tabitha, and few had spoken to Gill more than to say hello. Of course it was terrible, they said, and wondered who could do such a thing.

A clean stab wound doesn't hurt much more than a stiff punch, at least initially. Police sources said the wound in Tabitha's side had probably been done first, then followed by the severing of the subclavian artery. Pain and immobilization, then a merciful slash to the base of the throat.

The police were interested in any help they could get from the community to solve this vicious crime.

They'd get it.

Forty-Four

At eight thirty I left the office. On the Granville Street Bridge I saw the Navigator hove into view behind me. Nagy at the wheel, no pretense of tailing.

Instead of turning off to Granville Island, I let the street carry me up past Broadway, down the ramp into a parking garage near a Chapters. The SUV followed, stopping behind me, pinning the Cadillac between concrete pillars.

I stepped out of my car and waited for Nagy. He took his time approaching me.

"He wants his check back," Nagy said. "Seeing as you're not smart enough to play along."

"How do you know I wasn't on my way to cash it?"

"By now you'd've done it. Turn out your pockets."

I didn't move. "Turn out your pockets," he repeated.

He came forward, the cold light of the caged fluorescent overheads giving him a gaunt, sickly color. I shifted my weight to my back foot. Nagy reached to the small of his back and unsheathed a blade.

It was plastic-handled and coated with carbon fiber, and didn't gleam or reflect anything. He held it loose in his left hand, chest-level, like a conductor's baton. He stood between me and the exit ramp.

"Where's Winslow tonight?" I asked.

"Worry about this."

I'd once taken a knife away from someone. She'd been unskilled and drunk, and we'd both needed stitches.

Nagy looked comfortable holding the weapon. Faded red letters were tattooed on his knuckles. At this range they were unreadable.

"Jailhouse ink?" I asked.

He grinned and stepped forward. The right caught me on the temple. It wasn't the hardest I've ever been hit but it stunned me. The second one sent me hard against the Cadillac.

Holding the blade in front of my eyes, Nagy reached into my pockets, removed my wallet and took the folded check. There were two twenties in the billfold. He took those, too.

"That's just petty," I said, the taste of blood in my mouth.

He flicked out with the blade. I recoiled. My head banged into the car. Nagy laughed.

"Next time," he said.

He got in the SUV and drove up the ramp to Granville.

Forty-Five

You'll know you're insane when the world starts to make sense. When the blood and chaos coheres into a logical, sensible framework. It could be coincidence that Qiu's thug happened to favor a knife. That Qiu demanded his bribe back the same moment I should've been meeting Dana Essex.

I drove wildly through the rain back down Granville. Instead of taking the bridge I went under, passing the motorcycle shop with its row of glimmering Kawasakis, and headed through the cluster of boutiques that surrounded the Granville Island market.

It was eleven past nine and the market itself was closed. The buildings were lit only by security bulbs. I parked near the wharf and scanned for Essex. The waterfront was empty save for seagulls withstanding the downpour to peck at waterlogged trash and food scraps.

I waited forty minutes. Across the water lights blinked on in the high-rises. No boats on the water in the dark, other than the moored, canvas-covered rentals bobbing along the jetty.

At ten fifteen I risked a phone call to Essex. No answer. I circled the market, checking for movement. Nothing, no signs of life beyond the odd scavenging gull.

I left the market and drove over the Burrard Bridge into the West End, to the address Essex had provided. No one seemed to be following—or rather, every car seemed a potential threat.

She lived on Haro, a second-floor apartment in a mid-rise called the Threadgill Arms. I parked and left the lights on. Her name wasn't on the buzzer but I hit the number and waited. When no one answered, I stood near the entrance, hoping a resident would come in or out, allowing me to catch the front door. No one did. I watched the rain pour off the canvas awning above the apartment door, spilling into a muddy flower bed.

I tried the landlord's buzzer. I tried the side door. I tried phoning Essex again. I thought of taking my chances and climbing onto one of the second-floor balconies, hoping it was hers. I phoned the school and importuned a groggy-sounding registration clerk to check her office. He reported back that everyone had left.

Finally I dialed Sonia's number.

On the eleventh ring she picked up. "Dave. Didn't we agree not to—"

"I need a favor," I said, half-shouting over the rain. "I'm at this woman's apartment and I need to get inside. Come down here and pull come cop shit so I can break in legally."

"There's an easier way," she said.

"Yeah?"

"Sure. Stand in front of her balcony with a boombox and play Peter Gabriel."

"Other circumstances that'd be hilarious," I said. "I'm worried something's happened to her."

"She's a friend of yours? Or a client?"

"Friend," I said.

"I'll come down."

Twenty minutes passed. A small, frail-looking woman entered the apartment with her keys, but quickly pulled the door shut behind her.

Sonia's car passed and slowed. I stepped out into the street and waved. She pulled over and walked back to me. She was wearing a dark blue slicker and carrying her collapsible baton.

"Some police shit," she said. "What did you have in mind?"

"Break the door down, shoot somebody with a Taser. What do you normally do?"

"Call the landlord," she said. I watched her try the buzzer and get no response. She rapped on the glass door. When that didn't bring anyone she moved to the side of the building, shot the baton out to its full length, and began tapping on windows. That brought lights. Someone on the third floor opened their window to complain.

"Who the hell is doing that?"

"I'm an off-duty police officer," Sonia said. "We're getting no response from a tenant in the building and we're concerned for her well-being. Could you tell the landlord we're here?"

"Landlord's in Hong Kong."

"Maintenance person."

"Who?"

"Main-ten-ance. The janitor."

Pause. The voice said, "Why don't I just let you in?"

After a moment a lumpy man in a bathrobe, boxers, and slippers opened the door. He had whispy white hair predominantly in and around the ears, and the ruddy bulbous nose of someone who drinks sherry by the quart.

"You're police?" he said. "May I see your badges?"

Sonia held up her ID card. I showed him my security license. He nodded and let us pass.

"Who is it you're worried about?" he said.

"Dana Essex."

"Who?"

"Two Oh Four," I said.

"The teacher. She's a bit frigid, huh?"

We took the stairs. The resident puffed behind us. "Me, I try to know everyone. That's what we did where I grew up, got to know the people we lived with. Vancouver's a bit different from Medicine Hat. Not enough community anymore. Too many immigrants. No offense, ma'am."

"I was born here," Sonia said.

"Then you know what I mean, right?"

"We could always tell the coroner he slipped," I said to her.

We banged on 204 to no avail. Mr. Good Neighbor trudged to the elevator and found the maintenance person, a thin man who'd put his shirt on inside out. He jingled the keys. Whether he'd use them for us was another matter.

"Mr. Tsao—the owner—he told me not to let anyone in—less it was an emergency, like a fire, or if the tenant told me it was okay. You don't have her permission to do this, right? See, that's a problem."

Sonia said, "As a police officer I'd appreciate if you'd open it. We'll do a quick search and leave. We won't disturb anything."

"But Mr. Tsao said. And this is my job."

"The tenant could be injured," Sonia said.

"How 'bout this? Tomorrow I'll call Mr. Tsao and see what he says."

"Do you have any cash?" I asked Sonia. To the maintenance man I said, "Does fifty bucks get us in?"

"I can't, it's my job."

"You'd open up, the place was on fire, right?"

He thought about it and nodded.

"So tell Mr. Tsao you saw smoke. Then you can take this lady's money and sleep the sleep of the righteous."

A moment later we were standing in Dana Essex's apartment.

Forty-Six

The maintenance man and Mr. Good Neighbor waited in the hall. Sonia and I walked into the dark kitchenette. I felt for a light switch.

No dishes in the sink. Walls bare except for a framed master's degree from Carleton University. Cheap table and chairs, a paisley love seat, and a small television.

"What are we looking for?" Sonia said.

"The other case I was working. The target was murdered. This woman, Dana Essex, she's a part of things."

"Meaning she's your client," Sonia said.

"And my friend."

Passing behind me, Sonia said, "Is there anyone you won't lie to, Dave? Because I'd really love to meet that person."

I opened the bedroom door. A mattress and box spring rested on the floor, the box spring still in its plastic. A hamper. A closet full of muted tones, olives and oatmeals and tans. Behind the door, a pressed-wood bureau. I opened the top drawer and rifled through.

"Panty sniffing?" Sonia asked.

I moved to the hamper and lifted the lid.

"Of course," she said. "Why sniff the clean ones?"

I moved to the washroom and checked under the sink. In the closet, I pushed aside a peacoat and some bulky rain gear.

"She's gone," I said, "and she left on her own steam."

"Underwear and toiletries," Sonia said to herself, nodding. "Is that what you hoped?"

"I hoped I'd find her," I said. "But after my run-in with Nagy tonight, I think the best thing she could do is get away, lie low. Wait till I sort this thing out."

"Since when are you detailed to Homicide? And what exactly happened with Nagy?"

"Thanks for your help," I said, moving to the living room.

Books dominated the space. Crates of them were piled against the lengths of wall not taken up with bookcases. One case was dedicated to fiction, one for criticism and philosophy, the middle case double-stacked with slim handbound chapbooks and multivolume anthologies. A single space amid her Ishiguros where *When We Were Orphans* had sat.

"Find her?" the neighbor said as Sonia and I exited. He looked a tad disappointed when I told him no.

"You can lock it up," I told the maintenance man.

He did. He shuffled his feet. "There's the matter of the, ah, money."

I looked at Sonia. "Nagy took my last forty," I said.

She held up three twenties. "Anybody have a ten or two fives?" Then sighed, "Of course not," and handed it over.

Outside I thanked her and walked to my car. She followed me.

"You don't get to do that," she said. "Ask me for help and then not tell me what it's about. Should VPD be looking for this woman, to make sure she's safe?"

"I'll take care of it."

She seized my arm. "Tell me."

"Sure," I said, "after you tell me why you wanted Chambers followed."

She bit her bottom lip and moved as a pair of bicyclists came down the center of the road, tires hissing on the rain-soaked pavement.

"You don't have to," I said. "I figured it out a couple days ago. You weren't worried for Chambers. You didn't suspect he was corrupt. You knew. You saw the same thing I saw. You saw him tune somebody up."

She wouldn't meet my gaze.

"You have firsthand proof he's strong-arm muscle for Qiu, and you weighed that against what it would cost you career-wise to speak out against him. Not enough sense of justice to stand up, just enough to send your ex-boyfriend on some half-assed errand, to see if I'd do what you wanted without you having to say a word."

"You have no idea what it's like," she said, her voice breaking.

I said, "Chambers arranged to bump into me in the street. He offered me ninety grand from Qiu to end all this. I took the check, Sonia. Couple hours ago, Nagy held a knife on me and took it back. Guess Qiu thought if I hadn't cashed it by now, I was holding it against him as proof of a bribe.

"Truth is," I continued, "I was on the fence until I figured out the game you've been playing. Then, honestly, I was inclined to take the cash. If the Sorenson case hadn't got in the way, I might've done it. Now I've got a gangster and a beat cop and a couple of goons to watch out for, on top of the homicide dicks who probably think I knifed her or know who did. So thanks, Sonia, next time just put a gun to my nuts and—"

She struck me on the face with the baton. The steel crossed the bruises Nagy had left, sending a shriek of pain through my skull. One eye lost focus. I looked up to see Sonia backstep, sobbing, then turn and run to her car. I watched her taillights disappear over the hill.

My head knew what I'd said to her was true. My heart told me something else. That of all the people I'd driven away from me—and that list would be Dostoevskyan in length—here was someone who I'd spurned when she'd needed me most. You can be right and still find yourself sinking, and your rightness will not raise you up.

Forty-Seven

I woke to pain and sunlight. I was on my couch, still dressed. I'd passed out spinning my father's old country albums. I dropped the needle and made breakfast to Merle Haggard, "Old Flames Can't Hold a Candle to You."

Dana Essex would call today, I was sure of that. In the meantime I needed to figure out what to tell Triplett and McCurdy.

At ten o'clock I was parked in an uncomfortable chair in the reception area of Shauna Kensington's law office in Gastown. Above and behind me was a panorama watercolor of Burrard Inlet, the jagged tops of the Coast Mountains looming in the painting's background. The office was underground, the windows offering a view of legs clipping over the Water Street concrete. The receptionist told me Shauna was booked solid, but could probably spare a moment before lunch.

"That's why we generally make appointments," she said cheerily, before turning her attention back to her computer.

At ten thirty-five the inner door opened. The receptionist waved me through the assistant's annex into a high-ceilinged office replete with plush furnishings, the floor a minefield of Duplo and Richard Scarry. Shauna's youngest was sitting on her desk, his mother concerned with unwrapping a straw and using it to puncture the foil target on a juice box.

"Dave," Shauna said. "That's a hell of a shiner."

"She's a hell of a woman."

The kid tromped off to play in a yolk-yellow plastic igloo. "Adorable," I said.

Shauna Kensington smoothed out her blouse. She was broadshouldered and heavyset, spoke rapidly, and had a habit of rubbing her eyes when she sensed you were bullshitting her. Whenever we talked she'd be dressing or feeding or grooming one of her offspring, her responses precision-targeted though her gaze turned elsewhere.

I told her about Tabitha Sorenson and Dana Essex. She read the news reports on her computer. Her kid walked over to read with her, but lost interest and picked up a gold-plated fountain pen set, tomahawking it through the air. Without looking up, Shauna took it out of his hands.

"What do I do about the police?" I said.

"Depends what your client wants to do. And more importantly, how far you're willing to go for your client."

A good question, one I hadn't resolved. I said, "She went off the radar last night. I broke into her flat. She'd packed before leaving."

"You think Ms. Essex is connected to this murder?" Her attention left the pen set in her hand long enough for the child to snatch it back and run to his fortress, giggling.

"I think she's running for her life," I said. "This was a friend of hers who ended up murdered in her own house."

"So you haven't talked to her since the incident?"

"Briefly on the phone yesterday. We set a meeting that she didn't make."

"What was her state when she called?"

"Upset. Calm."

"Which?"

"We only spoke for a moment. She was whispering, or next thing to it."

"But not crying, not audibly upset?"

"She's introverted," I said. "She's not a rending of garments type person."

"Or an afraid for her life person?"

"I don't get it," I said.

"Oh, I see that." Shauna smiled, massaging an eyebrow with her thumb. "You and this woman have a closer than usual relationship, correct?"

"We slept together. I was consoling her, we were drinking."

"What's funny," Shauna said, "is you would be the first person to see this if you weren't in the center of it."

"See what?"

"You call this woman, tell her the news. She agrees to meet you later and then doesn't show."

"She got scared," I said.

"That is entirely possible. But let's look at what else is possible, Dave. What do you know about her?"

"Like I said, she's introverted, bit of a romantic—"

"Do you know those things, Dave, know-know them? Or is that what she told you?"

"I'm pretty good at reading people. That's an important part of what I do."

"Sure."

"And I wouldn't've taken the job if I'd got a sense she was violent, or after money."

"Your pride is hurt."

"She's not fucking involved," I snapped.

Shauna's kid looked up, looked at his mother and then grinned at me. The grin said, you're in trouble now.

I apologized. Quieter, I said, "The night of Tabitha's murder Essex and I were together. She ended up in bed with me. She was drunk and upset, and horny—is horny okay to say?"

"Horny," the kid said, giddily. "Horny."

"Sorry. The point is, I was with her, so I know she didn't do this herself, and she wouldn't hire it done, not out of jealousy, definitely not for money. I'd stake my reputation."

"You might have already," Shauna Kensington said. "In that case, isn't Ms. Essex lucky to have you as an alibi?"

Forty-Eight

From the phone bank in the lobby of Shauna's office building I dialed Surrey Polytech, looking for word of my client. The head of administration knew nothing, and suggested I call the Arts and Social Sciences director tomorrow at nine. I thanked her and said, "Sorry to be a bother, but could you tell me please what times Ms. Essex's classes run?"

"This semester?"

"Yes ma'am."

"All our class schedules are available on our web site."

"Yes ma'am. Next time I'll check there, and thanks for looking it up."

As I cradled the phone, out on the street, the Gastown steam clock tolled. Usually there would be tourists to capture it on video, but today there was no one. Thunderstorms were forecast for tonight, though so far the day was dry.

The receptionist came back on the line. "You did say this semester."

"Yep."

"Because Dana Essex has no scheduled classes this fall."

The gears of invisible machinery started to uncouple, derail, spill onto some nonexistent engine room floor.

"She's contracted for two sections of One Oh Three in the spring," the receptionist added.

"Thanks for your time."

There was a bench along the wall by the door. I sank down onto it, but immediately stood up. I needed air and solitude. My office on Pender Street was eight blocks east.

I made it without incident. Once inside the stairwell, though, I felt it all coming apart.

Caught in the flap of the mail slot, along with the usual flyers for Safeway and the Army & Navy, was a plastic parcel envelope with no address. I took it and the flyers upstairs to my office.

I put the envelope down on a chair. Judging from its heft and the deck-of-cards shape of its contents, it held some sort of electronic device. A bomb wasn't a far-fetched possibility. Whatever it was, I knew I wouldn't like it.

I punctured the envelope with my car key, tore it open, and dumped a cell phone into my palm. A cheap burner, the kind we used at the office. I fired it up and listened to its tinny jingle.

A dozen numbers saved in the contacts, including my own, Kay's, the office line, Jeff's. Photos were stored on the phone, candids of Jeff and Marie outside the office, Kay and Greg in the van, Kay standing in front of my apartment.

The message had to be that whoever took it could get to us. Message conveyed. I wondered if Tabitha Sorenson knew exactly who she'd been running away from, what kind of people. And Essex: if she wasn't who she said she was, how far had she been pulled into this?

Penned on the inside flap of the envelope was an eleven-digit number. I punched it in and heard it ring. No one picked up.

I thought of calling Sonia and trying to unburn that bridge. I touched my bruised and swollen eyelid, winced. As I tried to think of someone else to call, the phone jumped. A different out-of-town number appeared on the display.

I opened the phone and said, "Hello, Dana."

Forty-Nine

"I owe you a profusion of apologies," she said. "If it hadn't been necessary—"

"Why'd you kill her?" I asked.

"I was with you, Dave. From the bar to your apartment. All night, I never left your arms."

I said nothing.

"You performed perfectly," she said. "In your profession, I mean. Although the other was enjoyable, too."

"Was it really just money?" I asked.

"Not to me."

"Then explain it. 'Cause I don't get why you'd go to such lengths, not to mention ruin your career and make yourself a fugitive. For a couple hundred grand?"

"You'd find it more acceptable if it were billions?"

"More understandable."

"What if it can't be understood, Dave? Must there be a history of tortured animals and forest fires in my past, do you think?"

I leaned into the wall, my eyes fixed on the door. "What did Tabitha do to you?"

"I'm not going to give you a motive," she said. "I've decided I like the idea of you circling around me in your mind, thinking of me as a mystery, a—what do you call it, that hackneyed term? A femme fatale."

"You're just dressing up a common mugging in words," I said.

A pause. "I will tell you something. Two things, actually. I did not lie to you when I said money wasn't the deciding factor. You'd be surprised by how little I lied to you."

"Bullshit nobility. You had Tabitha murdered for money."

"You won't provoke me through feigned disbelief. Would you like to hear the second thing?"

"No."

"I didn't lie, but I heightened certain aspects of myself to give you the image you wanted. What you'd react strongest to. A damsel in distress. You came striding up the block that morning to save me, and I knew you'd want to save me again."

"Skip to the fucking end," I said.

"There's a connection between us. In spite of everything, I haven't felt as close to anyone in a long while. Which is why I regret that the burden of silence falls on you."

"If you think I'll stay silent," I said emptily.

"You'll have to, Dave. You've seen the photos? Imagine others for your partner's family, your friend Sonia, yourself if need be."

"And you'd be fine with that."

"I have very little sway over the man who'd do it. The steps have been taken already. All that holds him back is your silence."

"The police—"

"Can be lied to or ignored. I imagine you're an expert at that. Mentioning me wouldn't help you much, anyway, since I'm your alibi as much as you're mine."

"You confessed."

"Little that you didn't already know. And who knows what you confessed to, in bed, about other matters? Who but us could say how complicit you really are?"

I was preparing retorts, vows of revenge, all of them dying before I could speak them. Essex's voice was kind. Sisterly, even.

"Let things rest, Dave. Your livelihood will suffer, but you'll soldier through, I imagine, once you accept there's no profit in pursuing this further."

"You know I can't."

"My father once said to me, we don't win every engagement. It took Tabitha's betrayal to teach me that. For the sake of everyone who knows you, let this be the end. Accept that it's over. Please. Don't make us harm you."

I put the phone down on the desk without hanging up. Then I smacked it off. It hit the wall. I stomped on it. When it was in pieces I tossed the desk into the wall, leaving a deep gouge. I busted the chairs to splinters and left spiderwebs on the window. When there was nothing left to break I kicked at the steel doorframe. My kicks went wild and I tripped, falling back onto wood shards and broken glass. I lay there for a while, panting.

Eventually I sat up. Then, when I could stand, I walked to the window. I looked through the cracked pane at the gray-yellow sky, at the clusters of people shuffling up the block.

The world would have been more tolerable if it had been raining. Rain is a great equalizer, falling as it does on the just and unjust. It says so in the Bible, I believe, or maybe in Shakespeare. But it was dry, dry and darkening, and after a while I went home.

BOOK TWO
Dead Romantics

One

The poster in the display case read:

TONIGHT ONLY

FROM THE CLOVERDALE FAIRGROUNDS

LEGENDS OF THE RING IN ACTION

"DANGEROUS" DAN DOOLIN

CHIEF RED STICK, MASTER OF THE ATOMIC DROPKICK

AND HIS BEAUTIFUL VALET SPIRIT WIND

TERROR SCORPION KOBAYASHI

"THE RABID BADGER" BRIAN TOUSSAINT

TAG CHAMPIONS THE APOLLO BOMB SYNDICATE

AND MUCH MORE!

The person I'd come to the fairgrounds to see was part of the much more.

Cloverdale is a sleepy agricultural town an hour from Vancouver. The main drag is quaint, bordering on rococo: no surprise that it doubled as Smallville in one of the *Superman* TV shows. The fairgrounds host swap meets, farmers' markets, the odd classic car show. And professional wrestling.

The local promotion drew a solid crowd, though only maybe an eighth of the Alice McKay Building's capacity. Five rows of folding chairs around a worn-looking ring, with extendable bleachers coming out of two walls. Cotton candy and nachos and other assorted poisons in the far corner. Programs and merch by the door.

I took a seat high up against the wall. The opening wrestlers were rough and uncoordinated, the Irish whips and piledrivers lacking the grace of professionals. They did five-minute spots and received polite applause. Three matches in, the costumes became gaudier, the technique more polished. These jobbers knew how to stir up a crowd. The heels cheated and shook their fists at an old lady in the front row. The babyfaces slapped the canvas and reached to the sky, imploring the heavens for strength.

In match six an obese man in a leather daddy vest heaved himself onto the canvas to the tune of Slayer's "Here Comes the Pain." He strutted and posed. Audience favorite, maybe a local boy. He leaned back in a corner, waiting for his opponent.

Queens of the Stone Age blared over the PA system, "Feel Good Hit of the Summer." Tim Blatchford bounded through the dressing room curtain wearing a gold and black singlet, both hands raised to welcome the jeers of the crowd. He ran laps around the ring, then rolled under the bottom rope and shoved the ref to the mat in his eagerness to get at the man-mountain.

For seven minutes the leather daddy tossed Blatchford around the ring to the delight of the crowd. He squashed him in the corner and choked him using the ropes. Blatchford tried to muscle out, but the big man's grip kept him on his knees.

His break came when the leather daddy launched him into the ropes for a lariat. Blatchford ducked the ham-hock, bounced off the ropes. The other man turned just as Blatchford catapulted himself into the man's arms, tipping them both over the top rope, dumping them onto the floor.

On the outside Blatchford was an animal. He used whatever came to hand, or what the crowd passed him—a cane, a trash can lid, someone's souvenir belt. The leather daddy fought back and busted him open with a folding chair. Blatchford fell and covered his face. When he popped back up his head was slathered with crimson, but by then the ref had called a double count out. They fought all the way back to the dressing room, which took some nifty footwork.

At the intermission I went outside. Blatchford was standing by my Cadillac, posing for a photo with two smirking teenagers. He wore a butterfly bandage on his forehead. His own smile was almost painfully sincere and intense. When the kids left he joined me in my car.

"How you doing, Dave?" Blatchford appraised my new beard and longer hair. "Some disguise. Going for a Bruiser Brody thing, uh?"

"That was impressive," I said.

"Yeah. The kid can move, for that size."

"You cut yourself every night?"

He nodded. "You do it right, it barely leaves a mark. Do it wrong like tonight—" he shrugged. "Fuck it. 'S only a forehead. And you know what they say about getting color—about bleeding—'red equals green.'"

I wondered how much green he was actually clearing. I said, "Other than these shows, you've got time?"

"Nothing but. Same as you from what I hear. How're you enjoying retirement?"

"I stepped down. Jeff and I thought it'd be best for the business, putting some distance between me and it right now."

"But it was his idea, uh?"

"I can't blame him," I said. "I managed to fuck things up on my own."

Blatchford took a vial of pills out of his pocket. He popped three in his mouth, dry-swallowed, and offered the vial to me.

"Soma," I said. "Aren't those to sleep?"

"Shit, I need these just to drive home. My heart's still jacked from the match."

"Not for much longer."

"Nice you care," he said, and tucked the pills away. "'Splain to me how you put distance between yourself and a company that's part named after you?"

"Disney did fine without Walt."

"That's the kind of world it is," he agreed. "Nobody taking responsibility. But if you got all this time on your hands, what d'you need with me?"

His tone was chiding, but there was less scorn than the last time we'd seen each other. Maybe it was the high of performance, or perhaps Jeff had provoked his ire. In any case, buried in Blatchford's mockery was some small note of concern.

"I need you to find two people for me," I said. "A woman named Dana Essex, and another person, a man, I think, whose name I don't know."

"You can't do it yourself?"

There was no better time to tell him. I explained what had happened, what the consequences would be if they learned I was looking for them. Blatchford listened, taking swigs from his flask.

"They sound like they don't fuck around," he said. "You got no idea on this second person? Nothing at all?"

"Someone good with a knife," I said.

He nodded, as if accepting the fact. "Why me?"

"Because you're the bestest detective in the world, Tim."

"Since when did you figure that out?"

"Jeff is married and expecting. Kay's family. I wouldn't go to Bob Aries for any reason. You're competent and you're off the radar."

"Not to mention expendable," he said.

"I need your help, is what it comes down to."

He allowed himself a moment to enjoy my supplication. "I should tell you to go fuck yourself, Dave," he said. "'Cept you seem plenty fucked already. What's this job pay?"

I handed him a bank envelope stuffed with twenties. "Plus your daily and expenses."

"I'm not much of a record keeper," he said. "Make it the same as what you or Jeff would charge—plus a dollar."

I didn't argue.

Blatchford put the envelope on the dash. "You got a place to start with this woman?"

"Two," I said. "She works—worked—at a college in Surrey. She did her graduate work at Carleton."

"Hell," he said, "you're sending me to Ontario?"

"Somewhere her life intersected with this killer. You don't meet many of them in libraries. Look back till you find someone incongruent—someone who doesn't fit."

"Thinks I don't know what incongruent means," Blatchford muttered. "What else?"

I handed him a slip with six sets of numbers. "The top one was Essex's Vancouver landline. Next one is the number on a parcel the killer sent me. I dialed that, she hit me back on the third number. And then the others, she's used those, too."

Blatchford flicked the paper with his fingers. "This crazy broad calls you?"

"Every week," I said.

Two

It was nine days before I heard again from Dana Essex. That morning I'd gone to the office on Pender to patch the drywall and repair things as best I could. The landlord had seized my damage deposit—for a building that would be rubble in six months' time—but had let me handle the repairs myself.

I was grateful for the distraction. Every so often the news belched up a rumor or accusation about Tabitha Sorenson. I kept silent, distanced myself from Wakeland & Chen business, unburdening Jeff and appeasing any skeptical clients. Sonia hadn't called, and I'd had no further dealings with Chambers or Qiu. Without work to keep me busy, there was nothing to push down thoughts of Tabitha, the horror of her last moments. In a way, even Essex's call was some relief.

She phoned from an area code in southwestern Washington. Her gloating rang hollow, betrayed a lack of purpose. I'd said so.

"I admit I'm at a bit of a loss," Essex said. "I'm on the precipice of freedom, waiting for certain things to happen."

"I guess having all that money must help. How much did you end up with?"

"Would you believe I don't know the exact sum? Several hundred thousand, at least. Perhaps more."

"Not much for someone's life."

"For my life."

"You could come back, turn yourself in."

"Be serious, Dave."

Her tone was dreamlike. I could imagine her spread across a motel bed, contemplating the ceiling, midday traffic passing outside her room.

"I've been thinking about what happened with Tabitha," she said. "Analyzing my reaction. Taking stock of things like remorse, misgivings. It was more brutal than I'd expected—but then how does one 'expect' a murder? There really is no reference for it. It's all very fascinating."

"Murder is common," I said. "It's ordinary. It's cheap."

"Not to me," she said. "I think I'll conduct a study of the post-murder mindset. Perhaps write a book."

"Like Edward Bunker. Or Jean Genet."

"Former prisoners, you mean. Do you honestly think, Dave, everyone in prison deserves to be? The United States jails more of its citizens than China. The prison-industrial complex is positively booming. It's big business. In Canada, too. Prison makes the North American underclass economically viable. So why should we pretend it's punitive, when in fact prisons are simply an instrument of finance?"

"Say that's true," I said. "How does it justify you murdering a twenty-four-year-old girl in her home?" Essex didn't answer right away. "It does explain why you got along with Tabitha. She could buy into that thinking, too, couldn't she, that society's wrongs absolve our own."

"We didn't get along as well as you think." A note of aggravation had crept into her voice. "Tabitha was headstrong. And very intelligent. But constantly feeling she had to prove so. You've met tiresome people like that—janitors who insist on regaling you with the etymology of obscure words they no doubt learned for exactly that purpose. Or cab drivers who think a display of trivia makes them an intellectual. So desperate to be taken seriously. That was Tabitha."

"So why partner with her?"

"Because what she did understand was finance," Essex said. "With her position, she could manipulate the accounts how she saw fit. I thought inflating events budgets was the extent of what could be done. I didn't realize how much money could be accrued by lending it to the right people."

"You said it wasn't about money."

"I did, and it isn't."

"Then—love?"

"Honestly, Dave. Do you think you'd have bedded me if my heart's balm flowed toward her?"

"I like to think my charms are universal."

She laughed. "You needed the idea of love as motivation to take the job. I worked hard to give that to you. It would have been an easier sell if the target had been male, but I improvised. By my looks alone, I wouldn't be miscast as a woman suffering from repression. So that was who I gave you."

"Listen to how proud you are of your acting ability."

"The effort more than the ability," Essex said. "It worked well, you must admit. Remember the distinction you made, that first day, between being robbed and being cheated?"

"You're right," I said. "You won. You were brilliant."

"Thank you."

"Except now you're discovering what it's like to live on the lam. Only you don't have the love to carry you that Tabitha found. You're alone, Dana, with a dwindling sum of money, and a name that'll be useless to travel under, soon as it comes out you're involved. You don't have what it takes to be her."

Essex said quietly, emotionally, "She expected me to do nothing when she took that money—*our* money. We'd worked out that plan together. She didn't realize who she'd used and betrayed."

"Maybe neither do you."

"You'll never be in a position to do to me what was done to Tabitha," she said. "You'd be dead before you finished contemplating it. Even if you're not intimidated by me, you know I'm not alone. And you most certainly are. I know all about you, Dave. You don't have a solid move remaining."

"You might be right about that," I said. "But if I'm such a dud, why phone me?"

"I don't honestly know," Essex said.

"I do."

"Oh? And why is that?"

"I'm not going to tell you today," I said.

"A bluff."

"Maybe."

"Tell me."

"Not now."

"Tell me."

"Good night, Dana."

After I hung up I returned to patching the dents in the drywall. I wondered if I should bother sanding them smooth. How much effort was a condemned thing worth?

Three

Essex continued her weekly calls like clockwork. Her tone became more exultant. She explained how Tabitha's death was merely a settling of accounts, "the delayed yet inevitable response to her betrayal." Our conversations ended with her saying I'd never hear from her again, that this was it. Yet her tone would soften and she'd linger over the parting.

In the meantime I sanded and painted the walls and did a satisfactory job on the rest, so that the superintendent, a Lebanese man named Amir, said I could pass on fixing the woodwork.

"Is all be gone soon anyway," he said one afternoon when he came by to collect the rent. We stood out in front of the building, watching the cage of scaffolding go up on a property across the street.

"Condos, too?" I asked him.

"Rentals. Three fifty square foot."

"Good size. Who doesn't like to take a piss and cook eggs without leaving your bed?"

He laughed and asked if I wanted to join him in his office for a drink. We sat in his first-floor box with its odd domestic carpeting and hodgepodge of furniture. A desk and file cabinet, sofa. I'd been transacting business with Amir for six years, off and on, and I'd never been inside.

Amir had quite the collection of single malts. "My brother, he works for the Liquor Control," he explained. He poured us each a dram of Arran Twelve into a paper cone.

The company he worked for had buildings up and down Vancouver Island. He'd be taking over the business there, moving his family.

"Think you'll miss the city?" I asked.

"Of course," he said. "My kids'll change schools. They lose their friends, it will be hard. But I miss change. I move a lot before I come here. When I meet my wife, we find a house and we stay. Thirteen years," he said sadly.

"The tower they're replacing us with," I said. "Any word on the low-income housing?"

"Thirteen units."

I scowled. "Not even ten percent." Meanwhile the rents of the surrounding buildings would skyrocket, pushing out however many hundreds of people.

"Is their building," Amir said.

"Is my neighborhood."

"You'll go back up the street?" he asked.

I held out my free hand, who's to say, and sipped scotch with the other. "I'm not sure Jeff wants me back. I wouldn't, I was him. My side of the business tends to operate at a loss."

"Is like a marriage, uh?"

"With worse arguments," I said. "And better sex."

As we were talking someone rapped on the office door. Through the slats of the blinds I saw a short and malformed silhouette. Amir opened the door to reveal a man in a dirty cream-colored dress shirt and slacks. He had an eyepatch, a cane, and sundry bruises decorating the exposed flesh of his arms, face, and throat. I recognized him as Miles, the man Chris Chambers had assaulted out back of the Crossroads Inn.

"I'm looking for David Wake-something," Miles said.

Four

"You people are assholes, you know that?" Miles leaned on the door-frame and pointed his cane up toward my office. "Make a crippled man try those stairs. Ever hear of wheelchair accessibility?"

Amir insisted we use his office and left. Miles hooked the arm of a chair with his cane and dragged it to where he could flop down on it.

"This chick told me when I got out of the hospital I should find you."

"She wouldn't be a police officer?" I asked.

He nodded. "Cryptic bitch. All she said was you'd want to hear my story."

"I could use one where the good guys win."

Miles looked at the bottle of scotch on the desk expectantly. I waited. He cleared his throat.

"Anyway, she said there'd be sixty bucks in it for me, that you weren't a cop, and that my story might help you fuck No-Frisk Chris in some way. And let me tell you," he added, "I didn't come here just for the sixty."

I produced the bills but didn't pass them to him. "Story first."

Miles had wanted to host a club night in one of the waterfront dives. Dance music, cheap beer, Ecstasy, and untaxed cigarettes. He'd worked out a deal with the owners, but needed a few thousand for the pills,

audio equipment, and supplies. With two prior convictions and a busted
credit record, he'd turned to Anthony Qiu for the loan.

"I got beat on the pills," he said. "Fucking baby aspirin. Was Qiu's
connect, anyway. Asshole Malaysians pulled a gun when I complained.
I told Qiu's guy, Wong, and he goes, 'Hmm, they're usually reliable.'
That bastard doesn't do nothing, so suddenly I owe five grand and rising
interest to a gangster who prob'ly set up the whole scam, the prick."

Miles tried to scrape together the cash. With the club night dead, he
had a grocery clerk's income and whatever he could make pulling petty
thefts. Plus a propensity for cocaine.

"I figured, snort some, sell some," Miles said. "When Chambers
heard I'd copped, he came around, broke my hand. Now I can't work
on account of this busted mitt, so how'm I s'posed to dig myself out?"

He'd gone to ground in New Westminster, sleeping on the floor of
a friend. Chambers eventually found him. Cuffed him, dragged him out
to his car, and forced him into the trunk.

"They let me out, I'm looking around and all I see is dirt. Piles of it.
There's me, Chambers, Wong, and this other, sick-looking guy. They
start whaling on me. Mr. Sick takes a chain, loops it under one arm
and around my neck. Takes the other end and loops it round the back
fender. He's grinning. They take turns doing donuts. I remember trying
to keep my back to the ground as they dragged me, but I got tangled
and ended up face down. I remember this pain in my eye and then I'm
gone. Woke up in Royal Columbia. Said I was unconscious two days.
Tell me that ain't sixty dollars' worth of story."

As I handed him the money I asked, "Any chance you'd go to the
police with this? New West is Mountie jurisdiction. Chambers has no
pull."

"All a them're the same. Now good-bye."

It took him a moment to stand.

"Any chance for that eye?" I asked.

"They say something'll come back some time. Fucking doctors."

I helped him up and held the door for him. He was a prick about that, too. As he left I asked him if he knew of anyone else who owed Qiu. Specifically people who Chambers collected from.

"We're a dying breed," he said. "Ha fucking ha. I heard he laid a real beating on a Vietnamese over some poker game. Wouldn't know the name, but I heard it happened downtown. Just rolled up, got out, and started pounding on the gook before anyone knew what the why was. Chambers half-enjoys that shit, you ask me."

"Power," I said.

Miles nodded. "Yeah. Some time I'd like to know what that's like."

Five

There was no word from Blatchford that week. I'd given him a cell phone and set up a private e-mail account. It felt strange to occupy the position of a client, waiting for results.

I thought of my own client Ritesh Ghosh, whose nine-year-old daughter had disappeared, who had exhausted every possible means, spared no expense. And for nothing. Jasmine Ghosh's whereabouts after leaving the grocery store near their house had yet to be discovered. I'd watched the store's blurred surveillance footage a thousand times, sometimes on a loop. See the girl walk through the aisles. See her pay for her sour keys and fuzzy peaches. See her go tiptoe to slide the change from the counter into her cupped hand. Then see her walk out the door, unhesitating and happy, into the bright white nothing of the next eight years.

I'd waited six days on Blatchford. I could hold out longer.

The next Monday I met Jeff Chen at the Congee Noodle House, Broadway and Main. He was already seated by the glass windowfront, tucking into a bowl of watery jook. His honeymoon tan was long faded. Bags decorated the undersides of his eyes from long hours spent mollifying corporate clients. Jeff shook hands and smiled pleasantly, which was not a good sign.

"Things happen," he said.

"How's Kay?"

"We're keeping her in-office, like you asked. Glad your lack of computer skills don't run in the family."

I sat down. Jeff had a glass of Coke with a lemon wedge floating in it. I ordered the same.

"No food?" Jeff asked.

"I don't think we're going to want to sit eating with each other, time the conversation ends."

He tilted his head slightly to acknowledge the point. "Good news is we only lost Solis," he said, "and they'd been talking about making a move anyway."

"That's a relief."

He grinned, still spooning up broth. "No, it isn't," he said. "You don't give a shit about that side of the business. The profitable side."

"You're right."

"This isn't even about the Sorenson case. I don't blame you. Ultimately we have very different philosophies on business."

"This does sound like a breakup, doesn't it?"

"And I respect your philosophy," Jeff said. "Really. I just—I didn't sign up for a crusade. Y'know? I've got a kid coming. After the miscarriage, Marie was worried she'd never have another. Now everything's finally on track. And I feel like, work-wise, I've compromised all I can."

"You've been more than fair," I said. "I seem to be hardwired to push things."

"And people."

"And people," I agreed. "It's not you, Jeff, it's me. So name your terms."

"You're not leaving broke. I'd buy you out. I could borrow a lump sum, or you'd have a non-participatory interest in the company, a percentage for a certain number of years."

"Either or. Could Kay stay on?"

"Long as she likes."

I held out my hand. Jeff said, "What about price?"

"Work it out later."

We shook hands.

"I don't want to feel like I'm abandoning you when you're down," he said. "I'm sure this shit'll blow over. What'll you do now?"

"Don't know," I said. "Start over, maybe."

"You'd have to sign a non-compete, at least for two years," Jeff said. We stared at each other. "Or maybe we could limit that to corporate security and home protection."

"Gigs I wouldn't get, anyway."

I finished my drink, dropped some coins on the table. I felt empty in the best possible sense. I didn't want to burden Jeff any further. We'd been close, maybe friends. We knew each other's secrets and sins. He'd accepted me unquestioningly, and I knew he'd told the truth; it had been the business that had ended our partnership. A small distinction, but it meant something to me.

I walked.

Six

East Vancouver depends on bridges to traverse the ravine that cuts diagonally through that part of the city. Train tracks run along the valley floor, while above, gray ribbons of Skytrain track sweep up and out from the city center. From the Commercial Drive Bridge, you look down on a rusty orange cage that shields the crisscrossing lines from falling debris. Or from bodies. Three days after my retirement, I stood on the bridge and watched a crew of forensic technicians clear a corpse from off the tracks.

"Most likely the fall snapped his neck," Detective Triplett said. Away from her partner she was more direct, as if she'd absorbed some of his gruffness, or felt free to let her own seep through. We headed away from the rubberneckers on the bridge.

Below, McCurdy was talking to a pair of techs in white Tyvek suits as they collected samples from the soot-stained gravel beside the rail ties. I leaned over the railing, looking down past the cage to the body on the tracks.

"The geometry is suspect," Triplett said. "It's clear he fell. From where, though, is another matter. Do you have any ideas, Mr. Wakeland?"

"Why would I?"

"It's your neighborhood," she said.

From thirty feet up it was hard to make out the features, but the cream-colored garments the corpse was dressed in looked familiar.

"No other marks on him?"

"You mean injuries." Triplett took the hint. "None I'd connect with his death, but older ones, yes, including one to the eye. Does that fit someone you know?"

"It does."

She paused for me to elaborate. I kept my elaborations to myself.

"Does the name Miles Irigary—"

"You know it does," I interrupted. "If you want me to be on the level, tell me how you knew to ask me."

From her pocket Triplett produced an evidence baggie, pressed flat, holding a note. Scrawled in pen, what looked like my name, followed by both office addresses. "This was in his wallet." Triplett's look demanded an explanation.

"He came to visit me," I said. "He wanted to tell me about the beating he took. It factored into a case of mine."

"And did he tell you who beat him?"

"Two thugs employed by a gangster named Anthony Qiu." I added, "They were working with—for—a police officer."

"Be serious," Triplett said.

"Would you like his name?"

She didn't hurry to respond. I nodded, I understood. Below, the corpse was laid into a blue body bag, zipped up dispassionately, like old hockey equipment.

"If what you're telling me were true," Triplett said, "there are channels you could follow to lodge a complaint."

"Sure."

"But you won't do that." Disappointment and relief muddled in her voice.

"I've seen people make those complaints before," I said.

"And had one lodged against yourself, as I recall."

"Yes."

"You didn't think justice was served in that instance?"

"I chose to resign," I said.

"Of course."

"If you can convince Chris Chambers to do the same—"

The name provoked a reaction. If I read her face right, she knew Chambers, maybe liked him, but didn't find the accusation absurd. Surprise but not incredulity. Triplett recovered by watching the swaddled corpse being carted toward the waiting van just to the side of the tracks.

"I'm not sure I believe you," she said after a moment. "You don't seem to think this is connected to Ms. Sorenson—other than through yourself."

"No guarantees, but I don't think so."

She nodded, then surprised me by taking a pack of cigarillos from her pocket and lighting one. The sweet smell offended the more health-conscious of the gawkers on the bridge.

"Getting anywhere on Tabitha's murder?" I asked her.

"We're doing what we can."

"Gill didn't see anything, did he?" When she shook her head I asked, "How's he doing?"

"Devastated," Triplett said. "As you can imagine. Keep away from him."

I told her I would. Triplett gestured down toward the tracks.

"Meanwhile, you may want to consider, whoever did this might know you spoke with Miles Irigary. Might even have picked this spot for its proximity to your home, as a message."

"I'm retired," I said.

A glimmer of a grin caught on her face.

"The kind of world we live in, these days, even retirees are urged to take caution."

Seven

The liquor store clerk in her drab beige outfit recommended several excellent and reasonably priced reds, stressing their local origin. I settled on a Similkameen reserve and asked her if she thought it would make a swell apology note.

"Depends on the crime," she said.

"I said some things, which may have provoked some minor fisticuffs on her part."

She nodded seriously. "Two bottles, maybe, just to make sure?"

With my purchases under one arm, I walked over the bridge toward Sonia's apartment. A thin mist rose up from False Creek to halo the globes of light around the street lamps. Below the bridge I could see onto the roofs of the waterfront condominiums, and across to the silver-domed Science World. I remembered viewing the Bodyworlds exhibit there with Sonia years ago, human bodies skinned and posed and lacquered. We'd gone in agreeing that it was a noble use for a person's discarded earthly husk. Two hours later, one of us felt it was obscene. I couldn't remember which of us thought that, only that it had become the source of a playful argument and teasing. All our best jokes had revolved around death and its utter lack of dignity.

I rang Sonia's buzzer and she let me in. She didn't apologize for clocking me, but said she was happy she'd missed my eye. I gave her the wine. She had a tea service ready and we had that instead. Sitting next to each other on the couch, waiting for the other to speak.

"I know what you saw," I said eventually.

"I should've said."

"You can say now if you want."

"All right." She started to fidget and then stopped herself, laying her hands on her knees. Her words came out as a recital, as testimony.

"We were heading East on Kingsway, Chris and I. I was driving. We passed Pho Sho, the Vietnamese place. Chris leaned over and grabbed my arm. He told me to hit the brakes. I did. He got out of the car and told me to wait. I asked if I should notify dispatch and he waved it off like it wasn't important. So I didn't. Chris went inside. He was maybe three minutes. When he came out he was leading an Asian male, Vietnamese, late twenties early thirties. He put him in the back of the car and told me to drive. I asked where and he told me the coffee shop on Victoria and Powell, near all the storage places. I drove there. I didn't ask questions because I was waiting for him to explain. The man didn't speak. He looked afraid.

"At the coffee shop all three of us exited the vehicle. We were in front of that storage place. Chris told me to order him black coffee and a chicken wrap. I asked about the man he'd handcuffed. He said it was nothing. That he'd arrested him before and he wanted to scare him a little to make sure he was 'on the up and up.' That was the phrase he used and he smiled when he said it.

"As I went in Chris led him around the side of the building, into the lot of that old transmission shop on nineteen hundred block. I walked to the door and doubled back and looked around the corner. I saw Chris grab the man's hair and shove him face-first into the brick wall until blood came out of the man's nose and mouth. I remember it left a splash on the white brick. Chris removed the cuffs and kicked the man several times in the ribs. Eventually he let the man stand up. The man took off southbound, running very fast. I noticed then that Chris had the man's wallet. I watched him remove some bills and toss the wallet after the man, who didn't stop to retrieve it. Chris didn't explain himself and I was too confused and afraid to ask."

"Ever see the man again?" I said.

"I looked him up but couldn't find him. I did hear Chris subsequently refer to him as Larry, no surname."

"What context made Chambers bring him up?"

"At the end of shift he noticed I was nonresponsive to some of his comments. He asked what was wrong. I didn't reply. He told me if it was about that business with Larry, not to worry. That Larry was a multiple rapist who had skated on a technicality. I asked him about the money—the only question I asked. Chris said he slipped it into the mailbox of one of Larry's victims, a young widow and mother who'd been paralyzed by Larry's attack."

"What else did Saint Christopher say?"

"Nothing. But he insisted on buying coffee for me all the next week." She watched her toes grip the carpet. "I've sworn to these details, Dave. My lawyer's holding a copy and I've got one here for you."

She handed me the affidavit. I flipped the pages, each of which had been signed by Sonia and her lawyer.

"Are you afraid for your life?"

"No," Sonia said evenly. "I'm going to let it go."

"Meaning what?"

"I thought I couldn't live with it, knowing what Chris uses our job to do. I didn't understand."

"His crew killed that guy you sent to me. Miles."

"I know," she said. "And I can't stand it. But there is nothing I can do that Chris Chambers can't escape, and he will ruin me so amazingly easily. Even if he lost his job off my testimony—even if he was convicted—he'd turn the department against me. I'd never be able to trust a partner again, and none of them would ever trust me. And that probably sounds terrifically selfish, but this is all I have."

I said, "Resigning wasn't the worst thing to ever happen to me. Though it felt like it at the time. People always say you'll have a bunch of careers in your lifetime."

Sonia was clutching her cup right below her chin so the steam traveled over the planes of her face.

"When I was a kid, Dave, all I wanted was to be white. I didn't want to be the only brown girl in school, the one who didn't have parents. When I got to high school I became Miss Indian Pride. I found others who looked like me, but they all ended up back east, in university or business, and married. Now I don't know who I am. When I come home with my dirty uniform in my gym bag, and I pass that mirror in the hall, I see myself and think: no family, no husband, no kids, no country. I have a city and I have a job and that's all."

I didn't know how to respond. I wanted to lighten the mood, or share something equally as raw. To put my arm around her and comfort her with something pat and life-affirming. There were true things I could say. But a truth mentioned in the wrong spirit is no better than a falsehood.

So I said nothing. I brushed her arm with my hand and waited. I waited until I could say the words "There's a way out of this" and have them not be a lie.

Eight

Pho Sho was a small restaurant with white bars over the window, an off-white awning, the name bilingual in gray script. I waited for the lull between late lunch and early dinner, ordered a *bánh mì* and Vietnamese coffee, and handed my card to the server.

"Larry around?" I touched my nose when I said his name, and told her he was wearing a bandage when last I saw him.

The server glanced at the clipboard hanging from the wall. Instead of answering me, she brought an older woman out from the back, who said Larry wasn't around and she didn't know where he was. A hint of maternal suspicion in her voice.

I stepped out of the restaurant and looked up and down the street. I didn't know if Larry was an employee or customer, casual or regular, undocumented immigrant or Vancouver homegrown. But I remembered what Miles had said about being a breed apart.

Towers were making inroads onto Kingsway, displacing the narrow restaurants and the shopfronts with their barred windows. But it was still Kingsway. There were two corner stores within sight, a Korean grocer and a cigarette shop with stacks of Asian newspapers out front. I tried the latter.

The man behind the counter was cutting keys. He was wearing a polo shirt, blue with white piping, with a crude approximation of the Ralph Lauren logo stitched to the breast pocket.

I asked for two cartons of Marlboros. He retrieved them out of the case. Tax stamped and still in their plastic. I looked at him, at the cigarettes, and at the floor behind him. He put the smokes back, disappeared for a moment and came back with two unstamped cartons.

"Turkish?" I asked hopefully. He nodded. "Nothing smokes like a Turkish Marlboro."

As he bagged one carton I opened the other and took out a pack. Tapping the counter absentmindedly, I said, "You know the guy who comes in here with the thing on his nose? You think you'll see him today?"

He nodded, grimaced a bit. Evidently Larry wasn't a popular customer.

"I left my wallet at home, 'bout a week ago. He gave me his last smoke. I wouldn't've done that for me, I was him." I pushed one pack back across the counter. "He comes in, would you give him this?" I slid over another one. "For your trouble. Thanks, man."

I found a café up the block with a few tables out front, from which I could watch the front door of the tobacconist's without drawing attention. If in fact Larry worked at the restaurant, and if he decided to stop into the store on his way, and if I could spot him—too many ifs.

But sometimes you get lucky. It was two hours later when he showed, and the cigarette ruse was all but unnecessary. He pulled to the curb in a lime-green Civic with spinning hubcaps, climbed out, working the door handle with a tenderness toward the machine. The cartilage of his nose was still noticeably askew. He came out of the store holding the cigarettes and a wad of shiny gold strips. Once he got his smoke lit, he held the pack in his armpit while he dug out change and attended to the strips. Scratch tickets. I watched him scratch and curse his way through four before I approached.

"Son of a motherfuck," he said, tossing another loser into the gutter.

"I'd like a word with you, Larry," I said.

He jumped a few steps back. When he realized I was between him and his car, he returned, wary. "You the Cigarette Fairy?"

"More lucrative than teeth," I said. "Another carton and a half if you let me buy you a drink."

"Jesus," he said, "you're not from—"

"Anthony Qiu and Chris Chambers? No."

"Good, 'cause I'm up on my payment. I'll even be ahead if a couple things work out." He paused. "You said no but you know their names."

I said, "You know the parking garage on Beatty, near Victory Square? Park there, second floor. I'll meet you in ten minutes."

"I'm busy, I got to work—"

"I got a picture of you, a description, and your license number." I aimed my cell phone's lens at Larry's face and snapped a shot. "I'm not going to hassle you and I'm not a cop. See you in ten."

Larry was late. I crossed the street to the Medina Café. There was always a long lineup, extending out into the street, hip young couples with money. I bought a coffee and a lavender latte and two Belgian waffles. Larry's green Civic pulled into the garage. I crossed the empty road to meet him.

"Not what I thought you meant by a drink," he said, accepting the coffee and waffle. I moved to enter the car and he stopped me and climbed out. "Nobody eats in her," he said.

Leaning against a concrete pillar I said, "A couple months back Chris Chambers beat the shit out of you."

"Only because my hands were cuffed behind me," he said. "My hands were free, or cuffed in front? 'Tirely different story."

"You owe him money."

"He collects for the guy I owe. Winslow."

"You were behind on installments."

He lit another cigarette, dragged on it thoughtfully. A tour bus rumbled down Beatty, the uncovered back section crowded, cameras hanging limp around the necks of tourists.

"That restaurant should be half mine," Larry said. "My parents put it in my big brother's name, but the profits were always 'sposed to be split. When my brother found out about my gambling addiction, know what he did? You think he offered to get me counseling, his little brother who used to sleep in the same bed with him? No. Offered me cash money for my share. You believe that?"

"And you took it."

"Well, way he runs the restaurant I figured I can't do worse."

"And?"

"Turns out I can do worse." Larry shook his head, thinking of lost fortunes. "The money got me into this table game, and that's where I met Winslow."

"Playing?"

"Working," he said. "Thought he was a bouncer or one of the guys' drivers. Who else wears shades in a dark room? When I busted out he stopped me at the door, offered to loan me another K. And then two more. I was into him for seven by the end of the night."

"Why'd he lend you the money? Just to pick up debt?"

"He thought my name was still on the slip for Pho Sho. When he found out I'm just another broke-ass prep cook, he gave me two weeks."

"Then he sent Chambers."

"Right. My brother gave me two—'gave,' fucking advance against my minimum wage job—and Winslow said not good enough. I told him I didn't have a cent to my name. He said to have another grand ready for Tuesday. That would let me put the rest on installments. I didn't know he'd send a cop."

"How bad did Chambers hurt you?"

"I've been beat on since I was little," Larry said. "My dad was against it but my mom—shit, she used to break spoons beating my ass. With the cop, I just wish I got a fair chance, y'know? Easy to whip on someone who's tied up."

"When's your next payment due?"

"Two C-notes every Friday," Larry said. "Only half of one counts toward the principal. I never missed a payment."

"Then why'd he beat on you?"

"This." Larry patted the hood of his Civic. "I won it off one of the other chefs—not that he had it legally. When word got back to Winslow that Larry Tranh had a new car, he sent his dog after me, even though it was him said I couldn't pay extra to work down the debt."

"Still pissed at Chambers?"

"Hell yes."

"Interested in payback?"

"Tell me where he lives, I'll roll by with a Molotov."

"I don't think so."

"Maybe handcuff him, too. Show him how it feels."

"Punk stuff," I said, shaking my head at his bravado. "I'm talking about really hurting him. That takes a certain skill which you possess in spades."

"And that'd be what?"

"You annoy people to the point they want to hit you."

Nine

Friday night I stood in Thornton Park, across from Pacific Central Station. I was reading a placard dedicated to the memory of the women murdered during the 1987 shooting at L'Ecole Polytechnique. Strange to be in a city known for its missing and murdered women, and see reminders of an atrocity in Montreal. But you go numb assigning priority to the dead.

The work van turned off Terminal onto Main. It parked in front of the station. I walked over to it and pushed my credit card into the meter, buying us four very expensive hours.

Kay opened the driver's side door and dropped to the pavement. She'd gone all out. Black lipstick, peroxide streaks in her hair, sequined dress and exposed bra straps. Heavy eye makeup and press-on nails. The getup was garish, almost comical. I watched her teeter on the stems of her stiletto heels.

Larry Tranh emerged from the back. He was wearing yesterday's clothes, but under a new leather jacket with an oversized collar. He'd gelled his hair into something like a pompadour.

I told them the route and went over the instructions again. Down Main to Hastings, then to Cordova, then to the Waterfront. I had them memorize the names of the bars. The Waverley, the Cobalt, Grand

Union, the Irish Heather, moving down to Steamworks and then to Docherty's. One drink each, pay up front, and have it at the bar. When you speak to each other, speak loud but not too loud, and make sure people can hear.

At Docherty's you stay at the bar and wait.

I told them not to look around for me. Text if anything goes wrong. And don't feel you have to finish every drink.

"Get sangria," I told Kay, "or something else low-alcohol."

"I can hold my liquor."

"I know you can, Hemingway. But not while you're working."

When they were out of sight, I locked up the van and took the Skytrain down to Waterfront.

Larry had been under wraps the entire day. He'd phoned in sick to work that morning, pissing off his brother. That alone probably sold him on the plan. The rest would be less enjoyable.

Docherty's was a dark, sparsely furnished bar with grimy tables and little in the way of décor. A video projector shone grainy, desaturated footage onto a wall beside the DJ booth and dance floor. The bar was owned and tended by a middle-aged couple, Rick and Steve, who rented it out to whoever would hustle to draw a crowd. Including Miles Irigary.

I'd explained to them what I wanted and why. I dropped the dead man's name. When I did, Rick paused from scraping frost off the inside of the ice machine to remark that, while Miles was a prick and a chiseler, he was *their* prick and chiseler, and they'd be happy to do something to honor the bastard. They acquiesced to all my camera placements, except the washroom.

"The alley, too," I said. "At the Crossroads Inn, that's where he dragged Miles."

"How many of these cameras will you have?"

"As many as it takes."

Rick thwacked his partner's arm. "Get a load of Stanley Kubrick over here."

Without looking up Steve said, "Ready for my closeup, Mr. DeMille."

"That's Billy Wilder, you fucking philistine."

"Pretty sure it was Gloria Swanson."

Rick rolled his eyes. Turning to me he said, "How bad do you think it'll be?"

"I'd count on blood."

Ten

Sitting by the half-crowded dance floor with a view of both entrances, I waited. I imagined Larry and Kay making their rounds. A drink at the bar. Kay saying she wanted something expensive. Larry telling her to get whatever she wanted, flashing a stack of fresh twenties when he paid. Her prompting him. Didn't he have to pay Anthony Qiu? And Larry's response: Fuck Qiu. Fuck Winslow Wong. Fuck Chris Chambers. This was his money and he was through paying those punk bitches.

Then on to the next bar, and hopefully word trickling back to Wong, then to Qiu, then delegated to Chambers.

And me, nursing a bottle of Dark Matter, waiting for my movie to unfold.

My phone buzzed, incoming text. Sonia's number. She was parked on a residential street near Boundary, waiting for the headlights of Chambers's white Lexus to snap on. Her text said: IN CAR. ALONE. LEAVING.

Chambers might be carrying a gun. He might also bring friends. There was no way this wasn't going to end ugly, but I didn't want a bloodbath. I had my flashlight. Kay had bear spray. Sonia would have her sidearm.

Out back people smoked on the wooden porch. The steep geography of the waterfront put the bar's entrance at street level and the porch

ten feet above an alley. I had a camera over the back door, four inside
the bar, and two covering the street out front. All of them feeding into
a laptop I'd stored in the bar's small office.

An hour passed. At twenty to two Larry Tranh and Kay walked in.
They made for the bar. Kay stayed in character, didn't look around,
didn't seem nervous. I felt a surge of pride. Tranh seemed jittery and I
wondered if he was having second thoughts. I couldn't blame him—it
was his head. I hoped the same cockiness he'd exuded for the last few
days would shame him into carrying through with the plan.

I texted Kay the words OFF THE HOOK, our code for "everything on
track." I watched her show it to Larry, laughing, as if it were a friend's
comment.

Sonia's texts became one-word updates as she shadowed Chambers
through the bars along Main. I bought another beer. My adrenaline was
rising. I began to fidget, tapping my feet against the club music emanat-
ing from the dance floor. That awful disco version of Gordon Lightfoot's
"If You Could Read My Mind." All the laws against secondhand smoke,
not a one for secondhand sound.

2 BLKS, Sonia texted. I thumbed the keypad of my phone, typing TIME
TO DANCE and sending it to Kay. I watched her peel herself off from Larry
and cross to the dance floor, joining the dozen or so dancers.

NOW, Sonia texted.

Staring over the mouth of my bottle I watched Chris Chambers
push the front door open and stride in. He was decked out all in black.
I watched him scan the dance floor and tables, then fix on Larry at the
bar, gabbing to Steve.

It was quick. Larry had turned around and Chris was already at the bar.
Something in his hand glinted, a gun, and he struck Larry full in the face,
knocking him back into the bartop. Chambers struck him again. Not a gun,
something else.

Larry sprawled. Chambers grabbed him by the hair and collar and
started for the back exit.

I could've stopped him from taking Larry outside. I didn't stand up. Didn't even look up, not until the back door had swung shut. I wanted that perfect image on film, the full entry and exit. When I trimmed that footage, it would tell a whole story.

When the back door swung shut I sprang for it and crashed through. I saw Chambers, his back to me, arms on Larry who was bent backward over the porch railing. Trying to throw him over. The porch and stairs had cleared out rapidly.

I seized Chambers from behind and pulled him off. We back-pedaled, hitting the wall. Chambers struggled free. Larry had sunk down to the porch floor, clinging to the guardrail post. Chambers kicked him, not even turning to see who'd restrained him.

"Off him." Kay's voice, followed by a blast of bear spray that caught Chambers in the face.

Chambers thrashed and fell forward, cursing, rubbing at his eyes. My own eyes watered. Kay pulled Larry to his feet and they ducked back inside.

I thought of tossing Chambers over the rail and to hell with the cameras. He deserved it and more. But I wanted him unscathed. Any contusions, he could say Larry had done it before entering the bar. It would be a cop's word, a white cop's word, against an Asian gambler's. Better that Chambers stayed unharmed. You want your animals healthy and clean before you slaughter them.

I moved inside and retrieved the laptop from the office. Kay and Larry had left, hopefully with Sonia in her Mazda. The bar patrons were animated with theories and stories of other fights. The dancers danced on.

Eleven

Kay and Larry called it The Escape. Sonia and I were more comfortable with Exit Strategy. Sonia had parked out front and stationed herself with a view of the club's front door. When Larry and Kay burst out, she hustled them into the backseat of her car and drove them up the block. Kay had a spare key, in case Chambers had come out and Sonia needed to walk away. Sonia dumped them by the van, which is where I headed.

Chambers hadn't seen me, though it didn't matter much. He'd divine things for himself in a week or so. I was ready for that. I didn't want him or anyone else connecting this to Sonia. When she drove Larry, she wore sunglasses and didn't give her name. I wanted him thinking she was just another operative.

At the van I found Kay dressing Larry's wounds. The blow to his face had bled wildly but didn't seem to have done any serious damage. I thought of Blatchford, cutting himself secretly to draw a reaction from the crowd. Getting color, he'd called it. All part of the show.

Two lacerations to the face, a deep bruise along the kidneys, various bumps and contusions and a close call with a second-story plunge. For that I paid Tranh five thousand dollars of Sonia's money. He received it grimly, perhaps knowing it would soon line the pockets of a casino owner.

He said, "You see how close he got to tossing me over the railing? What'd you do if that happened?"

"I'd try to summon the strength to go on living," I said.

"You're a cold motherfucker, know that?"

His anger diminished as he counted his money. I told him if he wanted me to try and smooth things over with Qiu, he could leave the cash with me. He politely declined my offer. I recommended he get out of town, maybe go up to the Interior, Kelowna or Penticton, or maybe Calgary.

"Nah," he said. "I got a friend in Malaysia said I could crash on his couch. He runs a junket, Singapore to Cambodia. The gamblers over there are serious. Round the clock, and the hotels know how to treat people. Catch you later."

I dropped Kay at my mother's, then returned the van to the Wakeland & Chen parking space underneath the Hastings office. Walking up the ramp I saw Sonia's car idling across the street. She wasn't supposed to be here.

"You were going to walk to your place?" she asked.

"It's hard to come down after that sort of thing," I said. "Walking gives me time to cool off."

She unlocked the door. "Let me drive you."

I did. Only when we neared Broadway and Commercial she missed the turn and drove southeast, rolling into the gravel lot near Trout Lake. The still, black water seemed to reject the moonlight, instead soaking up the darkness of the trees and their shadows. A few rowdies chugged brews from the bleacher steps.

Sonia undid her seatbelt. She fumbled with her purse and brought out a check for seven thousand dollars. I reminded her I'd talked Larry down to five.

"For your sister, then."

I pocketed the money. Sonia asked me if I had any qualms. "About using Tranh like that. Putting your sister in harm's way."

"Kay can handle herself."

"She risked something. You put her in that position. Larry, too."

"Once I explained that a repeat performance would cost Chambers his job, Larry was eager to do it," I said. "Maybe not eager, but the cash tipped him. With Kay, she needs the experience. I won't have her doing this job and holding back out of fear. You have to be willing to stand a beating."

"Just like her big brother," Sonia said.

"Only I tend to catch them from friends."

She looked at the steering wheel. "I'm not sure I apologized. I'm grateful, anyway. What do we do with the footage?"

"Your choice," I said. "Someone well versed in etiquette might forward it to Chambers's bosses quietly, demand his resignation."

"And what would a pissed-off, marginalized bitch like myself do?"

"Spread it like herpes."

She thought about it. I looked at the water.

"It has to be that way," she said. "If we let the department handle it, they'll do their best to minimize the damage. It has to be public."

"Better that way," I said.

"Chris won't face jail, though."

"And never will."

"It doesn't seem like enough, does it?"

"It's enough for me," I said. "But it's not about me."

Sonia's tired expression broke into a rueful grin. Hope sometimes hits us that way.

Twelve

Sunday night I watched Blatchford and his former foe, Leather Daddy, take on a pair of Japanese wrestlers whose synchronized kicks and takedowns possessed a balletic grace that elevated the bloodbath to tragic theater. For a solid twenty minutes the Apollo Bomb Syndicate demonstrated an economy of motion and raw athleticism that should have shamed their opponents, who stumbled around the South Surrey Veterans Hall in a coke-and-Soma haze. If it wasn't for the last-minute interference of a dwarf dressed in a leather vest and cap and wielding a kendo stick, Blatchford's team would have completely lacked an offense, and probably would have lost.

I caught up with him later at Charlie Don't Surf, a restaurant near the beach with a Margaritaville atmosphere. Blatchford was drinking at a corner table with the little person and his girlfriend. I caught the tail end of a story about Sweet Daddy Siki and Harley Race.

Blatchford downed his drink and made the introductions. "Johnny Camino, best little man since Sky Low Low, and this is Beverly. Dave here is a private eye."

"That'd be a great gimmick," Johnny Camino said. "Could get myself a trench coat."

"You're welcome to it," I said.

Blatchford excused us, out for a smoke. He stopped by the bar and allowed me to buy him another double Crown and soda, no ice, which he threw back before leading me outside. We stood at the very edge of the patio and watched a train slink past the beach on its way to Seattle, its klaxon resounding against the soft hiss of the surf.

Blatchford pointed toward the bar. "That guy's been doing this thirty years. No pension. None of that pay-per-view money. One-night stands in podunk towns like this, one or two hundred a year, sometimes more. Know what he's most proud of?"

I shook my head.

"All that time, he never hurt another wrestler. That's the benchmark for him. And he fought tough guys, too, dwarfs as well as regulars. Even a bear, one time."

"How many have you hurt?" I asked. "In the ring."

"Me?" Blatchford thought about it. "Three for sure that I know of. Fractured skull from a chair shot, another a broken rib from being side-suplexed onto the guardrail. Those were accidents. Third guy I broke his leg."

"Intentionally?"

"Called me a faggot." Blatchford smiled. "It was the way he said it. Looked enough like an accident, but I knew where I was dropping him."

With the train gone we could see the ocean, black waves rolling against the breakwater at the end of the pier. Blatchford dropped off the patio and started walking.

When we were halfway down the pier, alone with the rain, he said, "This Dana Essex is a smart girl. I read an article of hers, published in one of those journals they don't carry at normal libraries. The kind of words she uses—you ever hear the word palimpsestic?"

"A page hidden beneath a page or something."

He whistled. "Somebody owns a dictionary. Anyway, her titles alone have more words in them than a Tom Clancy book. She's big on ogicals and izations, our gal."

"That all you have after two weeks?"

"Easy there," he said. "I can't make hide or hair out of her writing, but I know anyone writing like that is afraid. Like if she doesn't work in enough Cadillac-type words, her peers won't think she belongs."

"You don't think that's just how smart people write?"

"I'm smart. I don't write like that."

He chained his cigarette, tossed the butt so it arced and disappeared among the crevices of the rock beach.

"Anyway, that's who she is—eager to be a part of the club, and also better than the club. Her first years at Carleton she won half the awards, spoke at research conferences and volunteered to taxi around university bigwigs at those same conferences. Fucking go-getter. And then by year six"—he exhaled a lumpy smoke ring—"no more awards, no presentations. Total shutdown."

We'd reached the end. Looking down I could see the barnacle-crusted beams that supported the pier, emerging out of the water. We leaned on the rail.

"Anyone remember her from school?" I asked.

"Guy who was in the program with her said Dana was an exemplary student, then just stopped everything. He didn't see much of her after that. I asked could it have been her shacking up with someone? He said he didn't know, but he was glad for it. Whatever it was kept her out of the running for the big awards. She didn't even apply."

"Is that what you think happened?" I asked. "She fell for someone?"

"I don't get the sense she's ever fallen for anyone. I had a long chat with her ex-husband over a few beers. He said she was always like that—kinda distant."

"Any family trouble?"

Blatchford shook his head. "Mom and dad sound nice as can be. They don't talk much with Dana, other than an everything's-fine type e-mail now and then."

"Any luck on the phone numbers?"

"All burners," he said. "Disconnected now."

"So next you fly out there. When you do—"

"Are you gonna tell me to be careful?" Blatchford grinned. "Don't pretend you give a shit, Dave. Like you said, I'm expendable."

He'd said it. I was about to correct him, but after using Kay and Tranh, I wondered if I might be getting a bit too comfortable relying on others. If there'd been another way—

But there wasn't. I needed the help, I'd asked for it, and now I had to wait.

Thirteen

The video went online Monday morning. Links were sent to the department's public relations liaison and the Deputy Chief Constable, all major news outlets, the mayor's office, the Minister of Public Safety. The video was titled VANCOUVER COP ASSAULTS ASIAN MAN UNPROVOKED.

I'd shaved it down to twenty seconds of brutality, corrected for low light and filtered for optimum sound. The footage cycled through camera angles, staying with Chambers's face. He'd used steel knucks on Larry Tranh, pocketing them after, but he'd pulled his punches. His expression had remained stolid and businesslike throughout. That lack of rage leant Chambers's performance the casual menace of a bully. It was a star-making turn.

Shauna Kensington insisted on watching the video before her office orchestrated the leak. With her child in the other room, we screened the fight. She nodded enthusiastically during the blows.

"This," she said, "opens up a range of possibilities. They'll have to investigate this."

"I hope so."

"How did you—" She broke off. "No, don't tell me. Is the other guy all right? Would he be able to stand up in court?"

"I'm hoping he won't have to," I said.

"You're looking for a public outcry. A call for this guy's head. You know it might not happen. People are pretty cynical."

"We'll risk it," I said.

That evening Kay dropped by my flat with a box of my possessions. Marie had taken over my office space on Hastings, awarding herself the title of senior administrator. That was unfair to her—she knew the daily workings of Wakeland & Chen better than anyone. As I surveyed the box, it was clear that I hadn't left behind much worth claiming, beyond some case files and a bottle of good gin.

Kay hugged me at the sight of the check. I disentangled myself to fetch glasses and ice.

"That's next semester paid for," she said. "Give me more cases like this."

"I don't think Tranh's face could stand another."

She folded the check and then decided she'd rather keep it smoothed. "Still, I'm glad he stood up for justice."

"He stood up for the five grand," I said.

"I just meant that the video will get that cop off the street, and I'm glad somebody got the truth out there."

"Chambers is finished," I agreed. "He deserves to be. But that tape is as much bullshit as whatever he comes up with to protest his innocence. Only we got there first."

"So why'd you do it then, if it's so wrong?"

"Sonia asked for my help."

When she left I took up her untouched mug and finished her gin. I tried to think through what Chambers's reprisal would be, once he figured it out. He could come after me with the last of his authority, or on the sly, maybe with help from Anthony Qiu. Would Qiu support him when he wasn't a police officer? He'd have to, I decided. Or else kill him.

But that was more bloodshed than Qiu would care for. He'd suggest caution. Patience. Would Chambers listen?

It was hard to say. After studying Chris Chambers for weeks, I didn't feel I knew him. Affable with colleagues, ingratiating to his superiors, a dispassionate brute to those weaker than him. Chambers was three people, none of whom I'd ever seen angry.

Chambers would try to cling to his job. It wasn't above a police force to close ranks around one of its own. How many favors would he burn through to get back at me?

The thought struck me that I knew an expert on the subject of revenge.

Fourteen

"Is this a bad time, Dave?" Dana Essex's tone was mocking.

She'd phoned as I was pouring out the last of the gin, almost as if I'd willed her to.

"I was just thinking about you," I said. "Want to run something by you."

"Please do."

I explained in rough terms the nature of Chambers and his actions, what I'd done to provoke him. She laughed at the novelty of the setup and excused herself to view the clip.

"It's quite a work," she said after. "Almost too well shot to be amateur. Very nice mise-en-scene. This will certainly provoke his ire."

"Given his nature, how'll he respond?"

"This is a violent man, so: violently."

"No waiting around months like you?"

"My target disappeared," she said. "Are you planning on disappearing?"

"No more than I already have."

"Then I suspect he'll come for you," she said, "if he's able to deduce your involvement."

"With Qiu's support?"

"Or in defiance of him. If Chambers has connections within the department he'll go to them in turn. Once he finds they're unable to prolong his career, he'll see your antagonism as even more personally directed. Cut off from them, he'll focus on you."

"On me directly? Or will he come after someone close to me?"

"Not unless he's completely without honor."

"You did."

"Threatened, Dave. Do you honestly believe I'd be a party to that?"

"They say the first one's the hardest."

"Murder? I imagine one develops a stomach for it, if not a taste."

"You're responsible for Tabitha Sorenson's death."

"I told you, I was—"

"Right, the instrument or the facilitator or whatever. Keep repeating it."

"We weren't talking about me," Essex said coolly. "Your friend will come after you. I imagine he'll act betrayed, as if you should have settled this more directly. He might want to fight you first."

"Before killing me."

"Yes. To reassert himself. If he's wary of more cameras he might try to lure you somewhere less conspicuous. If he can do that he'll vent his anger and then dispose of you."

"I've never seen him angry."

"Of course you have," she said. "It's there below the surface. The look of concentration on his face during the video—a mask. Those are targeted blows he's throwing. You can see there's a wellspring of fury for him to draw on, and it's a supreme effort to restrain himself and only incapacitate his victim."

Recalling Chambers in the video, I could see her point. "That's good insight," I said. "If you weren't so damaged and untrustworthy I'd suggest you come work with me."

Essex laughed, warming now. "Actually," she said, "he reminds me of you. I imagine that's how you fight—anger condensed and bottled, ready to explode. Hurt and confusion, frustrations sexual and otherwise. Is that what happened to you as a police officer?"

"Something like that," I said.

"Where does it come from? Do you even know?"

"I boxed as a kid. My foster father used to take me down to the Astoria gym. Once he died, I stopped going."

"And this anger, it simply built up?"

I stared at the white expanse of wall across from my couch. "I don't know. Maybe."

"I think that's a lie," Essex said. "From what I've seen, boxing shapes and disciplines violence, it doesn't create it."

"No."

"So even as a child—"

"It's always been there," I said.

I was moving to hang up when I paused. Thought, no. It was time to confide. And I knew who I had to confide in.

I said, "You're much smarter than I am, Dana. You understand me better than I do. Better than anyone, maybe."

"Does that upset you? Frighten you?"

"A little," I said. "But I know why you keep calling me."

"To convince you to come with me," she said. "Between the money we have and our skill sets, we could make quite a nice life. It's not like there's anything keeping you in Vancouver."

"What you really want," I said, "is for me to convince you to come back."

"You're being facetious."

"Maybe." I waited. She didn't hang up.

"By my reckoning," I said, "you're about halfway to the point of realizing everything's out of control. That there's no real running away. Tabitha found that out. Whether it's Costa Rica or East Van, it's only a matter of time. The money didn't help her disappear—and she had the skills to use it. She also had someone she loved, and when he got his dream job she moved back here to support him, no matter the risk."

I paused, could hear her breathing.

"You on the other hand are saddled with a sociopath. You've just about figured out you don't have control. You're trapped. And when you realize that, you'll be calling me to bail you out. Because who else do you really have, Dana?"

She disconnected, which felt like some kind of victory. I put down the phone and took up the tumbler, thinking of Tabitha, her company, and the brave decision she'd made out of love. Mi Mundo, her company had been called. I dropped the Rega's needle into the grooves of a Patsy Cline record. Mi Mundo solo. Mi Mundo solitario.

And where was her world now?

Fifteen

The next day I watched a well-coiffed news anchor question Shauna's colleague. Anchor and lawyer sat facing each other, the background a hi-def image of English Bay at sunset. The lawyer explained that the victim in the video had fled due to the anguish of the incident, and the fear of further brutality.

"The individuals who documented the incident are similarly afraid of the damage Constable Chambers could wreak," the lawyer said. "Anonymity is paramount to their well-being at the present. I can tell you, though, we should all want the same thing, which is for incidents like this to be met with an appropriate response from those in power."

"And what would that response be?" the anchor asked.

The lawyer smiled. "At this stage criminal liability has yet to be determined. Our clients aren't looking for financial remuneration, though."

"No?"

"Their concern is for the safety of other Vancouverites. Certainly the officer in question needs to be removed from any position in which he can inflict further suffering."

"Firing him."

"We fervently hope the police will take the appropriate measures."

A pretaped interview showed a police spokesperson flanked by flags. She said the department was working to ascertain if the tape was genuine, and wouldn't comment until that first step had been taken, other than to say a few bad apples shouldn't taint the legacy of an institution.

The next day the news anchor spoke with a witness to an altercation between Chambers and a young woman.

He'd allegedly struck her, taken her purse, and removed a sum of money. The day after followed allegations about the death of Miles Irigary. And then, Sunday night, the anchor announced that the officer had been suspended pending a full inquiry, to be handled by an outside agency, most likely the Delta detachment of the RCMP.

The week had felt like watching a chess match from the perspective of the first pawn to move across the center of the board.

While I waited for Chambers, I set to work on my mother's house. I had leftover drywall from repairing the second-floor office, and I used it to patch up her basement, the room I'd slept in, off and on, from age six till adulthood. Property taxes had reached the point where she couldn't afford to stay unless the upstairs and basement were converted into suites. Every other house on Laurel Street had been sold, subdivided, rented out. More people shared the same space now, and yet it was emptier, less of a neighborhood.

One night after work I mentioned it might be time to sell. She looked at me as if I'd blasphemed.

"Your father and I built this home," she said. "That means nothing to you?"

I was sitting on her couch, drinking a beer, wondering what I could say that I wouldn't regret. My biological mother had given me up to her much older sister, knowing that, whatever her faults, Beatrice Wakeland was reliable. She and her cop husband had proven so in raising me. That quiet, incomprehensible childhood had also proven that the woman I thought of as my mother would never willingly invite change into her life.

Kay, stretched on the carpet with her dinner plate on the ottoman, saved me from tempting my fate. "If you did sell," she said, "it'd make you a millionaire."

"And that's a thing a person should want?"

"I'm just saying, Aunt Bea."

My mother looked at me. "And you think she's right?"

"If it makes you happy being here, you should stay."

She nodded in a way that told me it did, and she would, and I hadn't needed to say so.

"And when I'm gone you'll live here," she said. "Maybe settle down by then. That nice girl you were seeing, Sonia."

"The one you told, first time you met her, she looked whiter than you'd expected?"

"I only meant she was pretty."

Kay slunk out with her dishes. I put the beer bottle on the carpet and stood up, ready to fire back.

I thought of Betsy Sorenson, how she'd described her fights with Tabitha, fights like the one I was gearing up to have. Tonight Mrs. Sorenson would be alone in her house, willing to give anything to have one more argument with her daughter.

I had no moral high ground. It was my mother's place. She could decorate it with whatever illusions she had left.

The days clicked by with no news on Chambers. Friday, nothing. The weekend, nothing. Monday morning, word from the department spokesperson that a decision on Chambers would be reached by the end of the week.

Tuesday Chambers shot himself.

Sixteen

Over the last week, a single frame of the video had accompanied each mention of Chris Chambers's alleged misdeeds. Now, his scowling visage gave way to a smiling headshot of the officer in his dress blues, younger and without the mustache. Innocent was too strong a word—his youthful self looked proud and naïve, spared two decades' worth of compromise.

Footage of a teary-eyed Misha Van Camp aired that evening, but the audio was the newscaster's paraphrase of her words. Chambers's sobbing girlfriend hadn't emitted a single quality sound bite.

Van Camp had seen no indication that her boyfriend was a violent man. His work was violent but he wasn't. The past week she'd noticed the stress take its toll on Chambers. She'd heard him making phone calls, sounding desperate, fidgeting as he waited.

She'd left for work that morning like any other. They'd been planning to go out for Thai food in the evening. The call had come while she was on her break. Her neighbor heard the gunshot and phoned Chris's cell phone first, since he was a police officer. When he didn't answer, the neighbor had phoned Emergency.

Police found Chambers's front door unlocked. A note on the stairs was addressed to the officers, apologizing, asking them to tell Misha, but to please not let her see him like that.

Chambers reclined in his bathtub, in his uniform, his brain matter blasted in a peacock's tail around his empty, slack head. He'd shot himself through the eye. No doubt he'd heard of too many accidental survivors to aim through the mouth.

There was some confusion as to whether he would receive a full police burial, but his fellow officers insisted. Whatever else he was, Chris Chambers had once been one of them.

Seventeen

"I assume you had a hand in this," Anthony Qiu said. We were sitting at a corner booth in the empty Monte Carlo. It was late morning, edging toward opening hours, though nothing was set up. He'd spread newsprint over his end of the table and was cracking peanuts, dropping shells onto the financial insert.

I didn't answer him. It was too early for a drink, and I didn't feel like I'd earned one yet. What I felt like was a cigarette, but I'd quit, a fact I needed to remind myself of.

"Chris was a good man," Qiu said. He raised his mimosa. "He will be missed."

"He was an asshole."

"Respect, David." Qiu looked less angry than dismayed at the lack of decorum.

"And so are you," I said. "Let's be honest, Tony, what the hell are you doing? Well into the two thousands, and you're shaking people down for shylock money? When there's a Quick-Day Loans on the corner of every poor neighborhood, you need to muscle chumps like Irigary and Tranh?"

"I inherited a business," Qiu began. He'd been too shocked to interrupt, but now his expression turned sullen.

"So did I," I said. "But I realized pretty early that I wasn't suited for that business, so I found something else. Why don't you just run your restaurant, water down your liquor, and overcharge on food like everyone else? You don't need the grief."

Qiu's laugh was brittle but sincere. "You have more nerve than anyone I've met, David. I appreciate it, though talk like that usually leads to a bad end."

I shook my head. "It doesn't have to. You could decide not to send your thugs after me. That way I won't have to deal with them, the way I've dealt with everything else you've sent. This could end right now."

"Let bygones be bygones? That what you'd recommend?"

"Either or," I said. "I've got nothing else on my plate. I'm out of the PI business for now. If you're really hankering for a blood feud, my schedule is wide open."

He grinned. "No one wants that," he said. "People like Chris are hard to come by."

"Bent cops?"

"Reliable bent cops—and friends. I hate to let any advantage go, no matter how small, and Chris wasn't a small advantage."

"I bet the pressure's tremendous," I said.

He looked at the rubble amassed beneath his hands, then cracked and shelled another peanut, adding to the pile. He sighed.

"Between the triads, the Malays, the Exiles, and the gangs from Surrey, it's a crowded playing field."

"So get out."

"Impossible," he said. "My father-in-law chose me. His people wouldn't let me walk away. They'd replace me. Their replacement might see less of the big picture, but he'd be much more ruthless. No, David, I hold a pretty weak position, but I'm holding it all the same."

I had to respect him, even if I knew what was coming.

He said, "I don't think we'll be seeing much of each other any more. I can't spare the people. You win, David. Truce it is."

"It's the smart play," I said, shaking his proffered hand despite the flecks of peanut shells on his fingers.

"Good-bye, David. Best of luck."

I left the Monte Carlo and walked toward my office on Pender. Qiu had lied about everything but the pressure he was under. That told me he was coming. He didn't care about avenging Chambers, but others expected it. At a certain point you become what they expect you to be. A reluctant gangster, a crooked cop, a disgraced PI. Most people bend without even thinking there's another option. Those who don't either break, or they find out what they're capable of.

Eighteen

A black unmarked Interceptor was parked at an angle beneath my office. An argument out front. As I crossed Pender I realized the man with his back to me, pacing along the gutter, was Ryan Martz. He was wearing a track jacket and jeans, his shaved head stubbled and a week's beard growth on his neck. Sonia stood between him and the door, hands in the pockets of her trench coat, enduring Martz's tirade.

Martz turned, saw me, and charged.

"The hell did you do to Chris?" he said, shoving me back into the street.

"You want an answer," I said, "or do you want to swing at me?"

He wanted to swing at me. His knuckles stung my left forearm. I backed up, warding off his fists with my own. He grabbed for me and I broke his hold.

"I fucking knew something was up when you asked about him," he said. He nodded at Sonia. "I didn't get it till I saw her here, waiting for you. Remembered she'd come to me for advice. I told her to ignore it."

"You were wrong," I said.

"So the right answer's killing him?" Martz's hurt was fueling his rage. "Can't fucking believe you two."

Car traffic was minimal but we soon picked up a small crowd of onlookers. Sonia hurried to put herself between us as Martz approached. I had my hand up to deflect.

He swung wildly. He was stronger than me, in better shape. His blows stung.

Sonia grabbed his arm. "Stop it, Ryan."

He shrugged her off. When she grabbed for him again he gave her a hard shove that caught her off guard, and when he turned back to me I caught him with a right to the face. It wasn't a great punch and it didn't land where I'd wanted it to, but he hadn't seen it coming.

He struggled up. "You want to do this?"

I pointed at the gun beneath his jacket. "Gonna shoot me?"

Taking shallow breaths he opened the car door and flung the gun onto the seat. When he turned I came at him. I tagged him with basic combinations, jabbing to keep distance. He bulled back, taking the punches to seize hold of me. We spilled out into the street, landing amid a ruckus of car horns and passerby.

He was first up and kicked me in the side, too high to catch the ribcage. His padded boots hurt like hell. He tried for another and I took that, rolling away and finding my footing. He was on me immediately, throwing haymakers.

I covered my head. His punches rained down, driving me toward the concrete. When I was nearly doubled over I swung for his ribs. The punch was low and wide, tagging the kidneys. An instant DQ if the fight had rules.

There was a lull in his flurries. Kidney shots fucking hurt. I hooked my left arm around his torso to steady him and pounded on his sweetbreads until he collapsed on top of me. I rolled, facedown in the street. Martz's hand snagged the back of my collar, raising me up. The ground collided with my forehead.

His knee was on my shoulder. The street was wet and tasted like spilt gasoline. I raised my head up and grabbed for the front of his shirt. The fabric was still. He'd stopped fighting.

Looking up I saw a patrol car, its blue and reds on. No siren.

One of the officers had a bemused look on his face. "Where's your sidearm, Ryan?" he asked.

Martz was having a hard time breathing. He pointed at the car.

"Whatcha got there?" the officer said, looking at me.

"Personal," I managed to say.

Martz nodded. The officer chuckled, looking from his unsmiling partner to Martz. "You two about finished?"

He let go of me. I sat up and looked at Martz, sitting back on his bent legs. He nodded. I nodded. I started to stand and he decked me. It was a good punch. A wonderful punch. It kept me from standing up in a hurry.

"Now we're done," Ryan said.

The officer helped him up. The other one helped me scoot over to the curb. I sat there and waited until all the cars were gone. Sonia had gone, too.

It took a long while to remember how to stand, but walking came back to me with relative ease. Inside my building I leaned on the railing as I climbed the stairs.

In my office I sat at the table and went through the equipment I'd relocated from Wakeland & Chen headquarters. Cameras, case files, a Smith & Wesson revolver, a first aid kit. I brought out the latter. Triangle bandages and medical adhesive, scissors and aspirin and a bottle of distilled water. I took the aspirin and wet the bandages for a compress. The water was warm as fresh blood.

Nineteen

Chambers received the works. Bagpipes and dress blues. A few words spoken by the deputy commissioner. The same service my father had received. Cautions about the stresses involved in police work pervaded the media for a few days.

The party line maintained that Chambers was a good officer who'd met with trouble and hadn't been able to deal with it. Maybe there was even some truth to that. In any case, Chambers had inspired some loyalty from the people he served. His funeral was a grand one.

No word from Blatchford. No word from Essex. I didn't see Nagy or Wong or their beige Nav. The bruises faded to dull yellows and the cut on my forehead began to knit.

In the meantime, I cleaned the office to where it looked better than it had before I'd wrecked it. I put time in on old cases that didn't pan out. I read the book Essex had left me, Ishiguro, but it didn't hold any clues. She'd personalized it, signing *To D.W.* in elegant blue cursive. *If it had to be someone, I'm glad it was you.*

The morning after the funeral I showed up at the office before three. Early rush hour traffic turned Pender Street into a circus, pedestrians streaming up the street toward the bus lines and Skytrain stations. As

I approached the door I saw Sonia leaning against it, a brown-bagged bottle in her hand.

"Suggested stress leave pending redeployment," she said. "After Chris, they're worried. I'm off for a month to recover my wits."

"Plans?" I asked.

She held up the bottle. "Just this. It's Tuesday. Time we come clean with each other."

"Everything?"

She nodded. I unlocked the staircase door and held it open. "After you, then," I said.

Twenty

"This is going to hurt, isn't it?"

"I think we both need this, Dave. Unless you have someone to confide in I don't know about."

"All right. Pour the whiskey. I'll go first."

"Absolute honesty."

"Nothing but."

"How often do you think about me?"

"All the time. You?"

"Sometimes."

"Honesty."

"More than sometimes."

"Ah."

"But not all the time. How guilty do you feel?"

"About Chambers? I don't know. I wish he hadn't've."

"Same."

"But it hasn't kept me up nights. Least so far."

"What does?"

"What do I feel guilty about? Tabitha Sorenson. I feel helpless. Culpable. I don't even know what I feel."

"What about your police career?"

"Ask me three drinks from now. And anyway it's my turn."

"Go ahead."

"When I left, did it ever occur to you to quit?"

"No."

"Just like that."

"When you lost your job, Dave, you were angry at everyone. Disappointed in me, in Ryan. I couldn't've helped you by quitting. You needed to go somewhere by yourself."

"So you think I deserved it."

"I don't know all the details."

"Honesty."

"Then yes. You seemed constantly out to live down your father's reputation. It made you erratic. And us sleeping together made you overprotective. I needed to get my hands dirty and you were always trying to mediate between me and the job. Like you didn't trust me."

"I don't think I like this honesty shit."

"I'm having another if you are."

"Pour. I guess I hate to ask—after I left, there was someone else?"

"Yes."

"And?"

"And what?"

"Who was better?"

"Oh please."

"Honesty, ma'am."

"You."

"I knew it. By a lot, right?"

"No. When you and Ryan were fighting you could've talked him down."

"Is that a question?"

"You saw him shove me and wanted to hit him. Right?"

"Yes."

"See what I mean by overprotective?"

"Do you honestly think, Sonia—know what, never mind."

"Go ahead."

"Nah."

"Say it. Please."

"Fine. We both know the objections about female officers are just excuses, old boys' club shit."

"But . . . ?"

"Do you ever think there's maybe a small, tiny, miniscule kernel of a point to that argument?"

"You obviously do."

"Why I didn't want to mention it. I know you're an amazing cop, better than me or Ryan. But if I took a door with him backing me up I'd feel less apprehensive."

"That's because you loved me."

"That's part of it, sure. But you're sympathetic-looking. Caveman bullshit kicks in. Just confuses things."

"Maybe things ought to be confusing."

"Maybe. Your turn."

"Did you help me because you hoped I'd sleep with you again?"

"Well."

"I fucking knew it."

"You make it sound like payment. In my head it was more like gratitude."

"Oh, David, dearest, you saved me. I realize now what a fool I've been. Could you ever see fit to forgive me for not recognizing your amazingness? Would it help if I took off your pants?"

"About that, but in reverse order."

"Jesus, Wakeland. You are fucking hopeless, know that?"

"Sure. But it's not like your head's bolted on straight either. One more?"

"About half. That's good."

"What would it take, just out of curiosity?"

"Seriously? I'm not sure. I don't think we can trust each other."

"Is that a prerequisite?"

"Yes, as a matter of fact."

"Then ask me anything."

"What've I been doing?"

"Ask me something I'd lie about or evade."

"I already did."

"The job."

"Right."

"You really want to know?"

"I do know. I want to hear you say it."

"Say that I beat the piss out of that guy. A suspect. For no reason. You want me to say that."

"The truth, Dave."

"All right. I did. I could tell you he was a scumbag, a bad human being, but fact is, I wanted to hit him and I did. Killing him crossed my mind."

"Why are you smiling?"

"Because I've never said it before."

"And it only took you seven years."

"The guy ended up with a concussion. I was called up to the fifth floor, asked if I wanted my rep with me. The bosses laid out how serious it was, how I should've been straight up fired."

"You told me you'd resigned."

"I tell everybody that. It's a funny thing."

"What's the truth? They forced you to?"

"No. Exactly the opposite. A slap on the wrist, a probation period, plus I'd maybe owe a favor or two."

"So the truth—"

"I resigned. My choice."

"Dave."

"I'm not a police officer, Sonia. I can't be one. In my heart I don't believe the rules apply to me. My saving grace, though, if I have one, is I recognized it. Saw that ten, twenty years down the line, I'd be Chambers. Worse—Qiu and his money controlled Chambers, aimed him. I'd be busting every head till someone killed me, looking for some kind of justice that probably doesn't exist. I—Christ, I'm a weepy fucking drunk."

"It's okay. It's good."

"I didn't understand it. Still don't. Maybe it plays into my own parents not being there. But I'll tell you, if I have kids of my own, I'll cling to those motherfuckers like lampreys."

Sonia was laughing. It sounded strange. I realized I was laughing too. Laughing out all the hurt, the guilt. There were still tears on my face, but I was beyond the pain of memory. I was lighter than I'd felt in years.

Sonia had her arms around my neck, in my hair. Holding me. I wanted to tell her I was glad but she shushed me with a kiss. Her arms tightened and I felt myself lifting her onto the desk, cupping her face, matching the warm hunger of her mouth. She broke the embrace long enough to shrug out of her jeans. I leaned her back, pushing papers to the floor and the revolver to the edge of the desk. I kissed down her throat, moving past the cumbersome clinging bra to her dark trimmed pubic hair and below.

I had my face buried in pussy when they broke down the door.

Twenty-One

Triplett read my statement back to me while I sipped cold tea. I knew Sonia would be going through the same with McCurdy in the adjacent interview room. Or perhaps cops used a more welcoming environment with their own.

"You and Ms. Drego—Constable Drego—were in your office talking prior to the incident."

"That's correct."

"What were you talking about?"

"Gardening. This and that."

"You noticed the men standing in the doorway. You recognized them."

Heard them first, their laughter. I turned my head to see Nagy holding the crowbar and Wong with an automatic rifle. I hadn't heard them break the door at the bottom of the stairs.

Disoriented, self-aware, still kneeling, I looked at them laughing at us. I froze. Then the gun went off, and I couldn't hear anything after that.

I told Triplett, "The caucasian, Nagy, and Wong, the Chinese guy, are known associates of a known gangster."

"Known by whom?"

"Known around the way." I added, "They worked with Chris Chambers."

Triplett had been writing in the margins of the print-out, but now she stopped, looked up at me.

"You saw they were armed."

"Yes."

"Before or after firing upon them?"

"Before."

"So you saw them, recognized them, opened fire, and then noticed the weapons?"

"No. I noticed the weapons, then recognized them, then saw them raise said weapons to fire."

"Both of them. In the doorway."

"It's a wide doorway."

She annotated the statement. "Did you say anything to them, or them to you?"

"I believe Nagy said, 'Get ready to die, bitch.' Talking to me, I think."

"And you didn't respond verbally."

"No."

"No warning, no attempt at discourse."

"There wasn't time."

I watched Nagy stumble, knocked back onto the stairs. I didn't hear him fall, but I felt the vibrations through the old wood flooring. Wong grabbed the door frame and managed to stay on his feet. He'd lost his grip on the rifle, but it was attached to a shoulder sling, and his hands grasped the barrel as he processed what was going on. His lips might've been moving, but I was focused on the rifle, the barrel swinging up toward me.

"The Smith & Wesson revolver is owned by you?" Triplett asked. "You have a permit for it?"

"I have a restricted firearms license and an authorization to transport."

"Not to carry."

"I wasn't carrying it," I said. "It's stored at my office."

"You store it loaded and within reach?"

"Never," I said. "When Constable Drego arrived I was in the midst of cleaning it and inspecting the ammunition."

"You two did some drinking."

"A memorial toast. Her partner passed away recently."

Triplett ignored that and said, "You didn't think it was prudent to store your firearm before enjoying your drink?"

"In retrospect it seems a poor choice. Although to be fair, it's the reason Constable Drego and I were able to defend ourselves. Lucky, huh?"

"Lucky," Triplett said.

Wong was still raising the barrel when Sonia shot him. He didn't fall. He bounced against the doorframe and fired two shots into the floor. By then Sonia had both hands on the revolver and squeezed off a second shot which caught him in the breast bone, and a third that likely hit his heart. He teetered and then fell. All told, maybe six seconds had passed.

It was a clean story, and close enough to the truth. I didn't know how much of it Triplett believed. Hopefully she'd be swayed more by the knockoff AR-14, the pistol and knife found on Nagy's corpse. Down the hall, Sonia would be telling McCurdy the same story.

"Just to clarify," Triplett said, readying her pen. "What was Constable Drego doing in the moments of the shooting?"

"My attention was on the guns, and the men carrying them."

"She seems to be favoring one of her arms."

"You've worked patrol," I said. "You know how heavy all that equipment gets. Probably pulled a muscle."

"And yourself? Constable Gupta noted that you had blood around your mouth when he arrived."

"Might've bit my tongue," I said. "That gun has a hell of a recoil."

Alone afterwards, sitting in my apartment, I told Sonia that it had gone all right. A clean shooting, unofficially. If Triplett didn't believe I'd pulled the trigger, she couldn't prove otherwise.

I asked her if she was okay.

"I don't know," Sonia said. "I just need to be alone with this for a while."

Us or them. It couldn't've been more clear cut. And yet after she'd fired, I'd approached the stairs cautiously, taken a few steps down, saw Nagy lying beneath Wong's corpse. Nagy's eyes were open. He gurgled, his arm reaching up, palm open. Afraid of me. I'd watched him stop breathing.

There was no lesson to take away. He'd been a danger to me and his death made things easier. If he'd shot me I doubt he'd've thought twice. That he'd gone out childlike and fearful shouldn't have mattered.

So people die. Some instantly and others gasping on their own blood. And the rest of us run on for as long as we can.

Twenty-Two

Tim Blatchford's report was about what I'd expect from someone nourished on sleeping pills, whiskey, and chair shots to the head. When we met for updates he consulted frayed napkins and the backs of receipts. His e-mail correspondence was usually late, often lacking punctuation and capital letters. That was if he bothered to compose more than one sentence.

Even so, his work brought Dana Essex into focus. So much that when she phoned, it was difficult to feign ignorance when she embellished events from her past.

She'd grown up in Gatineau, near Ottawa, just over the Quebec border. Her parents still lived on the Rue des Invalides, working-class and stubbornly anti-French. Blatchford had visited them, been served coffee and ginger snaps in their living room. He'd told them he was with a reunion committee. Everyone was wondering what happened to Dana.

Her parents were wondering the same. Essex had gone from a sullen, poetry-obsessed high school senior, a straight B student, to making the dean's list her first semester at Carleton. Scholarships and merit awards followed, a four point et cetera GPA. She'd met a research assistant,

Graham, and married him, her first real relationship. They intended to apply to grad school together.

They made plans to leave . . . and Dana never left. Her parents didn't know when or why she'd divorced Graham, but Dana was accepted into the graduate program and moved closer to campus. From there the story muddled.

She'd never matriculated, was still technically ABD—all but dissertation, her doctorate unfinished. Then she'd taken the job at Surrey Polytech, moved without talking things over with her folks.

Blatchford had asked and they'd flung excuses at him: Politics. Poor job market. Change of scenery. Met somebody. Enough excuses for him to believe that her parents didn't really know what had motivated their daughter to move west.

Next Blatchford had visited Essex's graduate supervisor, a professor whose specialty was "Poetry and the Long Eighteenth Century." The faculty webpage showed a photo of Dr. Tillie Metcalf, a birdlike, veiny-throated woman whose meek smile Dana had echoed the first time I'd met her. I wish I'd been present to see her reaction to Blatchford, to witness that meeting of the minds.

Metcalf told him that Dana simply lost focus. Her graduate work had been on Mary Darby Robinson, whose contributions to the literary canon were finally receiving critical reassessment. Dana had presented a brilliant conference paper on the subject. While the brains of students and faculty alike were being turned to mush by deconstructionism and semiotics, Dana Essex represented a bright new critical voice. Someone in love with poetry, with close reading, someone ready to take up the tradition of the life of the mind.

And then it had all crumbled.

She'd stopped working on her dissertation. She'd missed meetings, under-delivered when asked to revise passages. Metcalf had taken on other students and moved on.

Blatchford asked what caused that rupture. Metcalf had seen it before in other promising students. Pressure could make them crack, as could money troubles or an ailing relative. It was important to remember this period was also a transition into adulthood.

It was also around this time, Metcalf remembered, that Essex started her other teaching job. Dana had found working with those people fascinating.

"Those people?" Blatchford had asked. He'd spent the day wandering the campus, eating soup in the cafeteria, watching a down-with-something-or-other rally on the lawn. If Metcalf meant students, then Essex's definition of fascinating didn't jibe with his.

"Prisoners," she had replied. "Dana volunteered for two years at Milton Correctional. She was part of a group working with inmates on core learning skills." She added with a rueful smile, "I might've even recommended Dana for the job."

Twenty-Three

"Things certainly have taken a turn," Essex said.

She was referring to Chris Chambers's suicide, but she could just as easily have been talking about herself. Her call had come less than an hour after I'd booked my tickets, making the decision to defy her.

I stood on the balcony of Sonia's apartment, the phone propped on her wedge-shaped patio table, set to speaker. I wasn't above leaning over the railing, trying to aim my expectorate at the crest of the green awning below. I spat and missed.

"Those men who attacked you," Essex said. "They were friends of Chambers?"

"Associates. I don't know he had real friends."

"But dead now, same as Chambers himself. You must be relieved."

"I must be," I said, thinking of the night before. Sonia waking up under a perspiration-soaked blanket, bolting to the bathroom and barricading herself inside. I'd waited for her, held her when she came back. Our first night together in years, shared with the ghosts of the men she'd killed.

"She seems like a remarkable woman," Essex said. Her thoughts ran close to mine, always a discomfiting experience. "How much have you told her?"

"Everything," I said.

"Really."

I spat again. Bullseye.

"It's a funny thing," I said. "You spend so much energy keeping up this idea that you're self-sufficient, unique. No one can possibly understand. Then once that falls away, and you find yourself trusting somebody, it's a relief."

"So she knows about us?"

"She knows."

"And about Tabitha? She can be trusted not to speak of it?"

"I didn't swear her to a vow of secrecy," I said.

"One might think you're making her a target."

"You already said she was a target."

"With more reason now than ever."

I turned, my back against the rain-dampened railing, and looked at the phone.

"My feeling is, Dana, you're more worried about yourself, where you stand with your friend with the knife. I'm the least of your worries."

No reply.

"Adding another victim to the list won't help you get out of this."

"Who says I want out?" An adolescent petulance had crept into her tone.

"If you don't," I said, "then why are we still talking?"

A day earlier, Blatchford had visited the "Milton Hilton," a medium-max prison, old and gray with high chain-link fences and ramparts full of armed guards. Undeterred, he'd met with the warden and asked about the program.

"It was called Late Start," Blatchford relayed to me on a video conference. "What it was, a local priest decided to start an outreach program for felons with learning disabilities. There's a high school equivalency program inside, but he felt a lot of people got left behind. So he and a few other churchies, and some interning college kids, worked it out to meet with the felons one on one, teach them the three R's or whatever."

"Did you get to speak to him?" I asked.

"The priest? I'm getting there." On my laptop screen Blatchford popped pills and swilled beer against the backdrop of a dark motel room. His face was blue from the glow of the monitor, eyes roaming over the mess of papers on the desktop.

He yawned and said, "I got all this from the warden. She said the crusaders were put out of business. There's a proper bureaucracy now, the"—he checked a note—"Western Ontario Correctional Education Bureau, which reports to the—let's see—Ministry of Correctional Services."

"Dana Essex's time would have been before the change," I said.

"Right. The priest, Father Darian, he's still around. Operates a parish in Hamilton. Guy gets a community service award every couple months. He's in his seventies now."

"Can you get in to see him?" I asked.

"I had a thought on that." He coughed and covered his mouth with a wad of brown paper napkins, which might have been part of his notes. "Maybe somebody else would be better for that interview. Like Jeff, maybe, or Kay."

"Why's that?"

"The father's a bit upscale. Guy likes to golf. Not really the type who'd open up to me."

"Meaning you got yourself kicked out of his church," I said.

"I fucked up a bit, yeah." Blatchford grinned sleepily. "Got there early and dozed off during the service. When I woke up the place looked empty. I go upstairs, check his office. But here he comes up the stairs, catches me, says no one's allowed up here. Had the guards toss me out." He shrugged. "Just bad luck."

"Bad luck which occurred to you stone-cold sober?"

"Finger-pointing will get us nowhere," Blatchford said. "Important thing is, what do you want to do now?"

Confront this, I thought. Do what I couldn't do weeks ago. Accept my failure and my fear. Find Essex and her unknown partner, then figure out how to bring them to justice. Tabitha Sorenson deserved the attempt. I felt I owed it to her.

"You're still in Hamilton?" I asked Blatchford.

"Till you say otherwise."

"Wait there," I told him. "Kay and I will come to you."

Twenty-Four

Father Charles-August Darian had a sharp-planed face below a frosting of silver-white hair. His gray beard swept out to a point, improving on his chin. The pockets of his cardigan were weighted down with golf balls and a cell phone, which he showed me to make the point that he was busy, couldn't spend all day, but would gladly spare a few minutes for someone in the education business.

He received me in his office, a high-ceilinged, wood-paneled affair with a latticed window that looked down on the softball diamond across the street. An avid Blue Jays fan, the father had found space for a pennant and an autographed picture of himself and John Olerud, amid the commendations that dominated his walls. My impression of him was of someone very comfortable with being well thought of.

Once we were seated and he'd rung for coffee, he asked what he could do for me.

I took a deep breath and said, "I work for an attorney who's handling the paperwork for a teaching institute doing outreach to prisoners." As proof I placed one of Shauna's cards on his desk. "We're interested in the Late Start program you pioneered. We believe there are advantages to your model over the current ones."

He nodded as if that went without saying.

"We'd like your reflections on the program, and of course any advice you could share. We'd also like to follow up with some of its beneficiaries, assess their progress."

"The inmates, you mean?" Reclining in his chair, Darian furrowed his brow. "When I started the program, I'd been visiting prisons for a while. I realized, talking to them, how intuitive and perceptive they are. Not dumb men, not all of them."

"Sure."

"I believed that if I could harness those smarts for education, I could cut down on the misery they might create, trying to express themselves without the proper intellectual and emotional tools. Maybe we could change the trajectory of their lives." He seemed to speak without thinking back on the events—this was a sermon he'd given before.

The coffee came, delivered by an assistant about the same age as the priest, who poured silently and left us to perform our own additions. The father took cream and brown sugar.

"You can't judge our success only by the people we worked with," he said.

"Goes without saying."

"Late Start made other correctional education initiatives step up their game, so to speak. We wanted to help people who everyone said couldn't be helped. Some couldn't, of course. My feeling was, if we could help just one."

I nodded.

"Truth be told, I think the full effects of our work have yet to be felt."

"It must have been intense," I said.

"Like you wouldn't believe. Just imagine it." He sipped his coffee, leaving me time to imagine it. "You're in a small locked room with a violent offender, someone who might not have passed high school. A murderer, a rapist, who can barely read a Dr. Seuss or calculate a tip. And it's your job to challenge him, focus on the areas where he's ignorant, where he feels most vulnerable."

I marveled at that, and asked if there had been incidents.

"One or two. We were usually well supervised. One instructor was present during a riot, another threatened with a knife. We all received threats, of course. That went with the job."

I drank some coffee. It was caramel-hazelnut infused, not my thing. "I'd be keen to see your reports. We're interested in how you negotiated between results-oriented testing and customized learning objectives."

"We preferred tailoring the program to what they needed. Maybe to a fault. Without test score improvements, diplomas, and whatnot, it's hard to get administrators on board."

The father leaned forward to drink, a few drops pattering on his saucer.

"What really did us in, apart from funding, was students trying to involve us in their legal troubles. My name carries some small amount of weight, and I was asked repeatedly to serve as a character witness."

"The others must have been approached, too," I said. "Though obviously not to the extent of yourself."

He nodded. "And that's what scuttled us—too much working at cross-purposes, people getting a little too friendly. I don't know if you've ever visited a prison, but those people are sharp. Uneducated, maybe, but savvy, on the lookout for weaknesses to exploit."

"Was there a specific incident?" I asked.

"I can't go into details." I waited him out, and he added, "It's neither here nor there, really, but we found one instructor had gotten a little too close to one of her pupils. I'm talking about an ethical breach, you understand. Nothing tawdry."

"Of course not," I said. "Was she disciplined?"

"We separated them, of course."

"But nothing beyond that?" I realized that might sound confrontational and pulled back. "Under those conditions, discipline must be hard to enforce. How did you manage it?"

"Some advice," he said. "Make sure your own group lays out ground rules, and properly trains its educators. In our case, we were working on a shoestring, all volunteers. How can you discipline someone who's not getting paid?"

"It must be tough," I said. "I'd still like to see those reports, see how you managed. Did you keep lists of which volunteers worked with which inmates?"

"That I can't help you with."

He pointed his coffee mug toward the computer on his desk, its screensaver a slowly-undulating school of neon fish.

"A couple of years ago I had someone digitize the archives, scan all our papers—field reports, lesson plans, assessments. It's a jumble, and I haven't had time to go through it."

"We could help you with that," I said. "We have a number of employees with filing experience—"

"I appreciate the thought, son, but I can't do it." He stood, a sign for me to do the same.

Father Darian told me to call if I had more questions. He didn't walk me out. I drove off in my rental car, wondering how well the priest had password-protected his computer.

Twenty-Five

Hamilton had the feeling of a college town that had got its college in the nick of time, right before its industry collapsed. Once upon a time I'd applied to McMaster, never having visited there, but thinking college and a change of setting would improve things for me. Lives unled.

I met Kay and Blatchford at the Travelodge. We found a chain restaurant with a decent salad bar and tucked into a corner booth to discuss strategy.

"I want those files," I told them.

Jet lag had hit Kay, and she downed refills of Dr Pepper. Blatchford leaned over the table, looking somnambulant, as if at any minute he might use the plate for a pillow.

"There's an eight o'clock mass," I said. "If Darian leads it, and his assistant has gone home for the night, sneaking in shouldn't be a hassle."

"You're welcome to do it, then," Blatchford said.

"I figured I'd distract the sentry, keep him outside. Kay attends the service. Leaves you to do the sneaking—if you're up to it."

"Of course." He rubbed his face, waking himself up. "Looking forward to it."

I leaned out of the booth to check the clock on the wall. Five thirty, two and half hours to kill.

They both wanted to nap, so I walked with them back to the motel, then called Sonia from the lobby.

"How was your flight?" she asked.

"No complaints. Any more bad dreams?"

"A few. They're not as bad."

"No other nonsense going on?"

The sound of wind hitting the receiver, a sigh.

"There's talk of establishing a Chris Chambers Award," Sonia said. "A scholarship for low-income students studying criminology. Three thousand dollars."

"Maybe I'll apply."

When I returned to the motel, Blatchford and Kay were sitting on the beds in Kay's room. She looked up at me, stifling a laugh as I came in. I said, "What?"

"Tim was just telling me about when he met you," Kay said. "You never told me you worked for Aries."

"I apprenticed with them," I said. "It didn't last."

"You almost got Tim fired."

Blatchford was grinning. "I was telling her about the time you, me, and Jeff drove up to the Interior. You remember?"

I collapsed into the chair near Kay's bed. "No one wants to hear that story, Tim."

"I do," Kay said. "You never tell me this stuff." Asking Blatchford, "What was he like?"

"Dave? Just a kid." Blatchford turned to me: "Two or three months under your belt, right?"

"It's your story," I said.

"Aries hired us out to a chemical company. Trademark infringement case. Two farmers in the area refused to buy the company's genetically modified super-seeds, so the company goes off on them. Trumped-up bullshit—some of their neighbors' seeds blew onto their land, suddenly they're violating patents and encouraging others to do the same.

Nuisance suits, but they drag on long enough, the bigger company always wins."

"Shitty," said Kay.

Blatchford drank and grinned. "Dave thought so, too."

"What'd you do?"

"We were hired to follow the sodbusters around, wear dark suits and shades, act conspicuous. They go out for breakfast at the local waffle house, we're at a nearby table watching them."

Kay looked at me. "You did that?"

"He wasn't the only one," Blatchford said. "I was griping to Jeff, us three sitting in the hotel bar, saying maybe we should take pity on them. These sodbusters didn't have a clue—the company's got a legal department, for crissakes, while they're sharing a library copy of *Average Joe's Guide to the Law.*

"I say to Jeff and Dave, if someone just told them what they were up against, they could pack it in, sell the farm. Otherwise they're going bankrupt. Jeff's nodding, half paying attention. We're just talking about this as a theoretical. And Dave's sitting there looking thoughtful."

"What'd he do?" Kay looked at me. "What'd you do?"

"He showed them the surveillance file," Blatchford said, "and did the world's worst job of leaking it. The clients found out and Bob Aries was pissed. He never did pay me or Jeff. Said it was half our fault for not stopping him."

He paused to see if I wanted to add or dispute anything. I continued changing my socks.

"Anyway, Jeff and I always disagreed over that. He said Dave did the wrong thing for the right reason. Me, I thought it was the opposite—right thing, wrong reason. Because it wasn't about helping the downtrodden, was it? It was getting to Bob Aries, making him look bad. Right, Dave?"

"It can't be both?" I said.

He leaned back into the headboard and grinned. I was beginning to dislike that grin.

"I think," I said, "it was the right thing, for the right reason, just done the wrong way."

At seven thirty I pulled on my shoes and zipped up my hoodie. I took a swig from Blatchford's proffered mickey of Red Label, and passed the bottle to Kay. I said to Blatchford, "You coming?"

He slowly pulled himself up to a sitting position.

"Of course," he said. "Who else is gonna look out for you?"

Twenty-Six

At night the church had the look of a Bavarian chalet, its upper windows glowing gold against the cloud-darkened night. I could imagine it as a sanctuary—which begged the question why we had to break into it.

The southern edge of the church property was a strip of reddish clay, crusted by the autumn chill, bike tracks imprinted over its surface. We parked across the street and trudged through the mud. At the parking lot entrance, Blatchford halted.

"Cold feet?" I asked.

"Strikes me I haven't been inside a church in years. Not since Brendan Jorgenson and I got caught in the gym showers at St. Pat's."

"Other than when you tried to break in yesterday, you mean."

"Strikes me yesterday I might've wanted to get caught. Like psychologically."

I looked at him. He was staring at his feet.

"All right," I said. "We'll swap, then. Can I count on you to wind the guard up for half an hour?"

He smiled, looking relieved.

Kay and I walked to the door. "You up to this?" I asked her.

"Sure," she said. "I figure he'd want us to."

"Who? Tim?"

"God," she said. "I figure we're after someone who's breaking the sixth commandment. And if we just copy those files, we're not technically breaking the eighth."

In the hallway, a rustling sound reached us from the nave, hymnals being flipped open. Two-dozen-odd voices began a somber tune I didn't recognize. We took the stairs in single file.

The lights from the atrium below left the upper hallway in shadows. I turned the father's office door but it was locked, a brass deadbolt set in the antique wood. I tried using a laminated discount card to jimmy the bolt, but it was wasted effort.

"Maybe there's a window," Kay said.

Her sneakers made less noise on the wood floor than my Rockports. We skirted the office and tried others. The door to the assistant's nook wasn't as well protected. I dug the bent card between door and jamb and retracted the bolt.

We entered, closed the door. Kay held up her phone, illuminating the room under cool blue light.

A loud voice from outside—"*Stop.*" I craned my neck to look out the window. A yellow-jacketed man stumbled out of the mud, in pursuit of a darting figure that must have been Blatchford. The singing continued from below.

Kay hit keys on the assistant's computer. A floating password box appeared on the screen. She tried closing it but it sprang up again.

"Why did you think this would be easy?" she whispered.

"Check the desk."

Kay opened the drawers, directing the light down on their contents. Stationery, correspondence, a cash box in the bottom. In the top right drawer, nestled beside pencils and a three-hole punch, was a spiral-bound notebook. Kay took it, held it up.

On the front of the notebook was a piece of masking tape with ASSISTANT written on it in smudged black marker. Evidently the job had a high rate of turnaround. Kay flipped pages.

The music had stopped. Outside, Blatchford and the guard had faded to shadows on the baseball field.

"Yes." Kay tapped the back page of the book, a list of passwords. I thought I saw her roll her eyes.

A stentorian voice filled the silence, Father Darian preaching the word. His cadence was more lyrical than his parishioners' singing.

Kay had access. She searched "Late Start" and copied files onto the zip drive. Outside I saw the security guard start back toward the church, winded, limping.

I watched the progress of the files. The father had called it "raw data." No kidding—pages of documents with gibberish names filled up the Late Start folder, A27677_B and the like.

When the transfer was finished, Kay put the computer to sleep. She followed me out, down the stairs. The sermon was winding down, dulcet tones, love thy neighbor. Murmurs of approval, soft amens. We almost collided with the security guard coming through the front door.

He was shorter than me, maybe twenty years older, still out of breath. Shock fading to suspicion. I put my hand on his shoulder and leaned in, as Kay circled behind us, making an end run for the door.

"Thank God," I near-whispered, drawing him toward the stairs. "I don't know what's going on, but I saw a guy go up there just now."

His eyes widened, putting it together. "Big guy, wide guy?"

"Yeah, kinda looked like a wrestler. I saw him go up the stairs but I didn't know who to tell, and I didn't want to interrupt—"

He put up his hand, a calming gesture. "Thanks for telling me, you did good."

I watched him ascend, then made my exit.

Kay and Blatchford were already in the car, ready to peel out as soon as my door closed. Kay drove, letting out a yip as we pulled onto the highway.

"Holy shit," she said. "I was worried there for a moment, but holy shit, right?"

I accepted the flask from Blatchford. "No problems?" I asked him.

"Wish you'd've been quicker, but I made it work." He grinned. "You're out of practice. If I taught you anything, it's that, this business, you have to keep your chops up."

I closed my eyes and told him to go fuck himself.

Twenty-Seven

On the plane ride home, Kay sat in the middle seat, her laptop open, trying to make sense of what we'd stolen. There was no sequence to the documents. Some had been copied from dog-eared or coffee-stained originals, some wrinkled or mussed beyond legibility. It was less like piecing together a jigsaw puzzle than sifting through pieces from many puzzles. I leaned against Kay's shoulder and directed her sorting—by penmanship, format, or date, but always looking for the name Dana Essex.

In the window seat, Blatchford snored. Before going through the security gate, he'd ingested whatever was left of his pharmacy. Then shortly after takeoff, he'd slugged back two airplane bottles of Tulla-more Dew. He'd be comatose till touchdown.

As Kay scrolled through the files, a familiar blue script filled the screen. I pointed. "Looks like her handwriting."

"I guess you'd know," Kay said. "When I dropped by your place that morning, she was in there?"

"Yeah."

"You slept with her."

"How does that help us now?" I said.

"Sorry, it's just weird. You don't think it's weird?"

"I crossed a line," I said after a moment. "She knew I'd cross it, maybe helped push me, but it doesn't change that this is my fault." I added, "I'm sorry you got caught in the middle of this."

"Don't be," Kay said. "I'm having a really good time."

We looked at the paper. The middle page of a report, explaining how Essex had spent the hour working with her client on paragraph structure:

. . . *while he doesn't understand the logical development of supporting ideas, Mr. Henshaw is nonetheless a gifted raconteur. It's a matter of focusing him, reminding him of the rules. He defaults to upper case letters when excited. I've suggested as a stopgap that he continue to write in caps while observing proper margins and punctuation. This method may . . .*

—and done, and none of the surrounding documents seemed to pick up the thread.

"Henshaw," I said. "We've got a suspect."

"Only another thousand pages to go."

"There's no rush." I remembered something. "Back at the church, you rolled your eyes. What was the password?"

Kay shook her head disapprovingly, like Father Darian should have known better. "Would you believe, 'Jesus1'?"

Twenty-Eight

The day of our flight home, a pair of unidentified males, wearing matching black drawstring hoodies with THRIVE OR DIE decaled in gold sequins on the back, approached the rear entrance of the Monte Carlo restaurant. Carrying automatic pistols, they forced the busboy, on his smoke break, to let them inside. They swept through the kitchen and rear offices, herding employees into the walk-in freezer. The gunmen singled out Anthony Qiu and his wife, Susan Leung Qiu, ordered them to seal the freezer with the majority of the kitchen staff inside, then walked them toward Qiu's private office.

A nineteen-year-old serving girl from Szechuan province intercepted them en route from the restaurant floor. Her scream was met by two .45 ACP slugs to the chest that killed her instantly. The young men and the married couple proceeded into the office.

One of the staff members who had hidden in the prep area heard Mrs. Qiu's screams, and a strangely accented voice say, "Which one of you bitches wants to die first." As he told the story on the news, the prep cook said there were five gunshots. He made the sounds. Boom. Boom. Boom. Boom. Boom. Right after each other, he added. Then the sounds of the two men leaving.

Lying in Sonia's bed in the late morning, I told her it felt like something was ending.

"Qiu was a threat but he was reasonable. You could talk to him, sometimes, at least. I tried that with the Hayes brothers and it went south fast." I looked up at the dust-caked blades of her ceiling fan. "Question is, if they take Qiu's place, do they become more like him? Or does the world just get uglier and slightly more stupid?"

"You don't like change," Sonia said.

"A decade knowing me and you're just finding out?"

She was first out of bed and to the shower, which meant the coffee and tea making duties fell to me.

When she emerged from the bathroom she was wearing pajama bottoms and a tank top, and her hair clung to her forehead in wet tendrils. I felt a clenching of the chest but didn't mention it as I handed her a mug.

"The flipside of that," I began.

"Of what?"

"Things changing," I said. "The flipside is I don't feel as anxious as I should. I'm pretty okay with being out of the PI business."

She knocked her hip against my crotch as she passed to the living room. "You can't bum around here forever. Are you really thinking of changing jobs?"

I shrugged. "I might not have a choice."

"Have you thought about what you'd do? What exactly are you qualified for?" She sipped her coffee. "Certainly not being a barista."

"Rent boy, maybe."

"Yeah? You think I'd let you do that?"

"I'd give you a discount."

"You'd better."

I sat down next to her, looking at the papers I'd left spread out on the coffee table. Copies of the documents written in Essex's hand. Next to them the newspaper, open to the story about Qiu. His photo, an old corporate headshot, looked at me with bemusement.

"I don't know what I'll end up doing," I said, stroking her knee. "And I don't much care right now."

Smiling behind her mug, she said, "Know what I think? I don't think you could live without being a PI."

"I thought that way about being a cop."

"Maybe every ten years you need to burn your career down, start over."

"And arise from the ashes," I said.

"David Wakeland, professional phoenix."

She dressed in the bedroom without closing the door, discarding her pajamas and slipping on underwear, jeans. None of the movements studied or done for my sake, which made them all the more beguiling. The world could be what it was, as long as I didn't have to take it on alone.

"It's been nice teaching Kay these last few months," I said. "Maybe I'll get some kind of degree and go work for the Justice Institute."

"It's a thought," she said. "But I don't believe you could give it up."

"Some people didn't think Elton John could pull off a country record."

In the shower I kneaded something lavender-scented into my scalp and tried to remember the lyrics to "Burn Down the Mission." When I shut off the nozzle I stood, naked, and luxuriated in the mist-filled chamber that smelled so strongly of all things her.

Chambers dead, and Wong and Nagy, and now Qiu. I could forget them all.

"Dave."

In the bedroom Sonia stood holding the phone. Instead of handing it to me, she hit the speaker button and tossed it on the bed.

"Believe it or not I'm glad you're back with her," Essex's voice said. Her glib tone sounded forced. "She seems pleasant, if a bit weak for you."

"She's right here," Sonia said, "and she'll beat your ass if you ever show your face in this city."

"Maybe I never left," Essex said.

"Then give us your address."

"I need to speak to Dave."

"You're speaking to both of us. My fucking phone."

A tentative silence from Essex's end of the line.

"All right." Her voice sounded tired. "If you want to involve yourself, I accept."

"I wasn't asking permission."

"Dave," she said. "Is this really necessary?"

"Yes, she is. Go ahead."

A pause, a consideration. "You weren't wrong about the things you said last time we spoke."

"Double negatives get on my nerves," I said. "What do you want?"

"Have you been prying into my affairs? Asking questions?"

"You're the one who keeps finding reasons to phone," I said. "I've said my piece."

"This is important. This could be fatal. Now please answer me."

"He's been busy helping me with a problem," Sonia said.

"Have you sent someone?"

"Who would I send?" I asked her. "Jeff and I are on the outs, and Kay is locked up filing invoices until this is over. You won, Dana."

"I hope that's true," she said. "Because it's not me you have to fear. What you said about my not being fully in control, you weren't—you were right."

"Okay."

"And I hope you're being honest, because if you're not, what's coming will be so much more horrible than what you expect."

"Meaning?"

"Watch yourself, Dave." To Sonia, she said, "Miss?"

"What?"

"Take care of him."

"Turn yourself in," Sonia said, meeting my gaze. "We can take care of him together."

I said, "Sonia's right. You know who this is. We can all walk out okay if you come clean."

"I can't risk it," Essex said.

She hung up without a good-bye.

"So that was her," Sonia said. She rubbed her shoulders. "Why does she phone like that?"

"Usually to taunt me. This was different." I sat on the bed and finished dressing. "I have to find her."

Sonia said, "Yes, we do."

Twenty-Nine

Kay and Blatchford combed through the Late Start documents, compiling a list of inmates Essex had worked with. From there we pulled court records and scanned newspaper articles, piecing together who had been released and where they lived now. One in Halifax, three in Ontario, two more spread over the prairies. All possibilities that would have to be checked. But three other felons lived in the Pacific Northwest; we started with them.

Robert Gordon Henshaw lived in Creston, a brewery town near the Idaho border. He'd killed two people, shot them, a pair of brothers who'd insulted him in a bar. Henshaw was seventy-three years old now, had been released last year. He lived with his daughter and her husband.

Lee Henry Crowhurst lived in Redmond, Washington, on some sort of farm. He'd beaten a senior citizen to death, been caught coming out of the man's apartment. He'd given no reason for the crime, and hadn't stolen anything or known the victim. His IQ was low. Of all the possibles, Essex had seemed to make the least progress with him. He was fifty-eight.

The last was Dale NMI Petrie, fifty-four, who lived on Vancouver Island, near a town called Ladysmith. Petrie had ties to the Ontario chapters of the Exiles Motorcycle Club. He'd killed a woman, killed her for money, and used a knife to do it.

The woman's name had been Joanna Disher, a twenty-seven-year-old bartender who'd witnessed an altercation between another biker and a local businessman outside a bar in Toronto. Her body had been discovered weeks before the case came to trial.

Petrie had been released six years ago, and seemed to be retired. When he'd moved to the coast, he hadn't made connections with the local biker gangs. Which was good—the last thing I wanted now was trouble with the Exiles.

We sat around Sonia's table, the four of us, copies of Father Darian's records piled in the center. Blatchford thought Petrie was the most likely by far.

"You read the reports," Blatchford explained. "Our gal uses the same descriptions with Henshaw and Crowhurst—with all the others, really. 'Progressing' or 'not progressing,' 'putting in effort' and whatnot. But read Petrie's."

I did, and saw what he meant. With the others, Essex tracked what she covered in each study session. With Petrie, though, her reports were more psychological. She wrote of his poor attitude, his excessive off-topic questioning. She felt bullied by him, like he didn't take her seriously.

I looked around the table. Kay shrugged. Sonia said, "Being cranky and a bad speller doesn't make him our killer."

Our. I let the word pass.

Blatchford said, "It's how she wrote about him. He got to her. Some people thrive on being pushed around, bullied a bit. Right frame of mind, I'm one of them."

"Still doesn't make him Tabitha's killer," Sonia countered.

"Passion is passion. It's the people that agitate you that you're most drawn to. Isn't it?" Nodding toward me, he said to Sonia, "Who can piss you off quicker than he can?"

Sonia conceded the point.

"First let's cross off Henshaw and Crowhurst," I said. "Kay and I can look into Petrie, figure out a way to approach him."

"We take him out now," Blatchford said, "head on, we all sleep easier."

"If he's the most dangerous and the most likely, we have to be the most careful with him. Two days we'll know more."

Blatchford grumbled but agreed to check out Henshaw and Crowhurst first. I asked if he wanted company.

"Better you stay here," he said, getting up from the table. "This kind of skullduggery I do better without an audience."

Blatchford was probably right about Petrie. He did seem the most likely. He also seemed more than capable of cutting another throat—Tabitha's, Blatchford's, Sonia's, mine. Maybe it was inevitable we confront him. If so, two days wouldn't make much difference.

Thirty

Tim Blatchford didn't call the next morning. He didn't answer his cell. Part of me worried, part thought he was legitimately busy, and part thought he held off just to taunt me. Like it or not, I had to let him do things his way. So Kay and I focused on Dale Petrie.

The ex-biker's Ladysmith house was valued at two and a half million dollars. Satellite photos showed a fenced-in property near a golf course, in a wealthy subdivision of similar-sized homes. The property even had an outdoor pool.

Where Petrie had got the money for the place was unclear. He was currently employed as a groundskeeper and maintenance man at an RV park / camp site. The property taxes alone would bite significantly into that salary.

Petrie needed money, and he'd killed for it before. That made him the most likely candidate, though there was still nothing connecting him to the death of Tabitha Sorenson. Only Dana Essex knew.

But there was one person who might have seen Tabitha's killer. I dreaded approaching him, but after trying Blatchford once more with no response, I drove to Sabar Gill's house.

Gill opened the door wearing sweat pants and a baggy sweater, barefoot and unshaven. His hair had been trimmed, stitches visible along his scalp. He stared at me.

"You're not how I remembered," Gill said. His voice was emotionless and his eyes showed signs of sedation. "When they let me out of the hospital, I looked you up. I thought you'd have more money."

"You and me both," I said.

For a moment I thought he'd slam the door on me, but his head canted to the side in a defeated shrug. He let me in.

Once we were seated on his couch, he asked what I wanted.

"It's about the person who killed Tabitha. Did you get a look at them?"

"Like I told the police, I don't remember that night," Gill said. "Any of it. I just remember waking up in the hospital with my head on fire, and then the cops telling me Tabby was dead."

Perhaps sensing I was about to offer condolences, Gill closed his eyes. "Just get on with it," he said.

I had an envelope with photos of the Late Start suspects, Petrie first among them. "Would you look at these?"

"I told you, I didn't see him."

"Maybe the person followed you before that night."

"That was you who did that."

Gill took the envelope, flipped listlessly through the pictures. He held up Petrie's, paused, then set it down atop the others. He shook his head.

"I know you didn't stab her," he said.

"No."

"The news made it sound like you know who was responsible."

"It's delicate," I said. "If you can give me some time, hopefully I can answer—"

"I don't care about answers."

Gill let the envelope slip to the floor, the photos fanning out.

He said, "The police asked me about you and that cop who killed himself. And that lady cop, your girlfriend, who was with you when you shot those other two."

There were tears pearling at the corners of his eyes.

"It's just death everywhere, isn't it?" he said.

"Feels like it sometimes."

His head lowered, nodding slowly.

"She's dead, Tabitha, because of money. You all wanted it, and she paid the price—she was the price. You should've gotten paid better for telling them where she was."

"You know it's not that simple."

He shrugged, smiling, all bleeding sarcasm and raw grief.

"I'm sorry as hell," I said. "I know I can't make it right. What I can do is find the people responsible."

"Find someone else. Kill someone else. You don't get tired of that?"

"This is different."

"For a good cause this time," he said. "Unlike before."

Gill showed me to the door, passing me back the envelope as I crossed the threshold. I offered him my card. He took it, then let it flutter to land on the stoop.

He said, "I was going to tell you I hope you die, but I don't honestly want that. I mean it, I don't. What I hope is that you find out what real grief is like. Someone you love, losing them, being helpless. You should know what that's like, and I hope you find out soon."

Thirty-One

When Blatchford finally called, it wasn't from Creston. Around seven p.m. he phoned from the truck crossing near Aldergrove, stuck in a long line waiting for Customs to let him back across the border.

"Figured I'd get them both out of the way," he said. "Henshaw and Crowhurst. They're not our guy. Henshaw's in a wheelchair. He's a colostomy bag with an old man attached. I saw that and headed straight to Redmond."

"And Crowhurst?" I asked.

"Not much better. Guy's borderline special ed. Lives on the old family farm—'farm,' fucking place is all mud. I stopped by like I needed directions, how to get back to the highway, just to see how sharp he is."

"And he said what?"

"'It's about a half hour.' And I ask him which way, and he kinda frowns and says, 'whichever way you got here.'"

"Did you tip you were interested in him?"

Blatchford's answer was a muttered "fuck" and the sound of his truck engine gasping back to life. When he came back on the line he said, "I rented a car in Bellingham, like you told me to, with Washington plates. Guy didn't give two shits about what I was driving. I was keeping him from his cartoons."

"Nobody living with him?"

"Nah. He's got a sister who checks in on him once in a while. He works in some warehouse stocking shelves. No license, guy can't even drive himself."

"How about Henshaw's family?" I asked. "He has a daughter and son-in-law."

"And they're both sweet as punch, and they have two kids. It's not him, Dave. Not either of them. You know who it is."

Before I could answer, his horn sounded, crackling the speaker of the phone.

"I'm going, shitstain, all right?" He was speaking to whoever was behind him. Once he'd maneuvered his car, he said to me, "I'll head over tomorrow morning and scope out Dale Petrie. I won't confront him till you say so. You and Kay learn anything about him?"

"He keeps a low profile," I said. "But his money has to come from somewhere."

"You'd keep your head down too, you were going around shanking people. I'll call you when I get there, let's say around noon."

"Stay safe," I said to a dead phone. He'd already hung up.

Thirty-Two

Irritation to anger, to disappointment, to worry, falling finally into fear.

Tim Blatchford kept to his own unfathomable time code, which didn't accommodate my need for regular reports. He was also more than capable of defending himself. I kept both facts in mind over the course of the next day, resisting the urge to bombard him with texts, limiting my calls to once on the hour.

But by nightfall he still hadn't called, and it was clear something had happened.

Kay hadn't heard from him, either. "You're worried?" she asked when I phoned her.

"Getting there."

"How well exactly do you know him?"

"Why?"

"No reason, I guess." She hesitated before saying, "We don't really know what he's been up to. I mean, maybe he's—I dunno."

"Go ahead," I said.

"Okay. Back in Hamilton, at the church, when he refused to go inside. Remember?"

"He was fucking with me," I said. "It's what he does."

"Sure. But maybe he didn't want to be seen by the father, y'know? Maybe they'd seen each other before." She forced herself to proceed. "Maybe he's the person we're looking for."

I was ready to scoff but I waited, let the idea play out. It was hard to stomach—the thought that I'd unknowingly hired the man I was trying to find. I could be stupid, but hopefully not that stupid.

"It doesn't work," I said to Kay. "Tim's not whoever Dana Essex met at Milton."

"But he might know that person, or know Essex some other way. I'm just saying, he was at the office right before the murder."

"Looking for work."

"Maybe," Kay said. "Anyway, I hope you find him."

I called the wrestling promotion he worked for but the promotor said he'd no-showed. The promotor added, if I saw Blatchford, tell him there'd better be a good fucking excuse for blowing off his cage match with El Phantasmo.

I drove to Blatchford's address, a carved-up house off Renfrew. The house was squat but still taller than its neighbors, with a mansard roof that gave it the look of a beige-painted barn. Twenty years ago it might've been owned by a single family, who might've maintained it with something like love. No more of that in this neighborhood. Parked cars jammed the narrow street, but I was the only person visible. Together/apart, as only Vancouver could do.

There was no outside staircase leading to Blatchford's flat. I knocked at the door of the downstairs resident. I heard movement inside, and waited on the weatherbeaten patio, staring at the dead plants that hung from the chained box planters above the railing.

The door opened. A barefoot man in sweats and an unbuttoned dress shirt stepped out, nodded, and lit a cigarette. I told him I was looking for Tim.

"His place is upstairs but he's not here."

"When'd you last see him?"

"He got in late yesterday. He must've left early this morning. But that's normal for Tim."

He was smoking Belmonts and offered me the pack. I managed to decline. "You know him pretty well?"

"Sure." Letting me infer from that what I wanted.

"I'm a friend of his," I said, "and his employer."

"Two things that don't usually go together."

"I think he's in trouble. I'd like to take a look at his place."

"Trouble." The man smoked and considered the term. "What's he done and who'd he do it to?"

"He hasn't been in touch and he was supposed to be. And yes I know he's unreliable, but this is beyond that. I'm thinking he's hurt."

He took a last long drag on his cigarette. "I got his spare set around somewhere. Let's take a look."

Inside, up the stairs, a fumbling of keys. "Your name's Wakeland, right?" He examined the key ring. "Think he's mentioned you."

"All praise, I'm sure."

"I wouldn't call it praise, exactly." He forced the door inward to line up so the lock would turn. "Tim seemed happy to be working with you. Didn't tell me what he was doing, but sounded serious about it. Tim needs that—without a goal he just flails about."

"I know the feeling," I said.

"He said you had that in common." He got the door open, sighed in recognition of the effort. "Stuart Royce, by the way. Tim's on-again, off-again, guess you could say."

Blatchford's apartment shocked me in that it wasn't a shithole. The long narrow room terminated in a shower closet, and had a cramped, lived-in feel. Hot plate and fold-down bed. Clothes on the floor, neither folded nor strewn. A stool next to the washstand served as a catchall for papers, flyers, chopsticks, and bills.

Nothing on the walls save for a signed poster of Roddy Piper, sunglasses on, ready to kick ass and chew bubblegum.

"It's as he left it," Royce said.

"He didn't say anything to you, where he was going?"

"Let me think." He stooped to tuck a tendril of bedsheet back onto the mattress. "Something about the Island."

"When was this?"

"Yesterday night, after he got back from Creston. He phoned that guy and got into it with him, and then—"

"What guy? You're talking about Dale Petrie?"

"That sounds right." Royce's laconic indifference let up enough for a note of irritation to creep into his voice. "He told Tim to fuck off, and you know Tim. And when Tim called again, he said he didn't know where Tim was from, but where *he* was from, fuck off meant fuck off."

Before Blatchford had even made the trip to the Island, he'd tipped off Petrie. "Why would he phone?" I asked.

"If I had an answer for half the things Tim does." Royce didn't finish the sentence. I pictured Blatchford phoning while drunk, exhausted from the drive, thinking a quick wrong-number call would confirm that Petrie was the one.

I thanked Royce and walked home. Inside my apartment the lights were on, the stereo spinning a Joni Mitchell album. The bathroom door opened and Sonia came out, pulling back her hair and threading it through an elastic.

"Food's on its way," she said. "General Tso's and some of those green beans you like."

For a moment it all seemed wrong, a cruel joke. This wasn't what I came home to. It was what I wished to come home to. I allowed myself to be enfolded into the domestic fantasy, kissing her, feeling the heat from the shower roll over us as we stood in the hall.

I explained to her what I thought had happened to Blatchford.

"We could phone the Mountie detachment in Ladysmith," she said. "Then head over tomorrow morning."

Again, that hesitation. It felt odd relying on anyone, let alone her. Now firmly entrenched in this fantasy, I didn't want to lose my hold on Tuesday night Chinese, on curling up on the couch. But the truth wasn't a choice between those two worlds. It was accepting they could co-exist.

"We can eat in the car on our way," I said.

Thirty-Three

The ferry from Horseshoe Bay to Nanaimo weaves through fog-shrouded islands, crosses a gray body of water that bleeds into an equally gray horizon. We stood on the deck of the ship, forgoing the lounge and the crowded cafeteria. Above us, the charcoal-colored clouds parted in a long straight slice that exposed a seam of blue-black atmosphere. Gulls pumped their wings, arcing back toward shore.

"My friends and I used to take the ferry all the time," Sonia said. "First trip away from my foster folks, Nanaimo's where we went."

"To do what?"

"Drink and get laid, smoke dope, smash things on the beach."

"Bet you left that off your police application."

She turned to watch the western edge of Bowen Island diminish and slide into the gray. "I know so many people who see whales on this trip. Orcas. They come right up to the boat, they say. I've never seen shit."

In Nanaimo we got back in my Cadillac and headed to Ladysmith. I'd taken a pamphlet from the tourism rack on the ferry, and as Sonia drove, I read out the local sites. "An award-winning meadery and a glass-blowing workshop. We could move here, you know. You could request a transfer."

"Just try and hold me back," she said.

The drive took forty minutes, through the sleepy downtown core of Nanaimo, down the Island Highway that ran along the east coast of Vancouver Island. Petrie's house was built sideways to the winding street. Three stories and bracket-shaped, the back yard concealed behind high hedges. Windows closed and curtains drawn, what looked like tinfoil peeking out from the other side of the glass. From the curb, we could hear cursing coming from around back.

Petrie sat on a chaise longue beside an outdoor pool, lit by floodlights. He was reading a paper. His Hawaiian shirt was unbuttoned, tanned belly hanging out like a half-inflated beach ball. The red coils of a portable heater wafted warmth toward his face.

He noticed us and put the paper down. Heaved himself out of his chair, staggered, steadied himself by grabbing the back of the chaise.

"This is private property, fuckwad." He walked over to us.

I leaned over the gate. "I'm looking for a friend."

"Bet you are." Up close I could smell beer breath. He was missing one and a half fingers on his right hand. Something in the palm of his left, black and metallic.

"Can I ask if you've seen him?" I said.

"You can take your faggot ass back where you came from, the bitch too, before I get really pissed and decide—"

I grabbed a hank of Petrie's hair and pulled him over the gate. The top hinge snapped. Petrie somersaulted, his face introducing itself to the gravel bed that was his lawn.

I planted a knee on his back and shook the weapon out of his hand. A fold-out knife, wood-handled and dull.

Petrie sputtered and cursed. He looked up at Sonia, who stomped on his hand with the heel of her boot.

"Answer his question, shit-turd," she said.

"I haven't seen anyone. You two know the people you're fucking with?"

"Mmm-hmmm. Can we check out your place?" As he formed his reply I added, "Thank you so much, won't take a minute."

I pulled him to his feet and Sonia cuffed him. We marched him through the broken gate, shoving him back onto the chaise.

"You talked to my friend on the phone," I said.

"Did not."

"You didn't tell him that fuck off meant fuck off?"

"That guy?" His mouth pursed in distaste. "So what if I told him to fuck himself? Shouldna fucking phoned me in the first place."

Up close, his pool was a floating collection of leaves, feathers, garbage bags, and beer cans. "You didn't see him?" I asked.

"No." He looked between us. "Swear to fucking god."

The sliding door opened onto an apartment, hot and humid like the Amazon Room at the Vancouver Aquarium. Petrie's apartment décor: ashtrays and ancient stroke magazines, empty cardboard flats of Old Stock and the odd two-six of Stoli. A big chrome .45 on top of the fridge.

"I'll watch him," Sonia said. She had her own pistol concealed beneath her coat, but I handed her Petrie's. I went back inside.

Up the stairs, into the foyer. I saw why the heat. Every other room in the house had been gutted, plank shelving installed, hydroponics and tin foil for wallpaper. Rows of pot plants, hundreds to a room. Water jugs and pails of nutrients everywhere.

A pro operation, the Exiles or one of their rival gangs. And Petrie tending things for them.

No Blatchford, no Essex, nothing on Tabitha Sorenson.

I heard a groan and a scream from outside. Rushing down the stairs and out onto the lawn, I saw Petrie fetal-positioned next to the chaise, his forehead sporting a spiderweb of blood.

"Bitch," Petrie said.

Sonia had the gun pointed at him, breathing heavy. "He's lucky he's not in the fucking pool right now."

I checked his storage shed, which held bags of chicken manure, a few gallon jugs of Dyna-Gro, and little else.

"Are those department-issue cuffs?" I asked.

"They're a spare pair. I've got others." She blushed slightly.

"Nothing linking us to him, then."

"We're clear." She handed me the pistol. Petrie seemed very interested in it.

I shot the glass of the sliding door and ventilated the siding. When the gun was empty I tossed it in the pool. We walked out to a refrain of Petrie's curses.

In the car, speeding back to the ferry, I said to Sonia: "Shit-turd?"

"Like you could've come up with better."

Thirty-Four

At Departure Bay we stopped for coffee and waited for the next ferry. The coffee shop was between the help desk and the car rental office. Travelers milled about, watching through the glass walls as the lights of the ship approached in the dark.

"You're sure Tim was coming here?" Sonia asked.

"That's what he said. Seems like he didn't make it to Petrie."

I had a thought. At the help desk I asked if any cars or trucks had been left at the ferry parking lot. The clerk had to track down a supervisor, but eventually returned with the answer. A black Grand Cherokee. Blatchford's vehicle.

"Left this afternoon," the clerk said without looking up from her monitor. "It already went to the impound lot. The vehicle is yours?"

"My employee's," I said. "Which parking lot was it left in—long or short term?"

"It was left on the ferry, sir. Our people caught it during unloading. No one claimed it and it was taken in. Delayed the sailing thirty minutes."

In the coffee shop, Sonia had the Late Start files on our table. Dana Essex's comments on Henshaw, Crowhurst, and Dale Petrie.

"What do you think?" I asked.

"She has nice penmanship."

I told her about the car.

"They rolled it off here," she said. "On the Island. Meaning something must've happened on the trip over."

She brought out her phone, searched "ferry attack," "ferry stabbing." Nothing relevant.

I thought of the control with a knife the killer had displayed with Tabitha Sorenson. "Try 'ferry accident,'" I said.

She did, and there it was: "Unidentified Man Removed From Ferry Following Below-Deck Accident."

He'd been found unconscious on the car deck, a deep puncture in his side that had bled out, presumably from an exposed edge of jagged steel somewhere amid the restricted nooks of the hull's interior. Discovered during unloading on the mainland, removed from the ferry by ambulance.

Essex's warnings came back to me, the note of fear in her voice. Blatchford had run into danger, and I'd pointed him in that direction.

The news site didn't say which hospital Blatchford had been removed to. "Easy enough to find out," Sonia said.

By the time we were back at her apartment, she knew Blatchford had been taken to Lions Gate Hospital. The receptionist confirmed over the phone that he'd been admitted after suffering some sort of industrial accident aboard the *Queen of Nanaimo*. He'd had cocaine and tranquilizers in his system, and might have stumbled somewhere he shouldn't have. He'd lost a significant amount of blood and been unconscious upon arrival, and had been in and out for the last few hours.

Once she hung up, I told Sonia we'd have to drive back to North Van and check out the hospital. She vetoed.

"Is Tim someone who could take care of himself?" she asked.

"I wouldn't've picked him otherwise."

"So he's capable," Sonia reiterated. "And this person surprised him and stabbed him. Just like he stabbed Tabitha. That should tell you he's patient, and might have done this just to lure you out."

"I can't leave him there."

"That is exactly what you should do," Sonia said. "Let me handle this. I'll go and see him. I'll make sure he's safe."

The sound of her leaving, her locking the door, felt like being submerged underwater with no guarantee of surfacing. It was all I could do not to call her back.

Instead I called the crime desk of the *Sun* to find out what the paper knew about Blatchford's incident. Next to nothing, it turned out. "The only thing anyone talked about was the amount of blood," the journalist said. Her name was Holinshed. "You wouldn't think a person could hold that much. Are you thinking it's foul play?" Excitement in her voice. "Is this connected to that Sorenson thing?"

"Not sure," I said. "But if you can wait two days, I'll give you the exclusive."

"Exclusive," she scoffed. "One major news corp left in the city. Who else would you give it to?"

But she agreed. I asked if she knew anything about the Anthony Qiu killings at the Monte Carlo.

"Drugs and turf, what else? The Leung family was getting weaker and their rivals pushed them out. League of Nations, maybe, or the Exiles. Hard to say till we see more bodies."

She added, "You know we'll have to start looking into the connection between Sorenson and Blatchford. I'll be expecting an interview with you. The full sordid tale."

"I'll get to work on an ending," I said.

Thirty-Five

Sonia didn't come back until three. I stayed up watching an Eastwood marathon, *Firefox* followed by *Two Mules for Sister Sara*. Not having cable at my own flat, I found the commercials and the bowdlerized films a comforting parade of colors.

She patted my neck to see if I was awake. I sat up and made room for her on the couch. "He's alive?"

"Recovering," she said, "though it's slow. I watched him for an hour or so to see if he'd wake up. I didn't see anyone suspicious, and I checked the entire hospital."

"By yourself? At night?"

I hadn't meant to say it out loud. She pushed away slightly on the couch.

"You need to find a way to accept that I know what I'm doing. You helped me, Dave, and now it's my turn."

"You're right," I said, with little to no sincerity. Her look told me she'd caught the subtext. "I shouldn't be afraid for you?"

"Afraid is okay, but you have to have faith. Otherwise"—she spread her hands—"we can't go on."

"Makes sense. Going to bed?"

"Unless there's something on."

"*Eiger Sanction*'s coming up. Eastwood as a mountain-climbing hit man."

In the morning I woke up to find her at the kitchen table, rereading the Late Start files.

"You and Blatchford had it narrowed to three," she said. "Henshaw in Creston. Crowhurst in Washington. Petrie on Vancouver Island. One of them is likely the cut man."

"Or put Essex in touch with the cut man," I said.

"Blatchford thought it was Petrie. Essex wrote more on the entries about Petrie. See?" She tilted the screen to show me the scanned pages. Dana's blue cursive filled a report template that looked like a photocopy a few dozen generations removed from the original.

"Petrie acted out, sounds like."

"A lot. The other two, the reports are more rote. Subjects studied, progress or lack of. Less writing."

"Maybe she thought more of Petrie."

"Maybe," Sonia said. "But reading them, it seems she was trying to get her bosses to pay attention to Petrie's antics. Like she wasn't being heard." She tapped the screen. "Here. The part about this tantrum 'being a continuation of last week's, resulting in a similar lack of progress, to the point where lesson delivery itself is impeded.' That's the voice of someone, a woman, struggling to get her bosses to see what's really going on."

"You'd know," I said.

"You never told me how Blatchford got hold of these," she said. "Do all PIs steal?"

"No," I said. "Only Blatchford, and me once in a while. Bob Aries, I guess. Pretty much everyone except Jeff."

"And he's the successful one, which should tell you something." Before I could retort she said, "Look here."

On the screen was a session progress report on Lee Henry Crowhurst. Essex had ended the report with a request:

While slow and barely literate, he is NOT in this writer's prognosis develop-
mentally disabled, and in fact demonstrates tremendous powers of ratiocination
and problem-solving. I humbly request to amend my course plan, elongating
the curriculum and increasing the total number of sessions, in order to aid
Mr. Crowhurst in adapting his fundamental skills to academic pursuits.

"Only a grad student could write 'in this writer's prognosis' without
a hint of shame," I said.

"She asks to spend more time with him. She's denied. The next
bunch of reports are all rote. 'Mr. Crowhurst made little progress. Failed
to meet his monthly goals.'"

"Sulking," I said. "Saying I told you so to her superiors."

"Right. Petrie's a nuisance and Henshaw's plugging away, but Crowhurst is all unrealized potential. She can see there's a thought process
with him. She's intrigued."

"What's their connection like?" I asked.

"I don't know. She resents administration, and Crowhurst comes
across as a victim of his own psychology. Felons are pros at sizing people
up. Maybe he manipulated her into thinking she saw the real him."

"What if it works the other way?" I said. "Maybe she's using him.
When Tabitha double-crossed her, maybe Dana got back in touch with
Crowhurst, promised him a cut of the—what?"

She was looking at me with the patient expression of a teacher waiting for a student to come around to the right answer on his own.

"We know someone who knows," she said.

"She phones me. She changes numbers every time."

"Try the one she called from last."

I dialed. No answer.

"Least it's not disconnected," I said.

"She'll call," Sonia assured me. "Until then, we have to figure out
what to say to her."

Thirty-Six

When the phone did ring, it was the journalist from the *Sun*, Holinshed, telling me to type a long, backslash-heavy URL into my browser. A live stream, shaky handheld footage of police milling about outside a familiar-looking house. Petrie's grow-op setup was being carried out.

"Dale Petrie's house," Holinshed explained. "Name familiar to you? He's connected with the Demon Wolves, an Exiles feeder gang."

"An ex-con's not the cleanest front for a grow-op," I said.

"No kidding. Yesterday someone turned a gun on Petrie's house. RCMP showed up to a shots-fired call from the neighbor. Petrie wouldn't let them inside, but the cops checked the meter. Electricity use off the charts, extra wiring. The cops got a search warrant first thing this morning, and now the top brass are acting like this was all part of some narcotics strategy, take a bite out of crime."

I wondered about Blatchford. The journalist was thinking the same thing. "This happens on the Island soon after your friend is left bleeding out on the ferry. Those shots fired could've come from someone connected to Blatchford."

"Anything's possible," I said.

"This is where you drop me a hint, Mr. Wakeland, save me some legwork."

"It ties back to the Sorenson case," I said. "I wouldn't be surprised if the person who gutted Blatchford turned out to be connected to Tabitha's murder."

She let out a soft "Jesus." Then, "Do you know who it is?"

"Working on it."

"If I start looking into this, does it step on your investigation?"

"No," I said. "Run with it."

I walked around Coopers' Park, keeping Sonia's apartment within sight. I thought about how I wanted this to play out. Petrie or Crowhurst, whoever it was, had murdered Tabitha Sorenson, nearly killed Tim Blatchford. If Essex would flip, this could resolve itself lawfully. If not . . .

I found myself running a catechism in my head.

Did I want Tabitha's killer brought to justice?

Absolutely.

Did I feel some responsibility?

Overwhelmingly yes.

Was I willing to do everything I could to stop that murderer, break the law if necessary, risk myself and the woman I loved?

If I was honest, the answer was no. If Petrie or Crowhurst or whoever decided to fade away and trouble me no more, I would take it. I'd live with my guilt—with Sonia—and live happily.

Back at the apartment I asked Sonia if Essex had called. No, but Sonia had phoned Lions Gate again. Blatchford was doing better. "He wants to talk to you," she said.

"Then let's go."

"Don't be silly. I've arranged with his nurse to Skype."

"He's a half hour from here by car," I said.

"I don't want you near him. I talked to his doctor and one of the nurses. They both emphasized how lucky he was—an inch or so and the blade would've hit a major organ."

"He caught a break."

"It was an incision. The person who did it knew it probably wouldn't kill him."

"Why show Blatchford mercy and not Tabitha?"

"It's not mercy if Blatchford is bait. Think, Dave. What is the question no one has asked yet?"

"They all thought this was an accident."

"And?"

"Blatchford's car was pulled off the ferry on the Island, but he wasn't found till the ferry returned to the mainland. Meaning this person must have followed Blatchford onto the ferry and stabbed him. Which means—"

"Which means he might be here," Sonia said. "In town. Waiting for you."

I picked up the phone and dialed Essex's number. It rang and rang. I hung up, dialed again. Hung up, dialed again.

Finally I heard the breath of a live connection, only to have it cut off into silence. This time when I phoned, Essex picked up. She said, "You're killing me."

"We need to talk," I said. "Your time's up."

"It will be if you keep pursuing things."

"We don't have a choice," I said. "Neither of us, when it comes down to it. You're not a master criminal. You haven't vanished without a trace. You're across the border, aren't you, probably less than a day's drive. Your hold over your accomplice, whether it was money or sex, is dwindling, and day by day you're seeing just how unstable he is. The real him, the side he hid from you years back at the Milton Hilton when you tried to teach him his three R's."

"So you did pry into our lives."

"Like you knew I would, Dana. Like you counted on. Your phone calls have been your attempt to throw yourself a lifeline."

"You can't protect me," she said.

"The police can." Sonia had been standing beside me, listening. She said, "As a witness you would receive protection round the clock."

"Do you know what my life would be worth if I testified against Lee?" Essex's words were spilling out amid frantic breaths. As if uttering the idea was a danger in itself.

"What's it worth now?" I said. "You've got Lee on one side, the law on the other, me on the third, and now the press."

"The—"

"In two days a story will appear linking Tabitha to the ferry stabbing."

"You can't."

"Has nothing to do with me—but if Lee was mad about Blatchford, this will push him over the edge. He'll cut every tie 'tween him and them."

"He'll kill me," she said. "I can tell he's considering it."

"There's one lifeline, Dana but you have to take it now. Find a cop and turn yourself in. Come clean—remember what clean feels like?"

"There's no way," she said.

"You don't have to believe in forgiveness to take the help offered. This works in your favor. A short time in jail, a dangerous offender locked away. And safety."

"Your help," she said. "You'd help me?"

"You can help yourself by turning yourself in."

"To you."

"To the police."

She said, "You. I trust you. I'm your client."

I paused and looked at Sonia for guidance. She nodded.

"Right," I said. "Meet me and I'll go with you to the cops. We'll explain everything to them together."

"You'll come get me? Take me there?"

Sonia said, "We'll come get you and bring you back, then you and Dave can talk to the authorities. We'll make sure Lee doesn't harm you. Tell us where you are."

"Tacoma," Essex said. "Near Seattle. Lee told me not to leave the state until the money was cleared."

"How did Lee get the money, anyway?" Sonia leaned closer to the phone.

"He stabbed her, Tabitha, and told her to transfer the money using her laptop. He said he was going to kill her but if she gave up the money he'd leave her boyfriend alive. He explained it all to me after. He said she didn't hesitate. Didn't even beg for her life."

I pushed the image of a dying, bloody Tabitha Sorenson from my mind. There wasn't time.

"We'll meet you in Tacoma in a few hours," Sonia said. "Can you find a safe place until noon?"

"There's nowhere safe," Essex said.

"Find a hotel. Let the front desk know not to give your information out for any reason. Call Dave at twelve. We'll be in town and we'll take you home."

"All right," Essex said. "I should thank you."

"Just phone on time. Will you promise?"

"I will."

"And keep the phone handy so we can call you."

"This is so different from how I wanted things to go," Essex said. "I thought it would be freeing, but it cages you in, tighter and tighter, until—" she broke off. "I don't see how Tabitha lived with it."

She didn't, I thought.

Thirty-Seven

Blatchford's face against the hospital bed was wan, his features relaxed by medication. Eyes unfocused, he looked toward the laptop camera and smiled.

"I should charge you per stitch," he said.

"Do you remember being attacked?"

"Not a thing. Something about a smell, maybe. Like wet coals after a beach fire."

"That's very poetic, Tim."

"I just remember that smell, then trying to walk and not being able to." He yawned. "Dale Petrie is not our guy. That I'm sure of."

"It seems to be Lee Henry Crowhurst," I said. "You met him. What put you off him?"

"Wasn't playing with a full set of chromosomes. Took him a long time to answer anything."

"Could it be an act? Or affectation?"

His head slumped side to side. "I know acting."

"Says the pro wrestler."

Blatchford hit the button on the beige remote that hung from off his guardrail. "Almost time for my medicine. I gotta get dinged up more often, this morphine shit's great."

"Crowhurst," I redirected.

"Lives on a mud farm outside Redmond. Lots of secondhand shit."

"Knives?"

"He had a kitchen. Nothing stuck out. Get it?" A corner of his mouth raised, forming a lopsided smile.

The nurse came, pushed the laptop away and adjusted his dosage. When we resumed, Blatchford was drowsy, his answers even less specific. I got ready to sign off, but something told me to ask once more about the smell.

"Can you describe it? Do you mean *he* smelled?"

Blatchford's mouth barely moved. Spit bubbled on his lips.

"Not sure 'zactly," he said. "Smoky but not like cigarettes. Not dope, either. I recognized it, but I don't know from where. Might've dreamed it."

"I don't understand."

"He needs to sleep now," the nurse said. She'd been sitting off-camera and now began taking down the apparatus.

"Sounds stupid," Blatchford said, "but I had this dream once about my dad coming back. He made it out of Vietnam and had me when he was older. Shot himself when I was in my teens. In my dream he'd sit me down and say, I've got something really special for you. You're a man now. This is yours. Holds out the cartridge, the one from his bullet. He used to reload his own cartridges, had the machine in our basement, sacks of powder and all that shit. Said this'll be a special load. 'Zactly the same. I watch him re-make the bullet he did himself with. Measure out the powder, tap in a primer cap. I had that dream a few times and never made it to the end. But that smell, on the ferry, that was the smell of my dad pouring in the powder. I don't want to smell that again. When I kill myself—I mean, y'know, if—it won't be with a fucking gun."

Thirty-Eight

We set out for the border. Over the Oak Street Bridge and down the long strip of highway that led past the airport, past Surrey, to the curved hilly lanes that fed into the Peace Arch Crossing. The dollar was still weak, and traffic was minimal.

Sonia drove. I played disk jockey. Once we were through Bellingham, I asked her if she wanted to hear the song she'd be playing at my funeral. I scrolled to Bobbie Gentry, "He Made a Woman Out of Me."

"You don't have 'Beast of Burden' on there?" she asked.

What struck me driving down through the Pacific Northwest was the lack of grandeur of so many of the towns. To put up a Vancouver or Seattle seemed understandable. But to carve deep into the endless green and blue, to clear-cut forests and redirect waterways, all to erect a dirty brick train station, a plastic coffee hut and yet another outlet mall with a drive-through bank and family restaurant, seemed the choice of an insane creature that would rather stare at its own feces than a perfection it had no hand in shaping.

And yet I loved it. When we gassed up in Everett I walked through the aisles of the convenience mart, admiring the English-only labels and the strange brands that never seemed to catch on up north: Skoal, Payday, Whatchamacallit. As we drove, the fast food billboards we passed seemed to cycle and recycle in indecipherable patterns, like the colored symbols on a slot machine wheel.

We crossed the Puyallup River on I5 and continued into Tacoma, the highway bifurcating a sprawl of gas stations, car lots, and casinos.

It was eleven forty. We pulled off and had brunch at a Denny's. We split plates of bacon and eggs, pancakes, hash browns, biscuits, and toast.

"White or brown?" the waiter asked Sonia.

"Excuse me?"

"Your gravy."

Sonia looked at me. "Who has gravy for breakfast?" I shrugged. She looked back at the waiter and smiled. "Little of both on the side."

At noon we both watched my phone stay perfectly silent. I took a sip of tea, which had been served as a cup of water, a tea bag, and a plastic thimble of cream.

"Could be a late riser," I said.

"You would know."

Her attention drifted away. I asked what was wrong.

"I don't want to search for her," Sonia said. "She's not worth it."

"What do you want to do?"

"Hand this over to the Pierce County Sheriff's and go home."

"Leave Essex out there with Crowhurst."

"She chose him. They deserve each other."

She broke off pieces of biscuit to sample the gravies.

"I have no problem helping someone who wants to be helped, especially someone who's risking her life to do right." She found the brown passable, the white made her pause. "But if she's planning something, I want no part of it, and if she's lost her nerve, well, that's not our problem."

"Or he got to her already," I said. "I'll phone some hotels. If I get nothing, we go to the sheriff and head home."

"Fine." She pointed her fork at the two gravies, together on the saucer. "The white is basically mushroom soup."

"We'll probably serve it at our wedding. Maybe have the service here."

"Planning our wedding now?"

"Just speaking words. Why, you have other designs?"

"Why no," she said, batting her eyelashes. "It's every girl's dream to get married at a diner in Tacoma."

"You're a haughty cosmopolitan."

"That's me. One gravy's just not enough."

The phone jumped. I opened it and read a text message from an unknown number. ARE YOU HERE?

I showed it to Sonia. We thought it over. I punched in, WHERE IS HERE?

IN TOWN came the almost instant reply. Then: TACOMA and finally, THIS IS DANA.

YES, I hit back, IN TOWN.

YOU SHOULD LEAVE. STAY AWAY AND BE SAFE.

WHERE ARE YOU?

Nothing for seven minutes. The check came and I laid down cash. The waiter asked Sonia what she thought of the gravies. She replied with tact if not sincerity. In the parking lot the phone buzzed again.

HES BACK IN TOWN, was the message.

L H C

YES

HE CALLED YOU

YES

FOR WHAT?

A minute's hesitation. We were back in the car now. I dialed up a question mark to emphasize my last point, HOW DO YOU KNOW?, but before I could send it Essex beat me to it.

HE PHONED. HE TOLD ME HES GOING TO KILL YOU.

A minute ticked by, and then the last text she sent.

BOTH OF YOU.

Thirty-Nine

Two years ago I'd done Vancouver legwork on a custodial interference case, daddy grabs junior and ducks over the border. I was some small help to the Pierce County Sheriff's. Deputy Kim Farraday remembered me, and agreed when I told him I needed the favor repaid.

He met us at a strip mall, in the window booth of a Seattle's Best. Kim Farraday was at least fifty, and cultivated the look of a retired soldier: silver mustache and swept-back silver-white hair. He wore slacks and a gray blazer cut to mask his shoulder holster.

"You two got no idea where this lady is, uh?" Farraday's voice was surprisingly high-pitched and carried the hint of a drawl. "She's not necessarily in Tacoma."

I showed him the texts. When he returned the phone his hands rested on the table, grasping his takeaway cup.

"You said this Crowhurst is for real and I'll take your word on that. Now I can run you two back up to the border and see you across safe. I can look into this Crowhurst, find out what I can."

I said, "The last person I asked to do that is studying his guts in a hospital bed."

Farraday nodded slightly, as if conceding a point. "I don't much like knives," he said. "Don't know how it works up north, but here, a fellow

comes at you with a knife, you put him down. When I worked for the
Wisconsin State Patrol I had a ticketing go wrong. Passenger came at
me with a screwdriver. I told him stop, told him I'd shoot. His choice."
He looked over at Sonia. "You're on the job. You know what I'm talking
about."

"I found out recently," she said.

He waited for her to elaborate, but she only stared into her coffee.

"What kind of evidence is there on this Crowhurst?"

"Scant," Sonia said. "Nothing the police would hold him on."

"Now that depends. There's ways to find something, if you just want
him off the street for a couple days."

Sonia shook her head. "Delaying the inevitable."

"I guess I'm not sure exactly what you want," Farraday said.

"We have to find Dana Essex," I said. "If we find her we can convince
her to put Crowhurst on the spot for the Sorenson murder. That ends it."

"Finding people's your specialty," Farraday said. "I'd be more inclined
to visit this Crowhurst, have a talk with him. What are you thinking?"

"Essex could be anywhere," I admitted, "but I think she was on the
level. Which means wherever she is now, she started from here."

"Only so many hotels," Farraday said. "You could probably run 'em
all down in a couple hours. Meantime I'll check out this Crowhurst's
place, see what I can see."

Sonia and I agreed.

"You kids carrying?"

"I have my baton," Sonia said. "Pepper spray."

"Wits and personality," I said.

"Can't have you empty-handed."

We followed him out to his Wrangler. He'd parked where he could
see his truck from the window, and as he dropped the tailgate I saw why.
A pair of pump shotguns, an AR-15, a Colt Python and a palm-sized .22.
A fireaxe, machete, rope, and sundry other tools filled the cargo space.

"Pick your poison," he said.

I tapped the lid of the Python's lockbox. Farraday looked almost reluctant. "My favorite," he said. "If the shoulder rig wasn't so damn ungainly, that'd be my carry weapon."

"We get stopped with this, it's a crime," I said to Sonia. "Could cost you your job."

She thought it over, then picked up the case.

"Better than the alternative," she said.

Forty

The strip of highway near the Emerald Queen Casino boasted seven motels. Even the run-down flops with their antiquated neon signs had modernized the check-in process, requiring credit cards and photo ID. We drew nothing on Dana Essex's name and another nothing on her photograph.

I wondered if she'd changed her appearance. If your natural look is nondescript, what do you change it to?

The sixth place we visited was especially run-down, and had the look of being stalled in mid-renovation. The neon letters on the roof spelled out U N K I N. A half-dozen canary-yellow Town Cars were parked near the front door. Police auction specials. It looked as if the owners were starting a taxi company, too, their ambition outrunning repairs.

The lobby was a tiny box stuffed with cab paraphernalia, meters, and roof lights. The clerk had spread a newspaper across the front desk and held a soldering iron in one hand. He looked up and smiled. "Welcome to the Sun King," he said. "A single?"

I told him I was looking for a woman named Dana Essex. He consulted his ancient computer and said there was no one registered by that name, now, yesterday, ever.

I sidled up to the desk, held up my cell phone with her photo displayed. The shot from the Surrey Polytech faculty website. "She's maybe not using her real name," I said. "You insist on credit card?"

He shrugged. "Slow economy," he said. "But I did not see her today. My son works the mornings. I can ask him."

He picked up the phone, pressed a single digit, and had a quick back and forth with someone in Hindi. A moment later a drowsy younger man in a checked shirt entered from the front door.

"Sanjay," he said. We shook hands.

I showed Sanjay the picture. He squinted and pawed sleep dust out of his eyes, looked again and nodded. "What's this for?"

"She's in danger," I said. "She might've been using a different name."

Moving behind his father Sanjay tapped the mouse and scrolled down. "Darby Robinson," he said. "She booked a room early this morning. Paid up front in cash."

"She still here?"

He shook his head.

"Any idea where she went?"

"I drove her," Sanjay said. "Train station, other end of the city." He checked his watch. "Eleven fifteen I dropped her, right before I went to sleep."

"Did she have a train ticket? Did she talk about her destination?"

"Nothing like that. I had to wake my pops to cover the desk while I drove." Gesturing to include the motel and cab service, he said, "We're just starting out. Things are slow. Have to take business as it comes. You're not police, are you?"

"Vancouver PD," Sonia said. "It's important that we find her. Do you remember if anyone visited with her, or maybe asked about her?"

Father and son conferred, both shaking their heads.

"Anything else weird about her stay here?" I asked.

Sanjay thought it over. "It's probably nothing."

"Anything helps."

"It's just, she gave me an address to drive to, originally. Then when we got there she changed her mind, told me the train station instead. That's where I dropped her."

"This first place was a residence?"

"Restaurant, I think. Close to the water. Not all that far from the train."

"Any chance you can recall that address?"

Sanjay looked at the stacks of gear on the shelves opposite the desk. He picked up a GPS unit and fished a cable out of a margarine tub full of stray wires. Plugging the device into the wall, he tapped down, retrieving the last few addresses. His father had gone back to soldering.

"Here." Sanjay held out the device. 416 Eldridge. I copied it down.

"If she comes back, let us know immediately," Sonia said.

"We don't like to get involved," Sanjay's father said. But his son nodded to us above the older man's head.

We headed to the train station to show around her picture, to no result. The ticket agents had no record of a Dana Essex or Darby Robinson. The earliest train left at one, an hour after she was supposed to call us. It was past that now, almost three o'clock.

"Maybe she picked up something from that address," I said.

"Or met someone there. Crowhurst, maybe."

Sonia punched the address into her cell. A picture of a restaurant with a purple awning appeared on the screen.

"Could be she skipped out before meeting him," I said. "Had second thoughts."

"It's worth checking out, at least."

We called Farraday from the parking lot to let him know where we were headed. Before I could speak, he cut me off.

"I might have something here," he said. I could hear dogs barking on his end.

"Where are you?"

The phone burped static. I repeated the question.

"Sammamish," Farraday said. "Near Redmond. Just drove up to Crowhurst's place, and it looks like there's a woman inside."

Forty-One

Crowhurst's property was a half acre of muddy and overgrown land, outside the city of Redmond and far from its prosperous industrial parks and software companies. The house was a two-story colonial, mossy and paint-stripped. A second building had been thrown up, sided with corrugated aluminum, one dirty window and a salvaged door. The husk of a wrecked muscle car, a Torino or Galaxie, separated the two buildings.

We found Farraday parked on the gravel road leading off from the highway. He was talking with a blonde woman in sleeveless black denim and enough silver pendants for a mall kiosk. A pair of rambunctious dalmatians had been locked in the back of her minivan, and she leaned against the vehicle, posture defensive, arms crossed. The conversation broke off as we approached.

"This is Mr. Wakeland and Ms. Drego," Farraday said to the woman.

"More of you," she said. "You're just making a bigger molehill outta this."

Farraday said to us, "This is Arlene Crowhurst. Henry's sister."

"And landlord, as I was explaining." She shook a cigarette out of a pack of Dunhills, mostly it seemed to give her hands something to set fire to and her teeth something to gnaw. "Henry doesn't own this place.

He pays what he can. Sometimes he pays for three or four months up front. One time he paid for ten."

Her match burned out and she swore. Farraday held his lighter cupped for her to use. "Your brother ever gripe about his job to you?" he asked.

"He works in a warehouse," Arlene Crowhurst said.

"Doing what, 'zactly?"

"Drives a pallet jack, forklift, that kind of thing. Keeps inventory. Why?"

Sonia said, "We're worried your brother is involved in a dangerous situation. We'd like to take a look around his place."

"That's up to Henry."

"Actually it's up to you," Sonia said, "you being his landlord and these being exceptional circumstances. You can observe us."

"Otherwise we gotta go through official channels, get us a warrant and whatnot," Farraday added. "This way's easier on all of us."

Arlene Crowhurst relented. She led us up the gravel road, over the chain strung between two posts that barred the driveway, and onto the porch.

"You'll have to take your shoes off out front," she told us, before unlocking the front door.

Nothing about the house was flat or square or true. The hallway was a ramp leading down a good two inches, the floorboards sunken and warped, a minefield of knotholes and nails. Hell with taking off my shoes. Runs and water damage beneath the paint in the living room. An antique television set, a VCR, stacks of cassette tapes in blue plastic cases. I opened a couple. *Barb Wire, Bloodsport, The Birdcage*. Stickers on the tapes—MONTY'S MOVIES AND ONE DAY DRYCLEANING and BE KIND PLEASE REWIND. No cable hookup. A recliner and a garbage bag full of takeout wrappers, a slashed-up can of High Life repurposed as an ashtray.

Smoke hung in the air, the pungent, woody smell of pipe smoke. It seemed to cling to the walls, yellowing the furniture, masking other smells. I recalled Blatchford's description—wet coals after a beach fire.

"I had no idea," Arlene Crowhurst said. She seemed more ashamed than worried.

"What's your brother like?" I asked.

She'd picked up the trash bag, squashed down its contents, dumped out the makeshift ashtray.

"He's a good man, though he's had his share of troubles. Shy, not very social. Some people think he's slow, but it's just how he is around people."

"No close friends, girlfriend?"

"Shy," she repeated.

The other rooms were similarly foul. One greasy coffee cup lay in the kitchen sink among a collection of dishware and utensils. Several knives but nothing incriminating. I drew one out and held it up. The handle was cheap chipped plastic but the blade itself had been honed.

"May we see the shed?" I asked.

We came out the back door, over a patch of waterlogged ground. Crowhurst had laid down car mats to create a path.

The shed door was padlocked. Arlene Crowhurst tried every key on the small ring but none fit. She held the keychain up by its orange plastic Husqvarna fob. "This is all he gave me," she said.

I tried the door but it was solid, the hinges and latch rusty but strong. I looked at the window, reached a palm up to the pane and slid. It opened an inch and caught. Tiptoeing to look inside, I could see a twig propped into the window's trough. Before Arlene Crowhurst could say anything, I put two hands on the window and rammed it. The twig bowed and broke. With the window open I looked at Sonia.

"Alley oop," I said.

Farraday was speaking in a placating tone to Arlene Crowhurst. "Better to know now, clear up any confusion. Scandalous times we live in, where absence of proof can be proof of guilt. This way, least we know what we know."

I formed my hands into a stirrup and helped Sonia up to the window. The interior was dark and as she dropped through she seemed to vanish. Brown-gray dust roiled and danced through the open window.

"Light," she called from inside.

Farraday passed me a penlight. I reached through the window and felt Sonia's fingers grasp at my own. She took the light and played it over the walls.

"Some kind of workshop," she said.

Rusty tools hung from spikes on the pegboard walls. A wooden workbench and vise. Aluminum garbage cans, dented lids shut tight.

I heard Sonia exhale, the sound of muted frustration and horror so common with cops.

"Skins," she said, "hanging off a hook on the door. Maybe a half-dozen."

"Animal?"

"Deer, I think. They're moldy."

"His co-workers hunt," Arlene Crowhurst said. "I think they bring the animals here for him to butcher. Not a crime, is it?"

"'Course not," Farraday said. "I got a good-sized bighorn last season."

"Freezer," Sonia called out. "Meat inside." I heard a screech as she pried up a garbage lid. Sound of revulsion as she peered inside. "Help me get the hell out of here, Dave."

I held out my hands and she took them and walked up the wall. Crouched on the sill before dropping down onto the soggy grass.

"Now we know," Arlene Crowhurst said. She and Farraday started across to the kitchen. I closed the window and wiped my palmprint from the glass, removing all trace of our presence.

I hung back with Sonia as she breathed, hands on her knees.

"It's all dirty," she said. "All the meat had spoiled. I don't think the freezer was even plugged in."

"So you're not hungry?" I asked.

"Ugh."

"Maybe we should stop for some nice rare veal, huh? Maybe some haggis?"

"Ech."

"Or what's that British breakfast, fried pig's blood? Black pudding? Maybe some steak and kidney pie?"

She bent over and clutched her stomach. "I'm going to murder you so badly," she said.

Forty-Two

In the kitchen, nursing a beer, Arlene Crowhurst explained that her brother's murder charge had been just one of those things. People were always provoking him. A shy, shambling outcast. I held up a kitchen knife and asked if her brother had a fondness for blades.

"This used to be our farm," she said. "This and the two properties nearby. When our daddy died we parceled it out to pay off the mortgage and his debts. Well, I parceled it out. Henry was in jail by then."

"When you owned the farm," I said, "he did the butchering?"

"We all did. But yeah, he would've done more since he wasn't at school."

"Any violent behavior prior to his murder charge?"

"Nothing unusual. Once he got in a fight over me, sticking up for me against a bully named Tommy Riordan. He lived a few miles east, closer to the school. He used to pinch and grope me. I told Henry and Henry made him stop."

"He beat him up?"

"Badly," she said, smiling a little at the memory. "Knocked out two of his teeth. He gave them to me and said, 'Arlene, he ever does that again, I'll bring you the full set.'"

"Where's your brother at now?" Farraday asked. "Any idea what his schedule's like, when he'll be home?"

"He works on the receiving dock, Goldschmitt & Goldschmitt Logistics." Holding up her cell phone she said, "I made him give me the number in case of emergency." Sonia wrote it down.

"There was a killing 'cross the border up in Vancouver," Farraday said. He nodded in our direction. "These folks are looking into it. Young girl embezzled some money, found with her throat slit. A third party has implicated your brother."

Sonia had ducked out the back door to try the number. Arlene Crowhurst left her half-finished beer on the edge of the sink. Her hands covered her mouth.

"Henry's not capable of that," she said. "Not against a woman, especially."

Farraday spread his hands. "Respectfully, ma'am, this is the house of a fellow who's capable of just about anything."

We walked out across the muddy drive. Sonia was waiting by the cars. Arlene Crowhurst unlocked her minivan and quieted the dogs. The upholstery inside was scratched to tatters, but the outside gleamed, a realty company placard fixed to the sliding door. LOWEST COMMISSION IN KING, PIERCE, OR WHATCOM COUNTY.

"He came back from prison so much quieter," she said. "Not that he was ever talkative. I just remember how glad he was to get home, even if it was run down and smaller than he left it."

"Home is precious," Sonia said, trying to sound sympathetic.

Arlene Crowhurst looked at the mud on her shoes. "I feel I should defend him. He's my brother. But part of me feels I know how this will turn out. Be careful with him."

"It's our top concern," Farraday said.

Once she'd left, I leaned on my car and asked Sonia what she'd found out.

"I talked to the floor manager at the warehouse," she said. "Crowhurst is due at work in two hours. The manager told me he's been acting strange lately. The other day he pulled a knife on a co-worker."

"Jesus Murphy," Farraday said.

"The co-worker's undocumented, so no charges, but there's a meeting planned to discuss Crowhurst's behavior. It was going to be today, only they had three containers dropped off this afternoon, one of them a fifty-foot Maersk. They all have to be cleared by early tomorrow morning. Crowhurst will be working through the night."

"Gives us enough time to check out that restaurant address," I said.

Farraday rubbed the heels of his boots on the grass, scraping off mud. "Long trek back to Tacoma, just to come back here."

"Without Dana Essex there's nothing to hold over Crowhurst. And if he's working there all night, we'll be back before his shift ends."

"Someone should watch the warehouse," Farraday said, "case he shows up early. I can text you if and when he does."

We agreed to meet at the warehouse later. Drinks would be on me if it all worked out. We said good-bye, then followed his truck back to the highway, before Sonia and I headed south.

Forty-Three

Located in a one-shop strip mall a few blocks east of the Tacoma waterfront, 416 Eldridge turned out to be a Mediterranean restaurant called JJ's Taverna. Why Dana Essex would head here from the Sun King motel was a mystery. By the time we pulled into the parking lot the place was closed. Or maybe it had been closed for a while.

Along the side of the building ran a wooden staircase, painted the same dark purple as the awning out front. At the top was a small apartment. No one answered our knocking.

Sonia inspected the contents of the mailbox. At least a week's worth of flyers. A few envelopes addressed to a J. Bezzerides.

I knocked again, peered through the dark window. "Any strong objection to forced entry?" I asked Sonia.

"Maybe let's try phoning first—there's a Jon Bezzerides listed in the Washington White Pages."

She dialed. We waited, then heard from inside the faint chirp of a telephone.

I didn't have to break down the door; it was unlocked. I stepped inside, turning on the pen light, too late to notice whatever it was under my feet that sent me lurching, colliding hard against the tiled floor.

Sonia asked if I was all right.

My knee and shoulder ached. A cloud of cheap perfume filled the apartment. Drugstore perfume, a synthetic blossom scent. Below that odors of piss, shit, burnt flesh, tobacco.

I sat up and noticed the odd shapes of glass and plastic by my feet. Nail polish, tubes of lipstick, a compact mirror crushed by my knee. All new, still bearing their price stickers. A clamshell purse with its silk innards mangled lay scrunched up under the right corner of the door. Its broken strap had curled around my heel.

Sonia stepped over the cosmetics and helped me to my feet.

We were in the tight hallway of a bachelor's suite. To the right of the door was a narrow living space with a sofa bed wedged into the corner. An open suitcase lay on top of it.

A throw rug had been folded haphazardly and dragged away from the center of the room. In its place, a mildewed tarp lay over the tile floor. A figure writhed helplessly amid its folds.

I pulled the collar of my shirt over my nose and mouth to mute the stench, walked cautiously into the apartment.

It was a man, stripped naked and sobbing. He faced away from us, his legs and right arm bound together by zip ties, a wadded rag duct-taped into his mouth. Spiral-shaped burns covered his torso and thighs.

An extension cord snaked out from the wall, ending in a hot plate that sat near the man's head. Its coils glowed bright orange, seared in places with a coarse black crust.

I unplugged the plate and toed it aside, held my breath and squatted next to the man. Up close I could see his face and left hand had been worked on with a knife. Segments of him lay on the bloody tarp.

"Fucking hell," Sonia said.

The man's eyes focused. They lingered on me, moving to Sonia, finally settling on the stump of his left wrist.

"Mr. Bezzerides." I knelt down and spoke softly, trying to still him long enough for me to saw through the straps with my car keys. Once free, his hand groped at my arm. The tips had been cut off his forefinger and thumb. His movements were feeble, breaths shallow.

Sonia scanned the rest of the room, the bathroom and closet across from the door. "No one else here," she said. I heard her cough and spit, heard water running, the flush of a toilet.

Bezzerides seemed eager to speak. I leaned closer, peeled off the tape that held the gag. His fragmented hand pawed clumsily at mine. Beneath the blood I could feel the soaked fabric of a crude attempt at a bandage.

He opened his mouth and retched. Coughs erupted from his chest, blood burbling out, soaking his chin. I felt something solid and moist hit my cheek and tumble down my shirt. I picked it off the fabric, dropping it when I realized it was a two-inch piece of tongue.

The retching slowed and his eyes drifted from me, off toward the ceiling.

"We need to call someone," I said.

Sonia held the phone to her ear. "Already doing it."

As she informed Emergency, I rifled through the contents of the suitcase on the bed. A woman's clothing, ranging from overalls to negligees. A Greyhound stub from Seattle. A packet of twenty one-hundred-dollar bills, banking papers, a cell phone. And Dana Essex's passport. Nothing packed neatly, which suggested someone else had already gone through it.

"They're en route," Sonia said. "Find anything?"

"Her money and papers are still in the case," I said. "Might mean she couldn't come back here—which means maybe she got out."

"Hopefully," Sonia said.

I knelt on the tarp, feeling the blood slosh and soak my knee. I felt under the jaw of the tortured man. Light cuts dotted the folds of his neck, as if a knife had been held there. Bezzerides's pulse was weak but steady.

Maybe she'd rented the room from him. Thought she was safe. She'd come back from the motel, maybe, to collect her things. Seen Crowhurst or his car and told Sanjay to keep driving, to take her away. Meanwhile

Crowhurst had done this, for who knows what reason. Maybe just to pass the time.

"What did he think Bezzerides could tell him?" Sonia said, echoing my thoughts. "What was worth all—all this?"

"It's beyond me."

"Bezzerides could've been in it with her. Maybe Crowhurst knew that."

"And maybe he's already picked her up."

"So we pick him up," Sonia said. No hesitation or doubt in her voice. She pointed at the slightly breathing form. "After this, Farraday has reason to hold him."

"We should let him know. Tell him he needs to call in backup."

She phoned Farraday but there was no answer. She texted. I ministered to Bezzerides as best I could. The first strains of an ambulance could be heard above the noise from the highway.

"Farraday needs to be warned," I said. "If Crowhurst would do this to a bystander—"

"What about Bezzerides?"

"Ambulance is on its way. There's nothing we could tell the EMTs that would help."

I wiped the blood from around my eyes, looked at her. Her gaze was on the tortured man.

"You could wait here with him," I said. "Might be best."

"And you'd go alone? Fuck that."

We left the door open, the light on. In the car I opened the gun case and fed cartridges into the cylinders. We drove past the ambulance as we made our way toward the warehouse.

Forty-Four

G&G Logistics: a gray box lit with floodlights, giant containers on iron stilts lined up to the seven bay doors. A yellow cross-bar gate blocked the entrance to the property. The front door of the building was propped open, light from inside spilling onto a pile of garbage bags heaped at the bottom of the short staircase.

Farraday's truck was parked on the far end of the industrial cul-de-sac. We slid in behind him, killing our headlights. The truck was locked, empty.

We ducked under the cross-bar and entered the property. The Colt was heavy and I didn't trust myself to draw it from my waistband. I carried it at my side, the barrel pointed down.

We knocked, then stepped inside. The reception corridor was brightly lit but the desk was empty. Time cards were neatly stowed in their pouches on the wall, CROWHURST, L among them. We walked to the door that led out onto the warehouse floor.

The floor itself was dark. Lanes built out of industrial shelving held skids of shrink-wrapped goods, boxes, building materials. The offices to the right were a maze of drywall and plywood. A steep staircase and gantry led to a second floor.

We went through the ground floor rooms, using the penlight to locate light switches. Break room with table and soda machine. Front office, a controlled mess of paperwork covering each workspace.

No Farraday. No Essex. No Crowhurst.

"Maybe he's in custody already," I said.

"And Farraday had to leave his truck?"

"It's possible." The possibles and maybes and unknowns were piling up.

We checked the loading bays. The doors were all secured save one. A stack of dirty pallets and an ancient forklift flanked the mouth of the container. The penlight showed a wall of boxes a few feet inside. Crowhurst's work had been left unfinished.

"What do you want to do?" Sonia asked.

"Check upstairs, take a quick look around the warehouse floor. Then get out of here." It felt good to say it. "Leave it with the police and go home."

"I'll phone them," she said.

We walked back toward the stairs. Sonia had her phone out. I shone the penlight toward the warehouse shelves but it did nothing to illuminate the dark towers.

I called out, "Anyone here," and heard my echo return to me through the vast space.

"Signal's weak," Sonia said. "I'll try phoning from reception."

I watched her move toward the entrance, holding her phone up to catch a signal. I thought of calling her back. Irrational—we were alone, I had the gun.

Coming up the stairs I could see the second floor was one single room perimetered by a catwalk, an executive office with a long window that overlooked the warehouse floor. A bank of switches near the entrance probably controlled the warehouse lights. An intercom below them. The door was shut.

I opened the door and, startled, pointed the Colt at the bloody face of Dana Essex.

A deep gouge in her forehead spilled a curtain of red over her cheek. Her eyes were opened wide. I saw them look beyond the gun barrel and recognize me. She collapsed forward onto my shoulder.

"Thank God," she said.

"What are you doing here?"

"It's Lee," she said, straightening up, pointing into the office. "He's here, he dragged me here, something about his money. Dave— Dave—you've got to get us out of here."

"It's okay," I said. "It'll be all right."

I looked into the office and could see only shadows. My feet crossed the threshold and I saw an inert form splayed out by the desk, Farraday, his face perforated and throat torn open. And I felt a hand cross behind me to rest on my left shoulder, an almost avuncular gesture, and something cold punched into my ribcage.

I turned and struggled, lost my grip on the gun. I tottered off balance and fell backward onto the metal grate of the catwalk.

The pain in my side was watery and dull and I knew I was leaking blood.

"I told you to stay away if you wanted to be safe," a voice said chidingly. "At the very least, Dave, you can't accuse me of lying to you."

Forty-Five

"I was aiming for your kidney," Essex said. "Lee told me if you nick that, it leaks bile into the wound. From what I hear it's unpleasant, but it won't kill you immediately."

She wiped the blood from her brow, inspecting it with gleeful disinterest. Her fingers smeared it on the front of her dark overalls. She looked down at my hands, which gingerly touched the wood-handled blade she'd left sticking out of me.

"Don't try to remove that," she said.

Her foot nudged something to the edge of the catwalk and punted it off into the darkness where it clattered and echoed.

"What a shiny gun," she said. "Did you come here to rescue me, Dave? To take me back with you?"

I looked up at her and didn't answer.

"I suppose I should be flattered," she said. "And you brought your policewoman friend, too."

"No," I managed. "Alone."

"That's a lie."

She crouched over me, looking at the wound with curiosity, with scientific detachment. We were strangers. Her gaze absorbed details, made note of results, compared this experiment with data collected from others.

"You look so betrayed," she said. "You might not believe this, Dave, but I *was* coming back with you. I did as you said, rented that hotel room. I was waiting for your timely rescue."

Static shot across my vision. It was difficult to hear her over the onrush of pain. I ground my teeth and kept hold of the handle, wondering how much it would hurt to pull it out, whether I could sink it into her.

Dana Essex said, "I sat on that bed for an hour and seventeen minutes. I counted, I watched the clock. And at an hour eighteen I decided something. Lee didn't get to take my money, to frighten me into submission. He didn't get to win. Right then I had a cab take me back to my friend's apartment."

"I know," I muttered.

"How could you—" She reasoned it out. "Very clever. I was so eager to get started, I almost didn't catch the mistake. The driver dropped me at the train station instead—a poor recovery. I'll do better next time."

Her hands felt through my pockets. I felt the strength fading from my left hand but my right closed solidly around the handle.

"Lee was still sleeping when I got back. Still drunk. Since your friend visited him he'd become even more paranoid. I really mean it, Dave, I was very close to leaving with you. Last night when he came back, I knew he was contemplating killing me. I thought sleeping with him would buy me time.

"And that's what I thought of in that hotel room," she continued. "How yet again I'd given someone else, some man, what he wanted. All the fear I've felt because of men like Lee. Like you. But I saw, if I accepted that fear, I could put it to use. My mother used to say a girl with my gifts could do anything she put her mind to. Do you think that's true?"

"Murder," I managed. "Capable of that."

She looked toward the door of the office. I made ready to pull the blade but her head turned back.

"I didn't have options with Mr. Farraday," she said. "I merely stabbed him as many times as I could. It's odd, for a burly man his voice was remarkably dainty. He screamed like an actress in one of those horror films."

"And Bezzerides?" I asked. I lowered my voice so she'd bend closer. "You torture him, or did Lee?"

"I suppose I forgot about him," she said.

"You burned him."

"I—" Essex looked puzzled. She drew away from me, out of range, thinking it over. I heard her laugh.

"Of course," she said. "You were in my apartment. Did you take my things? No, it doesn't matter, I won't go back for them."

I heard the door echo from below. Essex lowered her voice.

"I didn't burn Mr. Bezzerides," she said. "That was Lee you found. *I burned Lee.* I burned him and made him tell me where my money was. And he did. You know he owns this building? This is his office. His safe is in there."

Essex felt my breast pocket, her hands moving down to my hips.

"I wish you'd come alone," she said. "Was your plan to flaunt her in front of me as you took me away?"

She found my cell phone in my hip pocket. As she pulled it out I reached up with my feeble left and seized her neck and with my right pulled out the blade, aiming for her throat.

Only the blade didn't pull out. I felt it catch on my flesh and tear open my side. Blood soaked my hand and I screamed.

She pushed me down good-naturedly and stood up holding my cell. "Did I not tell you not to pull it out? You don't listen. You're the worst kind of person, Dave, because you think you listen. You think you know. When really, what the fuck could you know?"

The pain was too much to respond beyond a whimper.

"Lee called that a skinning knife, with a gut hook on the end." She formed her free hand into a claw, demonstrating the shape and movement. "What he did was sharpen the curved edge, so it tears both ways, going in and out. He told me about his knives in great detail. Incidentally, I'd clamp that other hand over your side—unless you feel like bleeding to death."

I did as she said, balling up the torn fabric around the handle to staunch it. When I looked back up at her she was reading through my text messages.

"You and Tabitha would've gotten along," she said. "You both have contempt for those who care for you."

Breathing was becoming harder. I could feel blood pulsing out from the wound. My fingers slid from the knife handle. I heard the phone vibrate in her hand. She turned it toward me but I couldn't read the text, my eyes half-closed from pain.

"All she had to do was transfer that money," Essex said. She spat. "In the end, Lee had to promise to spare her boyfriend. That's what it took."

"And you. Had her killed."

She was punching something into the phone, but she paused and looked down at me. "Tell me how this sounds." She read off the text she'd written. "*Found her*, which she'll take to mean me. *Back door*." She punched it in and waited. I hoped the signal wouldn't reach Sonia, but after a moment the phone buzzed again.

"On her way," Essex said.

From her pocket she pulled a folding knife and unclasped it. "I'll let you keep that one," she said, digging the edge into the cut on her forehead, dragging the blade with a twisting motion until fresh blood flowed. She stepped over me and headed down the stairs.

I couldn't sit up or turn over. The darkness seemed to be leaking out of me, as if the wound was a navel, connecting me to all of it. A night made up of my own thoughts. I wondered if I could fall endlessly through it, if that was what death would be like. Falling.

Forty-Six

I awoke looking down on Essex, who waited at the end of one of the aisles of shelving. Light was streaming in from the opposite end of the warehouse. Squinting, I could see the fire doors open, the light from the street lamps filtering in. The interior lights off, Essex bathed in shadows.

I wanted to wretch. Sonia would come through the back door that Essex had propped open, she'd see me up there and head toward me. And the blade would find her, same as it had Tabitha and Farraday and who knows how many others. And I'd have to watch from the catbird seat as Essex cut into her and reduced her to the same nothing as the rest of us.

I didn't want to see that. I thought of Chris Chambers, sending his woman away before pulling the trigger. Hoping to spare her that sight.

"Dave?"

Sonia was calling my name. I turned my head and saw her in the doorway. Saw Essex approach her from the end of the aisle.

They met, Essex gesturing, playing the wounded victim. She pointed up toward me.

Sonia started forward, Essex lingering a few steps back.

Warn her—

I worked my leg up, drawing it toward my chest, and used its weight to turn myself onto my belly. The knife tore and did what it was going to do. I clasped the guardrail and pushed and pulled and shredded myself along the scaffold toward the bank of light switches by the door.

It was agony. I felt myself separate, smear across the steel. I could still hear Sonia's voice. Through blurred vision I saw the beam from her flashlight dance off the shelves.

I reached the wall, reached up and dragged my hand down across as many of the switches as my fingers could touch. I waited for illumination, for the war drum sound of stadium lights.

There was nothing, only a crackle of static. I looked back and felt light on my face, knew she was looking up at me.

I reached up and pawed the switches again. No light. They didn't work the lights. She was heading toward me. Essex toward her. I leaned up and held the switches down, and screamed into the intercom and heard my voice reverberate through the enclosed space.

> *Sonia*
> *it's her*
>   *run*
> *she'll cut you*
> *don't turn your back on her*
>   *get the police, get a gun,*
>   *please*
>   *don't*
> *take*
>   *another*
>   *step*

What came out was nonsense, anguished babbling. I fell back, my head lolling in her direction.

Sonia had stopped halfway down the aisle, looking back. Essex was nowhere in sight. Sonia started toward me with the penlight off, cautiously, but still looking at me. I heard myself whimpering. Just go.

I saw Essex dart out to her left, saw her free arm swing out and clasp Sonia's shoulder. Sonia leapt back as the knife shot toward her, catching her clothing, maybe catching her.

Essex came for her like a boxer, open hand jabbing for her eyes, for a handhold, for an opening, the speed of their movements madcap and Chaplinesque, charging and backstepping cartoonishly.

Then the blade swept out toward Sonia's face and I knew Essex had cut her. That open hand grabbed her hair and the blade came up toward her chest, and her arm took the force of the blade, and Essex pulled Sonia toward her.

I heard a snap and Essex reeled back, the blade falling from her hand. Sonia was clutching her baton. She'd extended it into Essex's eye. She spun and caught Essex in the face and dropped her. Essex's hands felt out along the cement for the knife and Sonia hit her again across the bridge of the nose.

When Essex reached again there was no force left in her. Sonia cuffed her, kicked the blade away.

Then I lost all focus and my eyes began to close. I hoped to hell I hadn't dreamed it.

Forty-Seven

Awake a day later, tranquilized and woozy, with a pint of my sister's blood sloshing through me. A screaming pain in my side beneath the drugs.

Apparently in the night I'd tried to escape. Torn my stitching and the IV drip, somehow made it over the guardrail of the bed. I caused the nurses all sorts of trouble calming me down.

I don't remember what exactly prompted the escape attempt, but I recognized a dull fear coursing through me. Fear of being helpless and being forever at someone's mercy, and knowing this wasn't paranoia. That fear branded on me, insinuated into the wound in my side.

In the end you can save nothing and no one. And yet.

When Sonia and Kay came into focus, sitting at my bedside, I felt the fear ebb slightly.

Sonia had a bandage on her brow from a laceration that would take seven stitches and slowly fade to an indelible furrow. She told me Jeff and Marie were on their way, and even Blatchford, up and around now with the help of a cane, wanted to come down. And anyway, Essex was in no condition to press the issue.

"She lost the eye. Sonia broke her hand, too." Kay spoke with the reverence of someone with a newly minted hero.

Within the week I was trussed up, released, and allowed to make the trip home. The hospital bill cost as much as a Linn Sondek turntable or a good used Chevrolet.

Jeff told me the company would pay. When I asked if that meant I was still a part of Wakeland & Chen, he grunted an affirmative.

"Next time you get yourself stabbed," he said, "try to do it at home."

Lee Henry Crowhurst's initial position was stoic silence. Once they got him to waive his right to counsel and begin talking, he confessed. And kept confessing. He put himself in for seventeen homicides, including Tabitha Sorenson, all on contract. Four of the victims were still listed as missing, and he offered to disclose the locations of the body dumps for fifty grand apiece. The State's Attorney's office bought it, on condition Crowhurst give up his clients.

He'd met Essex inside, impressed her with his matter-of-fact demeanor and candor about what he did. She'd contacted him months ago to find Tabitha Sorenson and kill her, with the two of them splitting the recovered money. He'd agreed, but didn't do legwork: you find her, he'd told her, or hire someone to do it for you.

When Essex furnished him with Tabitha's location, he'd taken the train up from Seattle, using a false passport to get into the country. Once in Vancouver he'd bought a cheap set of knives from the first department store he saw. Crowhurst waited for nightfall, then slipped in a back window, incapacitated Gill, and confronted Tabitha.

He explained how his banking contact had notified him the minute the money cleared. A green light for murder.

All told, Crowhurst made off with just under two hundred thousand dollars. Once it was in his account, he gave Essex nine thousand and instructed her to be patient. He swore he wasn't trying to rip her off, only being cautious to make sure the funds weren't traced back to

Tabitha. In the meantime he'd followed and photographed me, Kay, and Jeff, Essex telling him it would keep me quiet.

His testimony went on. Dates and wounds inflicted and sums agreed upon.

I'd study Crowhurst's evolution over the following years. The first leaked videos of his confession showed the genuine article. The scars on his face and the lisp from his mangled tongue only added to his credibility. Then, in later interviews, still plainspoken but now self-aware, playing a role for his audience. His slow, considered responses gradually tapering to phrases learned by rote, repeated on command. And finally cutesying himself up into a sound-bite-spouting talking head, available when an expert on psychopaths or hitmen was needed. A joke of himself, a paper tiger, and prison royalty.

Dana Essex pled guilty and didn't speak a word.

It was a Big Sensational American Murder Case, and Sonia and I found ourselves supporting players. It was everywhere. We endured it, head down and covered up, like a boxer on the ropes waiting for her opponent to punch herself out.

Months later, at the tail end of February, when a lull in work had left me feeling restless, I walked downtown to view the demolition. The Central Library was on my way. On a whim, I took the elevator to the seventh floor, where I asked for Sabar Gill.

"He's in the stacks," the Special Collections curator said. "One floor down."

I found Gill as he was shifting an electronic shelving unit back into storage position, a blue-bound book in his hand. His expression hadn't changed much from the last time we'd spoken.

"Got a minute to talk?"

He considered it and nodded. "I have to hand this book off. Just wait here and I'll be right back."

I stood by the guardrail, watching the pigeons in the atrium swoop up to the skylight. Gill returned, leaning on the rail to my right.

I said, "You probably don't want to hear this from me, but Essex told me all Tabitha cared about was you being safe. That she bargained her money away to make sure. And whatever else, the rest of your life, you're always going to have that."

He didn't answer, only stared across the atrium to the cables that held up the Milton quote.

"Anyway." I prepared to take my leave. "Felt you should know."

"What's weird," Gill said, "is even though I know it wasn't you, when I think about her and picture her killer, it's your face I see."

"I guess that's understandable."

He looked at my ribcage, noticed I was wincing. "The news said she stabbed you. Does it still hurt?"

"Not if I don't move or laugh or breathe."

We made small talk and I left. Outside it was a white-skied winter day, rain in the offing. I walked up Robson, bought a Japadog, then turned right on Richards and headed east to the building site.

A small crowd had gathered on the corner of Pender, where a lifetime ago I'd intervened between Essex and Gary. The crowd was more upscale than the neighborhood usually saw. Gary darted among them now, asking for change and cigarettes. The crowd looked past him, training their cameras and cell phones on the spot where my office had been.

The building had been reduced to a skeleton of exposed joists, scaffolding around it, blue plastic and cyclone fencing marking off the perimeter. The workers were carting out the building in pieces, loads of crumbling brick and timber.

Tied to the fence was a sign proclaiming the future location of THE LOFTS, with HOMES STARTING FROM $799,000, and below that the hashtagged slogan, YOU DON'T NEED A MILLION!

But beyond that, what the demolition exposed—a hand-painted sign on the faded brick of the neighbor building. A movie advertisement,

HAROLD LLOYD IN SAFETY LAST!, directing passersby to the long-gone Capitol Theater.

A white-gloved hand pointed up the street to where the Capitol had stood. My now-gutted office had preserved its neighbor's sign for almost a hundred years. The white paint looked pristine, a ghost emerging above the rubble, though the hand now pointed nowhere.

I made sure to slip Gary some money, enough to convince myself, at least for the moment, that I wasn't like all the others. He greeted me with a belated Happy New Year.

I limped home, thinking about how the past returns to us, how it folds back upon us. How it always seems to have the final say. And I thought, as curses go, there probably were worse.

Acknowledgments

While in some cases I've drawn from actual events, ultimately this is a work of fiction, and the people are entirely imaginary. Characters who misuse their authority are not representative of their real-world counterparts, or the institutions themselves.

I've taken slight liberties with the geography of downtown Vancouver, in the hope of more accurately reflecting the city's character, or what's left of it.

In writing this book I consulted the findings of the Kwantlen University College Student Association's forensic accounting investigation, made public by the KSA. Don Pentecost's *Put 'Em Down, Take 'Em Out!: Knife Fighting Techniques from Folsom Prison* told me all I wanted to know about stabbing someone and more. Kim Bolan and Nick Eagland from the *Vancouver Sun* took the time to answer questions about Abbotsford crime, and Jerry Langton's *The Notorious Bacon Brothers: Inside Gang Warfare on Vancouver Streets* also provided important details. Thanks also to David Swinson, retired police officer and author of the terrific novel *The Second Girl*, for some procedural advice.

I owe a tremendous debt of gratitude to my agent Chris Bucci of The Cooke McDermid Agency, and my editors, Craig Pyette at Penguin Random House Canada, and Amelia Ayrelan Iuvino at Quercus USA. All three made important contributions to the book, and I'm indebted to them.

Thanks to the publishing teams at Penguin Random House Canada and Quercus USA for their support. Nathaniel Marunas, Amanda Harkness, Elyse Gregov, Patricia Kells, Anne Robinson, Nick Seliwoniuk, and Anne Collins, among many, many others.

Thanks also to my brothers Dan and Josh and my parents Al and Linda; Sook Kong and the staff at Coquitlam College; Jade, Anne, Amber, Sam, Jenna, and Mark at the Vancouver Public Library; Alex Kennedy, Bruce Lord, Mike Stachura and Nicole Fauteaux for accompanying me during my wrestling "research"; my fellow Vancouver crime writers Linda Richards, Sheena Kamal, Ed Brisson, Dietrich Kalteis, Robin Spano, Owen Laukkanen, E. R. Brown, and Tricia Barker; as well as Mercedes Eng, Mel Yap and Mako Morris-Yap, Chris Brayshaw and the staff at Pulp Fiction Books, John McFetridge, Ashley Looye, Brian Thornton, Paul Budra, Torsten Kehler, Cecilia Martell, Neil Kennedy, Charles Demers, Benoit Lelievre, Janie Chang, and the late Brad Dean.

And thanks to you for reading this.

Sam Wiebe

Vancouver

About the Type

Typeset in Dante MT at 11.5/15 pt.

The result of collaboration between typeface artist
Giovanni Mardersteig and punch-cutter Charles Malin, the
Dante fonts were originally developed as hand-set punches in
1955. The fact that Dante was so easily recreated in machine-set
and then digital versions is a testament to its designers' skill.

6168